THE BEATING HEART OF A MIND

The Mind Sleuth Series Book 6

Bruce M. Perrin

First Edition

Cover Art by Courtney M. Perrin

Visit the Author at

brucemperrin.com

Mind Sleuth Publications

ISBN-13: 978-1-955114-05-9 (ebook)

ISBN: 978-1-955114-06-6 (paperback)

For my family and
their boundless love and support

Contents

The Beating Heart of a Mind 1

FRIDAY, MARCH 26 2

SEVENTEEN MONTHS LATER, SATURDAY, AUGUST 20 8

MONDAY, AUGUST 22 18

FRIDAY, AUGUST 26 38

SUNDAY, AUGUST 28.. 41

MONDAY, AUGUST 29 80

TUESDAY, AUGUST 30 124

NINE MONTHS EARLIER, THURSDAY, DECEMBER 9 136

TUESDAY, AUGUST 30 148

WEDNESDAY, AUGUST 31..186

THURSDAY, SEPTEMBER 1 224

FRIDAY, SEPTEMBER 2 297

SUNDAY, SEPTEMBER 4... 310

Acknowledgments 321

About the Author 322

*It's not what you look at that matters,
it's what you see.*

HENRY DAVID THOREAU
AMERICAN NATURALIST, POET, AND
PHILOSOPHER

FRIDAY, MARCH 26

Midnight, Jen's Place, Lone Tree, CO

Conditions were far from ideal for what Kyle Logan had in mind.

He pulled a pint of whiskey from a back pocket and leaned on the front fender of his battered brown pickup truck to consider his options. His gaze tracked up and down the lonely road. Empty, as he expected at this hour. So, he tipped his head back for a long pull on the bottle, his gaze following the tilt of his head. The moon, although only three-quarters, shone like a searchlight, its rays unfettered by the thin cold air of the high plains.

His eyes came back down to the ghostly outline of a massive old house across the road, previously the home of a local rancher. Now, it was Jen's Place, a temporary shelter for survivors of domestic abuse.

In the front, a porch ran the length of the building. Two sconces carved arches of light in the darkness cast by the porch's roof. Their rays revealed two doors—a larger main entrance to the shelter and a smaller door well to its right. Otherwise, the porch lay in shadows, the windows mere rectangles of still darker voids. Having seen the structure by day, however, Logan was under no illusion that the feeble rays of those two bulbs were the only security for the building. He'd seen two cameras—motion-sensitive no doubt—on each corner of the structure. There were almost undoubtedly other cameras on the sides and back of the building.

A gravel driveway cut through a xeriscape yard, ending in a circle in front of the house. The native shrubs and grasses of the plot were brown and brittle from the long winter, matching the vacant lots on either side of the building. The area behind was undeveloped, although whether it was just waiting for a new housing project or was part of the Colorado Open Space Alliance, Logan didn't know. And he didn't care because the wind that might have covered the sound of his approach through the dry landscape—a wind that had howled down from the mountains or across the face of the front range most of the month—was eerily quiet.

Yes, the conditions were far from ideal. But since the shelf life of Logan's information was limited—probably measured in hours rather than days—he had to act soon. And since he couldn't hasten the new vegetation of spring or command the wind to blow, tonight was as good a night as any. He drained the bottle of whiskey and tossed the empty into the bed of his pickup.

"To hell with sneaking around," Logan snarled into the darkness. He pulled a knife from its cover, admiring the sheen of the blade in the moonlight. Growing up, knives had been his weapon of choice against his peers who always seemed bigger and stronger. Now, it would serve him well once inside.

But to get beyond the front door, he needed another of his tools. He returned the knife to its sheath, walked to the back of his truck, and lowered the tailgate. Laying on the bed was a post driver—a thirty-inch, weighted section of pipe with handles used to drive metal posts into the ground. Though lighter than the equivalent law enforcement battering ram, it was much cheaper and considerably less incriminating. And unless the new owner of the ranch house had seriously upgraded its door, the driver would work. He picked it up and quietly closed the tailgate.

As Logan started up the drive, lights mounted below the cameras came on. The beams overlapped on the drive, and Logan had to pause a moment to shade his eyes with a hand. He broke into a slow jog. His quickened pace wasn't to limit his time in view of the cameras. After all, before the night was over, it would be clear to everyone who had visited the home. There would be no doubt because, one way or another, he'd be leaving with what was rightfully his.

Logan hit the porch steps at a full run, only slowing to ready his makeshift battering ram. He slammed it into the door just above the knob. The door held although he could hear the frame crack. He hit it again and the door exploded inward, splinters from the shattered wood flying across the entry hall. He dropped the post driver on the floor and pulled the knife from its sheath.

There were rooms on the right and left with their double doors open. Their interiors were dark, but even so, Logan could tell they were large communal areas with chairs, couches, and desks. Beyond the doors, the hall split with a stairway on the left while a narrower hall continued on the right toward the back of the house. From his surveillance earlier in the day, he knew he wanted a room in the front right corner of the second floor. He took the stairs two at a time, reversed direction on the landing, and sprinted to the door. He turned the knob. Finding it unlocked, he burst inside and switched on the lights.

A woman was sitting up in bed, covers gathered up around her neck. Her eyes blinked under a hand that partially shaded them, her understanding of the situation coming slowly. But when it did, she screamed. Logan sprang forward and slapped her hard across the face. With her head turned from the force of the blow, he grabbed her roughly by the hair, sat beside her, and held the knife in front of her eyes. She froze, her sobbing the only sign she was still alive.

"What the hell am I going to do with you, Linda? I thought after the last time you'd forget all this crap. You belong at home. With me. What do I have to do to make you see that?"

"Please don't hurt me," Linda whimpered. "I'll do better."

"Like hell, woman." Logan raised his hand again, this time slowly closing it into a fist. He drew his hand back.

"Don't you dare touch her," came a voice from behind him.

Logan spun around to find a rather petite young woman with light-brown hair standing in the doorway holding a baseball bat. He laughed once with contempt, then turned back to Linda. "This is between me and my wife. It's none of your business."

"This is my home, and Linda's my guest. That makes it my business. And I believe the police will agree; they'll be here any minute."

Logan turned to the woman. "You're a nosy little bitch, aren't you?" The woman said nothing. He turned back to Linda. "Let's go. We'll settle this at home."

"Stay, Linda," said the woman. "At least until the police get here. Then, you can leave with him if you want."

"And I said mind your own damn business," Logan snarled, his face turning red. He released his wife's hair, stood from the bed, and made a wild lunge at the woman. It was all for show, but it further stoked his rage when the woman held her ground and glared at him in response.

"I should go, Nicole," said Linda. "It's better for everyone that way."

Logan added his agreement with a sneer.

"It's better for me if you make that decision once the police get here," replied Nicole. "I want to know it's your call, not his threats speaking for you."

"I've had it with you ... Nicole," Logan shouted, hesitating a moment until he recalled the name. "We're getting the hell out of here, and you're going to shut your damn mouth. Got it?"

Everyone paused at the sound of a siren in the distance. Logan grabbed Linda's wrist. "Get a move on, woman."

"The police will be here in a minute, Linda. Stay."

"Shut your mouth or I'll shut it for you." Logan took a step toward Nicole, breathing heavily as his brain selected the first option from the fight-or-flight response. He swung the knife up in her line of sight, anticipating a flinch that he would use in a backswing to cut her. He wasn't going to kill her; he was just going to change her tone. Pain could do that.

Again, she didn't flinch, but rather, took a slight step backward. Logan stepped forward, planning to complete his maneuver even though the first thrust had failed to produce the reaction he wanted. But as the blade came back toward her, she swung the bat down on his wrist. The knife went skittering across the floor as he screamed in pain and grabbed his arm.

Logan could feel the heat from his face. He could hear the thunder of his heart in his ears. A drop a sweat ran down his forehead. "You're dead meat, you bitch," he hissed at Nicole through clenched teeth. He turned back to find that Linda had slid out of bed and was making her way around behind Nicole. "And you," he said. "I'm gonna teach you a lesson you'll never forget."

"Get out of my home," Nicole said. "You can wait for the police in my yard or run like the coward that you are."

Logan took another step toward Nicole, his one good hand forming a fist. But when he glanced at the bat, he thought better of it. "When you least expect it, Nicole."

He turned and ran out of the room.

SEVENTEEN MONTHS LATER, SATURDAY, AUGUST 20

Afternoon, Marte Investigative Services, St. Louis, MO

Nicole Veles stood outside the building that housed Marte Investigative Services, her thoughts wandering to the original purpose of the structure. Maybe it had been an automobile showroom with all the large plate glass windows on the ground floor. And if its art deco touches indicated its age, it could have been filled with cars from any of the big three at the time: Ford, General Motors, or Chrysler. Now, that floor was subdivided into several small shops filled with antiques and collectibles, the latter being much more common than the former.

The business she sought, however, was on the second floor. And though Saturday afternoons were not part of their published hours, Nicole had been in the area reminiscing anyway. It was close enough to her old neighborhood to have the feel she had wondered about, but far enough away to hold most of her uneasiness at bay.

She hitched up the small backpack she carried, entered the building, and took the stairs. As she approached the door of the company she sought, she vaguely heard voices, but as she neared, the conversation stopped. She tried the door. It was unlocked so she opened it slowly, a squeak in the hinges announcing her arrival.

The first room was empty, save an old desk that was bare and a chair of matching vintage. Through an open door into the room beyond, a woman appeared, leaning to look over the shoulder of a man seated with his back to her. Though her hair was longer and her features softer, Nicole had seen her picture. The woman was Rebecca Marte, a private investigator and owner of the company.

"Can I help you?" Rebecca called.

"Yes, you can."

The man spun around, nearly knocking the chair over. His face went pale. "Nicole," he said softly. "What is it?"

Nicole cursed her misfortune. It had not been that long ago when she swore that she'd kill this man if they ever met again. And now he was sitting right in front of her. Fortunately, that murderous rage had mellowed but only to be replaced by a deep-seated revulsion. It had been that disgust that had kept her debating with herself for days before deciding that she had to return to St. Louis and try to secure the services of Rebecca Marte ... even if the man and the private investigator were close.

She thought about saying she'd be back on Monday. Certainly, with as casually as she was dressed—a simple white shirt and cutoff jean shorts—they'd believe she wasn't here for a business meeting. But after a moment, she decided that if Marte wanted the business, he'd be the one to leave.

"Nothing that has anything to do with you, Doc," Nicole said, using the nickname she'd found too impersonal when they were engaged. Now, it sounded too familiar—and much too friendly. "I came to see Ms. Marte."

Doc turned back around. Both he and Rebecca were quiet for a moment exchanging glances, then he said, "I'll get out of the way, let you two talk business."

Facing Doc, Rebecca said, "Hold on just a second." Turning back to Nicole, she asked, "Can this wait until Monday? It's the weekend, and I was getting ready to go home."

To the point, thought Nicole, which was fine with her. She preferred the direct approach. But she'd gone this far and didn't like the idea of being dismissed without a chance to say a word. And she especially didn't like the idea of taking second place to a man she detested.

"I suppose that's up to you, but I wanted your help because ... I killed a man."

Rebecca blinked several times, her brow starting to knit.

"I'll call you next week," said Doc quietly as he stood and started for the door.

"OK," Rebecca replied. The PI's tone, however, sounded like Doc could have said "I killed someone, too," and he would have gotten the same response. Rebecca watched him closely as he retreated toward the door. Nicole, on the other hand, turned away, figuring he would read the loathing on her face if she looked at him.

When the outer door closed, Rebecca stood and came around her desk. She was taller than Nicole had expected—probably four or five inches taller than her five foot, six inches. And with her light blonde hair, blue eyes, and fair complexion, Nicole thought her even more attractive than her pictures had suggested.

Rebecca extended a hand, but Nicole didn't take it. In fact, she took a step backward.

"Sorry," she said. "A holdover from the pandemic."

Rebecca nodded. "Sure. I still find myself shying away when someone around me is coughing, and that's a habit I'm in no hurry to break."

"And if you'd lived for months with the belief that COVID was just the warmup for a plague that nearly wiped out the world, habits like mine get very deeply ingrained," Nicole replied. "Frankly, I'd love to break some of them."

Rebecca closed her eyes a moment, accompanied by a slow nod. "I'm sorry. I knew that was part of the fiction the kidnappers used to keep you under control. It just slipped my mind."

"There's no need to apologize. If you're going to take my case—which I hope you will—then you can't be worrying about everything that comes into your head. Besides, your knowledge of what I went through is the reason I came to you rather than some PI in my new hometown."

"Concerned that the past might complicate things?"

"No, I'm certain it would," replied Nicole. "No one is talking about my sordid history, and I'd like to keep it that way."

Rebecca nodded. "Fair enough. Please, have a seat."

Nicole did as Rebecca walked back to the other side of her desk. But when both women were seated, Rebecca hesitated.

"Maybe we should clear the air about something before we talk about your case," she said after a moment. "You may know from the news that Doc and I worked together on my last case."

Nicole did and nodded, but in her mind, she wondered where this was going. It sounded like the private investigator was probably going to say "I'm not giving him up without a fight," or less likely in her mind, "He's all yours." Both were equally absurd to her, but apparently, Rebecca had been too lost in her own thoughts to pick up on the disgust she felt toward the man.

"You may have also guessed that we are friends, but I want you to know that friendship is as far as it goes. I won't be in your way if you have any intentions ...." Rebecca held out a hand toward where Doc had been sitting to finish the thought.

So, it was the he's-all-yours option. Nicole couldn't help herself and laughed.

"How ironic. I was going to say the same to you because my only intention regarding Dr. Sam Price is to stay as far from him as possible."

Rebecca frowned.

"Yeah, I know my feeling is irrational, that it's built on the lies that the kidnappers forced into my memories," Nicole said. "None of the times I recall him raping me, hitting me, or leaving me for dead really happened—or at least that's what I'm told. But you know what? Information doesn't change emotion. In fact, it's mostly the other way around, isn't it?"

"Mostly?" Rebecca said, tipping her head back and forth as if weighing the options. "I'm not sure, but maybe you're right. Shall we talk about your case?"

"Sure."

"How about we start with a little background. You mentioned living in another city. Where?"

That was the first of two questions that Nicole dreaded but knew were coming. "Lone Tree, Colorado."

Rebecca drew back in her office chair, her eyes narrowing.

"Yeah, I know," said Nicole in response to her unspoken concerns. "Different state. Different laws. You have no private investigator license for Colorado, and it's not like you can drop by on the weekend and get one."

"I didn't even know if they had a licensing requirement for PIs. But as for complications, you forgot that I have a business here. I can't be running off to .... What was the name of the town again?"

"Lone Tree. I was hoping you could clear your calendar for a week or two. Think of it as a working vacation in a beautiful setting." Nicole paused, figuring there was little point continuing if even that much was impossible.

Rebecca folded her hands on the desktop, her gaze drifting to a corner of the room. Eventually, quite slowly, she said, "Maybe I could. I'm due some time off, and though I'm pretty much a city girl, a break in the mountains—even a working one—sounds pretty good."

Nicole thought about correcting her misimpression about the location, but bigger surprises were coming. This one would work itself out if everything else fell into place.

"OK, let's say I could free up some time," said Rebecca. "Working a case out of a hotel room is going to get expensive."

"It would, but unless you like living in hotels, I have an alternative."

"Such as?"

"I have a place where you could have your own bedroom and a private office." Nicole glanced around to confirm her impression. "The office is about the same size as this one. It has a desk, bookcase, and a couple of filing cabinets, and we can get whatever else you need. There's a nice common area, and if you're around at mealtime, the food's great. I don't do the cooking," Nicole said, smiling at the self-deprecating remark.

Rebecca, however, was looking more perplexed than entertained as she rubbed the back of her head with a hand. "A cook and a common area? Where do you live?"

"I run a shelter for survivors of domestic abuse— Jen's Place, by name."

"So, you're out of biomedical engineering completely?"

"Well," Nicole said, drawing the word out, "not completely. The purchase of the building and transfer of all the licenses for the shelter took time, so I was doing design work for a biomedical company called HealthVie. And since that was mostly computer work and they are flexible on work-from-home arrangements, I'm still with them part-time."

"And Jen? Is that after your sister?"

"It is," replied Nicole. "She kept telling me I should build on my experience, not ignore it. So, when this home showed up with the owners wanting to retire, I figured it was a sign."

"You say that like you believe it," said Rebecca. "I mean like it was preordained or something."

"I do believe that."

Rebecca lowered her head fractionally as if staring over glasses that weren't there. Nicole, however, knew there was no way she could explain. She did everything she could as a biomedical engineer to build physical aids for those who needed them. But on the other hand, she had no problem believing there were forces she couldn't explain that helped guide that work.

Perhaps deciding that no explanation was coming, Rebecca said, "OK, the question of where to live is at least partially answered. But the bigger problem is the Colorado PI license."

"With your background, it won't be a problem." Nicole paused to rummage through her backpack. After a moment, she produced an addressed envelope and pulled a card from it.

"We'll want to get the process started as soon as possible by submitting this fingerprint form to the Colorado Bureau of Investigation. Have the St. Louis PD complete it, then mail it and the check inside the envelope to the CBI. That starts the background search."

Nicole returned the form to the envelope and held it out for Rebecca, wondering if the PI would refuse even this minimal expression of commitment, but she took them. She glanced at the front of the envelope, then the contents. "OK, but there has to be more than a background check to this."

"There is." Nicole pulled a slip of paper from her back pack and handed it to Rebecca. "There's an online test. You register for it at this web address and I'll cover the fee. There are also sample questions there. If you want to get some additional study materials, we can do that, too. Passing the test, statements covering your education and experience, and a surety bond with $10,000 in coverage and you're done."

Rebecca studied the paper a moment, then glanced at the envelope again. "This all seems very well organized."

"Colorado's great that way," said Nicole. "It's the only place I've lived where you can schedule a driver's license or a license plate renewal online, and they actually get to you on time. At least, that's the way it worked at the office I went to."

Rebecca smiled. "Sounds like a step in the right direction for license bureaus, but I meant you. You either thought about getting a private investigator license yourself or you did your homework."

"The latter," said Nicole. "Running Jen's Place and working biomed design fifteen hours a week wouldn't leave much time for moonlighting as a PI. So, what else can I tell you?"

"Just the basics today. I'd like to wrap things up and get home. Can you come back into the office on Monday, say 9 o'clock, and we can work through the details?"

"Sure, but there are some things I need to clarify about the man I killed before we call it a day."

Before Nicole could say more, Rebecca held up a hand.

"You did your homework. Now, let me do mine. Just the man's name and the date for now. I'll do some checking online. We can avoid a lot of unnecessary questions this way."

"His name was Kyle Logan and the date was December 9 of last year. But ...."

Rebecca held up the hand again.

"That's plenty to get me started. I'll see you on Monday." Rebecca stood to walk her potential client out.

The second question that Nicole had been dreading since the start of the meeting was apparently going to be left unasked. That might be a mistake, but blurting out a long, unsolicited qualification about Kyle Logan's death didn't seem right either. And besides, Nicole would learn a lot about the PI from her reaction to what she found online.

Finally, Nicole said, "If you say so," and stood to leave.

MONDAY, AUGUST 22

Morning, Marte Investigative Services

Rebecca sat nearly motionless at her desk, her external calm belying the turmoil of her emotions.

Yesterday, as she had started her research into Jen's place, its owner, and the death of one Kyle Logan, she'd first been somewhat amused by her findings. Lone Tree, Colorado, it seemed, wasn't some quaint mountain hamlet tucked away high in the Rockies, but rather, a modern, thriving suburb of Denver. Apparently, her potential client wanted to have some fun at the expense of a Midwest flatlander. But Rebecca wasn't above some good-natured ribbing; she just intended to give as good as she got.

But as she read on, her ire began to grow. Nicole wasn't out on bond for a felony. She wasn't even a suspect in a murder case because there was no crime. Yes, Kyle Logan was dead. And, yes, he had died at Nicole Veles's hands but in self-defense. The District Attorney had dropped all charges almost six months ago.

Believing that Nicole had lied to her to force a meeting was almost enough for Rebecca to call and cancel. But her anger had eased. And although she was still simmering, that emotion had been joined by another—curiosity. Just what had the woman hoped to achieve by implying she was in some sort of trouble when clearly, all that was in the past?

Rebecca's outer office door opened, and she leaned over to see Nicole enter. She didn't stand. She didn't welcome her potential client. She just sat motionless behind her desk.

"I thought the door might be locked," said Nicole. "But then, if you didn't let me in, you'd miss the fun of tossing me out on my keister."

"And I may do exactly that," said Rebecca, the woman's quip rekindling some of her anger. "But first, why the hell did you lie to me?"

Nicole took a long breath. "I said I wanted to see you because I'd killed someone, and that's not a lie. True, I don't want your help because I'm under suspicion for his death; I need it because of what his death led to. Mind if I sit? It's a long story."

"You can stand." Rebecca knew it was a petty reaction, but Nicole claiming it was "a long story" did little to change her mood.

"You read about Kyle Logan breaking into Jen's Place and threatening his wife, Linda, at knifepoint, right?"

"I did, although I also read that he claimed he was just visiting and you overreacted."

"His lies aside, he was eventually charged with menacing, which in Colorado means his actions could be considered serious threats to life or limb. And when there's a deadly weapon involved, menacing is a class 5 felony. However, Logan's lawyer claimed that the knife had been a birthday present from Linda, and he was just showing her that he was caring for it. I barged in. He was startled and turned around with the knife still in his hand. I misinterpreted the situation and assaulted him with a baseball bat."

"So, was it?"

"Excuse me?"

"Was the knife a present from his wife?" asked Rebecca. "I don't remember seeing that claim in the stories I found."

"I suppose, in a manner of speaking. He didn't like the shirt she'd given him for his birthday, so he bought the knife and told her it was his present. That didn't come out at the trial, but Linda told me later. Anyway, his lawyer argued that Linda wouldn't have been intimidated by her own birthday present, and I was in no danger. Fortunately, the judge didn't buy the full load of BS the lawyer was selling, but he reduced the menacing charge to a class I misdemeanor. That's punishable by a year in jail, and Logan was out in five months."

"And that's when the harassment started? I did find that in the news."

"Correct."

"And you got a restraining order?"

"I did, but unfortunately, it just made me feel like a prisoner. I was safe at Jen's Place. He'd never go there again. But he kept popping up in public places and then acting like he was surprised to see me. He even showed up where I buy groceries one time. He literally shouted, 'Didn't expect to see you here' then turned and walked out of the store. Of course, he was stalking me. I'd see his pickup in the rearview mirror from time to time. But by the time I could turn around to confront him, he'd turn off on a side street and disappear."

"Until, one night he cornered you," said Rebecca, summarizing what she'd found online. "You fought back and ended up in the hospital. And he ended up dead."

"Sort of, but there's more that you need to know about that night."

"Actually, there isn't. The case was investigated and the charges were dropped. That's all I need to know."

"But if we are going to work together?" asked Nicole, her brow wrinkling.

Why would Nicole's actions that night be pertinent to anything Rebecca might investigate now? If Nicole had gotten away with a crime, she certainly didn't need or want to know. There was, of course, another possibility.

"If there's something you need to confess to, I'm not the right person," said Rebecca. "Find a counselor. Or a priest. Or whatever, but otherwise, I can't see how anything that happened then is relevant to this mysterious case. If that changes, we'll backtrack to December 9. All right?"

Nicole's brow furrowed. She took another deep breath and slowly blew it out through half-closed lips.

"OK," she said eventually with a slight shake of her head.

At least Nicole was cooperating, albeit reluctantly, but it was enough for Rebecca to relent. She extended a hand toward a chair and Nicole sat. "So, tell me about the case."

"About five months before the confrontation with Logan, Jen's Place gained a major benefactor—Ms. Eleanor Bethune-Peterson. Ellie feels very strongly about domestic violence and wanted to do whatever she could to help us. And since her husband, Randolph Peterson, was president and CEO of a very successful home warranty company called HomeRight, she was in a position to do just that."

"Home warranty is big enough for her to be a major donor?" asked Rebecca.

"The name of the company is a holdover from when it was founded. Since then, they've moved into related areas—real estate sales, construction, and homeowner's insurance. They do about a billion dollars of business a year."

"OK. That makes sense."

Nicole nodded. "Anyway, Ellie and I became friends. She isn't just a behind-the-scenes philanthropist, writing her checks and forgetting about the people. She's hands-on. She visits with the women and children about once a week. She even helped serve Christmas dinner last year and twisted her husband's arm into donating a bunch of toys for the kids. She's a little gruff on the exterior, but underneath, she's about the nicest person you'll ever meet."

"I'm not sure I'm following. You want to help a woman whose net worth is probably in the millions? She could hire a small army of PIs if she wanted to."

A frown formed on Nicole's face. "Yeah, I suppose she could if she wanted to. But she doesn't because she doesn't believe there is anything to investigate. I do. You see, on the same day that I took the life of

Kyle Logan, Randolph Peterson took his Glock 19 and shot himself in the head because he'd lost the company he'd founded. Or at least, that's the official version of what happened."

"But you think there was foul play."

"I do," replied Nicole.

Coincidence? Rebecca couldn't see that the timing of the two deaths was anything but a coincidence. But in the mind of this troubled woman, was it cause and effect? She had taken a life and gotten away with it, so the universe was exacting its revenge through a friend? It was a strange thought, but Rebecca had seen enough bizarre beliefs in her last case to think it possible.

"I learned of Mr. Peterson's death a day after it happened," continued Nicole. "I was still in the hospital from the injuries I received from Logan, and Ellie came in. Her eyes were red and puffy, and she kept apologizing for not coming to see me earlier. I thought she was upset about what had happened to me ... and in a small way, she probably was. But most of her pain was because of her husband.

"But even as she told me the story, I felt there was something wrong. And after I got out of the hospital, we continued to talk—not about the gruesome details of his death, but why he might have done it. Of course, he was depressed about losing HomeRight. But Ellie kept saying that the thing that really ate at him was the way people he had known and trusted for years suddenly turned on him. I'm convinced that those same people drove him to take his life."

Morning, The Whitten Residence, Lone Tree, CO

James Whitten stared at the ringing phone on his dresser, wondering who would be calling at this hour. Even the telemarketers weren't tormenting people this early. But then, he thought of his Saturday-night companion. Perhaps she wanted to express her gratitude for the evening and he'd like nothing more than to accept ... maybe several times.

He picked up the phone, a grin covering his face with the thought of her nubile, young body. "Hello."

"It's me," came the voice of a man on the other end of the line.

"Are you out of your freakin' mind?" Whitten snarled. "You know you're not supposed to call me here."

"It's an emergency," he said, the tension in his voice unmistakable. "It's Dan Milgrom. He's spiraling out of control. He's sure that what he did drove Peterson to his death."

"Which would be an accurate assessment, would it not?" said Whitten, his tone dripping sarcasm.

"Don't play dumb with me," hissed the man. "You know what I mean."

"Watch your damn mouth," Whitten shouted, then looked around. Though his wife was out of town, as usual, there was still help in the house. He continued more quietly. "I have to be in the office shortly, and I'll look into it. But you need to pull yourself together." There was, however, something else troubling about the call, and after a moment, he knew what it was. "Just how is it that you know Milgrom's falling apart?"

There was a long pause on the line. "I hear things."

Whitten shook his head. "Yeah, I'm sure you hear a lot about what Milgrom's doing from that palace of an office you have in Englewood. Want to try again?"

"We talk from time to time," he said slowly.

"How often?" asked Whitten, his anger starting to grow again.

"I don't know. Maybe a couple of times a month?"

It sounded almost like he was whining, which fit Whitten's mental image of the sniveling little man on the other end of the line perfectly. "What the hell are you thinking? Consider the optics. You're either a ghoul who loves to have people recount the loss of a friend or ...."

"We don't always talk about that," the man blurted.

"Oh. So, you learn he's panicked by talking about the weather. I feel so much better now." Whitten realized he was nearly shouting again and took a breath. "Look, we've been through this a dozen times," he said through clenched teeth. "Milgrom knows nothing, and there's no possibility of him figuring it out."

"He knows enough to agree to talk to a private investigator."

That stopped Whitten for a moment. "So, it's true," he said absentmindedly.

"Guess you don't know everything. That little busybody, Veles, is bringing in a PI."

"I know a bunch of them. What's his name?"

"I don't know. Besides, I think he's from out of town," said the man. "She's been gone for a few days now."

"Look, I don't care if Veles is bringing in a psychic from Shangri-La, they're not going to learn a damn thing from Milgrom."

"You said you could shut Milgrom up if it came to that. In my opinion, we're there."

"And in mine, we aren't. But if you disagree, you can handle it."

Whitten could almost feel the panic coming through the phone. "Pull yourself together," he said again. "To anyone but you, Milgrom is just a confused old man with regrets about how Peterson's career ended and in shock because he committed suicide. Now, I have to get to work." He hung up.

Whitten stared at the phone a moment, his anger building. "You're the one who's coming unraveled," he snarled at the device. Then, he smiled. "Maybe you need something else to occupy your mind for a while."

Morning, Marte Investigative Services

"Hold on a minute," said Rebecca, rubbing her temple with her fingertips. All she could think was that Nicole's damaged psyche was skewing her beliefs, and if so, she needed to get that issue settled fast. "Look, I'm no shrink, but it seems like you could be connecting two completely unrelated events. You'd just survived an attack. You defended yourself, killing the assailant. Then, later, you learn that the husband of a good friend was committing suicide at the same moment, and you end up feeling like something shady must have happened to him? Don't you think your pain from the first may be affecting your thoughts about the second?"

"That's possible," replied Nicole quite matter-of-factly. "And frankly, it's something you should keep in mind."

For a moment, Rebecca was completely taken aback. Was she supposed to accept a case that even the potential client thought might be the side effect of coincidental timing? But then, she had a thought. Perhaps the reason Nicole wanted her on the case—her knowledge of Nicole's past—was the key. She paused a moment collecting her thoughts because this was unfamiliar territory.

"I hate to put you through this, but I need a little more background on your kidnapping two years ago."

Nicole nodded but didn't look happy with this change in topics.

"It was widely implied that the trauma of the kidnapping affected your memory."

"Trauma did that?" said Nicole. She shrugged, then said, "Close enough."

"How much of it was affected? Everything or did they focus on some specific beliefs?"

"Most everything, but only the two or three years before I was kidnapped, as best as I can tell," said Nicole. "All of those years became sickness, death, and betrayal. You see, if you want to remove every reason for someone to escape, you make them believe there's nothing and no one to escape to. Why?"

But rather than answering, Rebecca asked, "So, if you remove the two or three years that they filled with lies, your impressions of the world are basically the same as anyone else's, correct?"

"Yeah, basically," said Nicole, although some of the conviction of her earlier words had disappeared from her tone.

"Well, I don't see how that can be true," said Rebecca. "You can't just pretend those years never happened. It's like you deciding not to shake my hand when we met. Logically, we both know there's some risk in contact. For me, it's acceptable. For you, with what you went through, it's not. The past that you know logically to be false still affects how you see and feel about things that happen today. And that's what I really need to be watching for, right?"

Nicole slowly nodded her head and let her gaze drop to her lap. Without looking up, she said softly, "It is, and it's not anything I can fix by going elsewhere. I wouldn't be able to stand the pain of sharing my past with a stranger. And I'm not sure they'd believe it, anyway."

If she took the case, Rebecca would need to guard against accidentally revealing what Nicole had gone through. What she knew, although not the full story, might still be enough to destroy her new life. But she also needed to remember that Nicole's history might be the only reason there was an investigation in the first place. Her dark past might be making ordinary, competitive business practices appear sinister and evil. Doc, with his background in psychology, might be able to expound on this idea with all the appropriate psychological theory and terminology, but Rebecca was certain she was right.

After a moment more to let the woman compose herself, Rebecca said, "Let's talk about the case."

Nicole looked up. "So, you're still considering it even though it might be a figment of my imagination?"

"Yes, I'm considering it." Actually, Rebecca had already decided that if there was any way she could make this arrangement with Nicole work, she would. The woman deserved the truth and that might even make her future better ... or at least, less affected by falsehoods. Rebecca just needed to get a few other issues resolved first. "How sure are you that Mr. Peterson committed suicide because of something that happened at work?"

"According to Ellie, that's what bothered him the most. He talked about his 'backstabbing, one-time friends,' as he called them, almost every day after he was voted out by the board."

Rebecca paused, considering that information.

"The crime of driving someone to commit suicide has gotten a lot more press in recent years, what with all the bullying and cyberbullying cases around the country. Most of them are at schools, but it can happen in business. It wasn't too long ago in Missouri when a manager of a Dairy Queen pleaded guilty to third-degree assault after she repeatedly humiliated an employee who eventually committed suicide. But most, if not all of the cases I know about involved young people—middle school, high school, maybe college. Proving that a mature, seasoned veteran of the business world was bullied to the point of turning his gun on himself? That's tough to believe, much less, prove."

"But we have a chance, right?" asked Nicole.

"Of course. It's just that evidence from the inner sanctums of a major business will be a lot tougher to get compared to cases involving, social media, texts, email, and eyewitnesses. And let's face it—debate and disagreement are expected in business, so it'll be a question of its viciousness, not just its occurrence."

Nicole nodded. "Well, if what Ellie told me is true, the pressures on her husband went far beyond his inner circle playing devil's advocate. It was a concerted, coordinated effort to defame Mr. Peterson professionally, apparently led by two of his subordinates. And while I'm not certain it's related, his problems spilled over into his personal life. About the same time his colleagues turned on him, there was a rumor about his sexual orientation. I'm not sure how much of that fiction the board believed or if they just felt the company couldn't stand the bad press any longer. But in the end, they voted him out."

"So, some of this made the papers?" asked Rebecca.

"Most of it. I've collected the stories and they run the gamut. Declining revenues. Mistakes at work. Missing deposits. There was also a very negative article about some of Mr. Peterson's marketing ideas. But according to Ellie, those ideas were from twenty-five years ago. Somehow, there were no dates on the report that was leaked to the press."

"Who would have access to a twenty-five-year-old report?" asked Rebecca.

"Apparently, just about everyone at HomeRight. Mr. Peterson kept it around to use in new hire orientation to show how far the company had come. If the newspaper had asked any employee, they would have gotten the full story, but instead, they took it out of context. The papers also picked up the story about the boy that Peterson allegedly propositioned. He was of age, but according to his statement to the police, Peterson was rather insistent. Some investors might be upset by the CEO's preferences."

"The sexual orientation of adults is newsworthy?"

"Apparently, it is when the company's already in hot water," replied Nicole. "Or at least, in the opinion of the editor, it was. And that story hit close to home for me because the young man and his mom were staying at Jen's Place before the news broke."

"There are males that old staying at Jen's Place?" asked Rebecca. "Seems like that might make some of the women uncomfortable."

"I would have made other arrangements, but his mom lied about his age. And he was small enough to pass as a fourteen-year-old. But when the police required a birth certificate, the truth came out."

Nicole's connection to the young man and his mother again brought into question her ability to separate fact from fantasy. Wouldn't she naturally feel guilty if she had given this boy shelter and food before he turned against a friend's husband? Wouldn't laying the blame for Peterson's death on his business partners lessen some of that guilt? An interview with the boy might help answer those issues.

"Where's this young man and his mom now?"

"She's moved back to California, but no one knows where he is, even her. Or so she says."

"So, you've talked with her?"

"Once. She said she doesn't believe anyone propositioned her son. And, according to her, he's run away before and now that he's old enough to take care of himself, she's washed her hands of the whole mess. In the end, all this incident did was raise a stink in the minds of some of the public."

In that conclusion, Rebecca tended to agree—it could be a smear tactic, pure and simple. But if any inconsistencies arose in the story, she'd verify the facts along the way.

"Do you know if Mr. Peterson kept any personal records of his business dealings?" Rebecca asked. "Maybe some sort of journal he kept at home?"

"I doubt it," said Nicole, "although we can ask Ellie. He had a computer at home that he occasionally used for business. When he was voted out, the company removed all the business files, although Ellie thought they might have deleted anything with the word HomeRight in it. She said it was almost wiped clean. But on the positive side, she knows a lot about the inner dealings of the company. She and Mr. Peterson started it together, and she worked there for years before retiring."

"If I take the case, I'll talk to her, of course. But if this case ever goes to court, the testimony of a grieving widow of a disgraced president and CEO isn't going to carry a lot of weight without corroboration. Specifically, we'll need to get details on the attacks at the office."

"Maybe you can get that from Daniel Milgrom," said Nicole.

"And he is?"

"He was the Chief Financial Officer of the company until he retired. And he was one of the two men who led the effort to oust Randolph Peterson."

Rebecca could feel her head jerk back as if this information had struck her physically as well as logically. "So, you're telling me," said Rebecca slowly, "that one of the conspirators against Peterson might actually discuss his attacks on his boss with me? That doesn't make any sense."

"To me either," said Nicole as a chuckle escaped her lips.

The sound of her laugh made the hair on Rebecca's arm stand up straight. To simply ask a suspect about an attack, verbal or physical, and expect a truthful answer didn't suggest rationality. But rather than getting into that issue again, Rebecca simply asked, "Are you OK?"

"Sorry," replied Nicole. "That must have sounded like I'd totally lost it. The thing is, I remember school and I believe my recollections of the first year or so at work are accurate. And during those times, as an engineer, I worked almost exclusively with men. It just struck me as ironic that everything I believe about this case comes from women. I don't know her nearly as well as Ellie, but it was Daniel Milgrom's wife, Miranda, who gave me the idea he might cooperate with us."

"Well, first, there is no us on this case. If I take it, I work alone."

"Sure," said Nicole. "I just thought I might do the introductions."

"Maybe," replied Rebecca. "So, what did she say that made you think Mr. Milgrom might work with us?"

"According to her, he remembers the smear campaign against Randolph Peterson, but now, he doesn't know why he did it."

That did seem strange, although maybe there was an explanation.

"I suppose Mr. Milgrom might wonder about his motives after his old boss took his life," said Rebecca. "Something like that has to make you question what you were doing."

"But that's it. Dan Milgrom retired and was questioning his role in having Peterson voted out before he committed suicide."

First, it was a potential client whose impressions of events might be flawed. Now, it was a potential witness who might admit to his actions but couldn't explain them? Was there something in the Colorado air? Or, she thought with an inward smile, maybe it was the lack of air. But even though this session with Nicole was proving almost as confusing as enlightening, there was one thing they could accomplish.

"OK, let's complete the cast of characters," said Rebecca. "Who was the other primary conspirator against Mr. Peterson?"

"That would be James Whitten."

"And is he going to turn into a witness for us, too?"

"Not a chance," she said. "He was Chief Operating Officer but took over as CEO and president when Randolph Peterson was removed."

Her matter-of-fact tone took a turn toward bitterness.

"I really don't know Whitten at all, but Miranda says that the company's official statement after Mr. Peterson's death is vintage Whitten. In part, it said that Peterson's misguided business vision was a cry for help, but with the implication that he wouldn't accept it when offered. So, he, Whitten, was left to clean up the mess."

"What a nice guy," Rebecca replied. But sarcasm aside, at least she now had one good suspect. Whitten had gained a position of power and wealth when Peterson was removed from his job, and if Nicole's summary was accurate, he had no remorse about the reversal of fortunes.

"So, I'll need to speak with the two wives, Milgrom's and Peterson's," said Rebecca. "And hopefully, Daniel Milgrom will work with me. Do you know of any other possible witnesses to the campaign against Peterson at work?"

"A man named Fred Reese is on the HomeRight board. I think he might be willing to talk about some of the information Milgrom and Whitten raised against Peterson."

"And you think he might help because ...?"

Nicole gave an exaggerated grimace. "Mostly a gut feel, I suppose. I met him at a function for another organization. It, like Jen's Place, supports victims of domestic abuse, but it's a lot bigger and does a lot more—things like manning a call line 24/7 and sponsoring dedicated children's programs. Anyway, with my friendship with Ellie and him on the HomeRight board, the conversation turned to the problems at the company. At the time, he thought the complaints about Peterson were exaggerated. But that was a while before the vote, so I'm not sure what he thinks now."

"I suppose if Mr. Reese can't or won't help, we can try some of the other board members. How about inside HomeRight? Do you know any employees who might be sympathetic to the case? It would be good if we could find out more about how each of Peterson's mistakes surfaced in the company. Or better yet, how they got leaked outside of it."

"No, sorry," said Nicole. "I don't really know anyone who works there."

"OK, that one falls to me. So, the last issue is my fee. We have some good starting points—Milgrom, Reese, the young man who is missing, and, hopefully, someone inside HomeRight who is willing to talk. Realistically, however, each of those ...."

Nicole finished the thought for her. "I know. Each of them has problems. The talk with Milgrom will just reveal he's getting old and forgetful. Reese won't be able to say anything because he's bound by a nondisclosure agreement. The trail of the missing boy is cold, and he doesn't want to be found. And no one in a position to know the inner workings of HomeRight is going to risk losing their job over a case that has already been closed by the police."

Rebecca released a single laugh. "I said realistically, not pessimistically. I don't think all those lines of inquiry will fall through ... although it's possible. I just wanted to make sure you understood there's no guarantee. And that getting anything could run into some serious time and expense."

"I understand," said Nicole simply. "And I'll take whatever I can afford of your best shot."

"OK." Rebecca pulled several sheets of paper from a drawer and pushed them across the desk to Nicole. "This is an estimate for the first two weeks of the investigation. I'll prorate the refund if the investigation runs shorter, which is doubtful. And after two weeks, I'll need to get back to St. Louis. If that happens, we'll see if I can package my files for another PI in a way that keeps you out of the spotlight."

Nicole leafed through the pages. "Do you have a pen?"

"Just like that?" asked Rebecca.

"Just like that."

"Then, I guess you've hired yourself a soon-to-be Colorado PI."

FRIDAY, AUGUST 26

Evening, An Alley in Englewood, CO

"How do you know he'll be coming through here?" asked Tucker Redd, glancing sideways at the darkened silhouette to his right.

It had been an unusually hot day and the alley was deserted. The setting sun hadn't yet delivered on its promise of a reprieve from the sweltering temperatures, and everyone except Redd and his companion had taken refuge in their air-conditioned homes. And yet, as the final pink and blue and gold of the setting sun faded, he knew it could be near 40 degrees before the night was over. After living most of his thirty-eight years in Alabama, he still couldn't get used to the temperature swings in the dry, thin air of his current home.

"And how do you know he won't be carrying a gun?"

"He comes this way every day," snarled James Whitten. "And he doesn't believe in guns, a holdover from his elitist, liberal upbringing on the East coast. Now, shut the hell up and keep your eyes open. Light brown pants, light blue short-sleeve shirt. I'm guessing his jacket will be thrown over a shoulder by now. His hair is gray, but it may look black in this light. He's about six feet tall, maybe 175 pounds."

It was the third time Whitten had offered that description and Redd knew it by heart. But he wasn't about to say that. Rather than a description, he would have preferred to have seen his target in the daylight—get a mark of the man—but he wasn't going to say that, either. Whitten called the shots. And for the little he was paid, he'd ignore these issues. Besides, assuming the description was correct, he had six inches and seventy-five pounds on his quarry. He wondered what his boss had against this guy because it wasn't going to be pretty. But like most everything else that had popped into his head, he wasn't going to ask.

"You still following Milgrom?" asked Whitten.

"Sure. Just like you said. I let him see me from a distance, then fade into the crowd." Redd paused, wondering if he dared ask his question. "Are you sure that's going to work?"

Whitten laughed softly. "OK, Einstein, let's hear your concerns."

"Well, it's just that I don't know when he's going out most of the time. I don't get many chances to spook him. And at least once, he came toward me. He's not as shaken up by all this as ... not as much as I expected."

He was going to say, "not as much as you expected," but thought better of it. Whitten, however, took offense anyway.

"So, it's my fault you don't know where he's going to be. Is that it?" Whitten hissed under his breath.

Redd cast another glance to the right. Although he could no longer make out the man's features in the growing shadows of the night, there was no mistaking the tone. "No, Mr. Whitten. That's not what I meant."

"Just use that muscle between your ears to do what I tell you. If stalking him doesn't work, it's because you've screwed it up."

Whitten paused. Redd hated these moments of silence. It usually meant the man was reloading with a fresh set of insults. But this time, Whitten said, "There's your target. You see him?"

"Yeah, sure. I got him."

Redd started forward, immediately sensing that his companion wasn't following. "Aren't you coming?"

"Don't you want to make sure I do it right" was the rest of the thought, but this, too, he left unspoken.

"No, you imbecile. I take no pleasure in your form of persuasion. Just make sure there's no permanent damage and nothing that shows. A broken rib or two should do the trick. I just want him to know he's not as high and mighty as he thinks."

"Sure, Mr. Whitten. I'll deliver that message."

But even before he finished the last sentence, James Whitten had turned and was walking back to his car.

SUNDAY, AUGUST 28

Late Afternoon, Jen's Place

"I really didn't expect you for another two days," said Nicole, coming out of Jen's Place to greet Rebecca on the circle drive. "The application for your license must have gone smoothly."

Rebecca was still sitting in the driver's seat of her car, although the door was open and she'd swung her legs out to rest her feet on the ground. She stood up slowly, stretching her back as she did. It felt so good, she groaned.

"I'd go home and come back when you expect me, but I couldn't stand that drive again. After Kansas City, it was long, boring, and flat, except for the Flint Hills. And they're not much more than flat. Not like that," Rebecca said as she waved a hand across a picture-postcard-worthy scene of the sun starting its slow descent through rows of wispy clouds toward the Rocky Mountains. "That, I have to say, makes the drive worth it."

"It's beautiful, isn't it? When you need to take a break from the investigation to clear your head, I can take you to some of my favorite spots. Some are in the mountains; others are down here on the plains. Say, are you hungry?

And your shorts and T-shirt are fine. We're very casual around here."

"Thanks, but no. I've been snacking since Goodland, Kansas. That's 200 miles of granola bars and an apple, so I'm good for today. And as for the license, yeah, it went smoothly. The Colorado Bureau of Investigation coordinates with the FBI on background checks. So, with the Bureau sending CBI my prints and my training and service history ... well, I was probably nearly done before I did anything. And the exam, like you guessed, was straightforward."

"Well, I'm glad you're here," replied Nicole. "Let's get you moved in."

Rebecca pressed a button on her key fob, the trunk opened, and the women walked around to retrieve two roller bags from the back. As they walked toward the shelter, Nicole said, "Your bedroom is in the back of the first floor. My room as well. In the front are the common areas—a dining room, a media room with two public computers and a television, and a small study for private meetings. The rooms for the women and children are on the second floor. Right now, I only have one child in residence—a small boy. But even when there are several kids around, it's never that loud."

"A result of what they've been through?" ventured Rebecca as they climbed the steps to the front porch.

Nicole paused a beat. "I'd guess so. I took some crash courses so I could run this place, but now that I have more time, I'm fleshing that out with some online classes. I just haven't had much on the developmental effects of what these children have experienced."

"Quite a change from biomedical engineering, I suppose?"

"Definitely. Why don't we check out your office first?"

Nicole turned to her right and walked across the porch. "The rancher who lived here had a pretty big operation, as you probably guessed already by the size of the place. He wanted an office to conduct his business, so he added an annex. It shares the porch, but otherwise, it's completely separate from the main house." She stopped in front of a smaller door, removed a key from her pocket, opened the door, and reached in to turn on a light. When she turned back to hand over the key, however, she found Rebecca staring at the door. "It's something, isn't it?"

"I didn't think it was anything special until I saw the four bolts that go into the frame," replied Rebecca. "But it's wood, right?"

"Steel clad in wood," said Nicole, as she handed the key to Rebecca. "There's also a bolt that goes up into the frame above and one that goes down into the threshold. It's the same on the main door, although with all the construction shortages and delays, I was three weeks too late getting it installed to stop Kyle Logan's midnight visit."

Rebecca stepped into an empty reception area. Beyond it was a second door and when she passed through, she found an office with a massive wooden desk, two file cabinets, and a bookcase all of a matching style. It was clear that each had been lovingly maintained, although they showed the inevitable signs of a long and productive life—a few scratches here and there, a slight discoloration from a liquid left too long on the desktop, a small chip on one corner of a file cabinet. The chairs were of a more recent vintage. Two dark blue upholstered wingbacks faced each other in a small conversation area, while four chairs with padded seats and backs of the same blue fabric were scattered around the room. One of them sat behind the desk.

"Very nice," said Rebecca. "And you're right. This office is as big as mine back in St. Louis. The previous owners just leave everything?"

"They did. The desk, file cabinets, and bookcase are all original. The only modern conveniences are the minifridge behind this wood panel"—she opened the door to show shelves already stocked with water and soft drinks—"and the coffee station in the corner with a bar sink. There's some coffee and tea in the drawers beside the sink.

"I thought about using the annex as my office, but I prefer things more informal. Everyone who stays here knows that if I'm on the property, I'll be in my room. And since it isn't safe to have residents walking back and forth on the porch at all hours, I've kept it locked up until I can have a doorway cut to connect the two spaces. Guess it's lucky that I haven't had the time to get that done."

"Lucky for me, anyway," replied Rebecca, although she was thinking it strange to be managing a shelter from living quarters. But then again, perhaps it wasn't that unusual. "I'll leave this bag here, since it has my work files, and take the other one to my room."

"I have it," said Nicole. She didn't wait for Rebecca to object as she spun on a heel and walked back out the door.

After Rebecca locked the office behind them, the two women went to the main door and entered. As they walked toward the back of the building, Nicole pointed out each of the common areas. After they passed the stairs, the hall narrowed and ended with two doors. "Your room is on the right and I'm across the hall." She pulled another key from her pocket and handed it to Rebecca.

Rebecca unlocked the door and started inside, only to stop so suddenly that Nicole bumped into her. Even so, Rebecca didn't turn around.

Nicole leaned over to look past her shoulder, knowing immediately what had rendered the PI immobile. Through two large picture windows directly ahead, the setting sun had dipped behind the mountains, painting the underside of the clouds a blazing yellow that transitioned to a brilliant orange and finally, a deep purple as they stretched toward the plains.

Rebecca turned around. "You didn't need to put me in this room."

Nicole smiled. "Trust me. I'm not making any sacrifices here. The sunrises are just as spectacular, maybe more so since the horizon for the plains seems to go on forever." Nicole paused. "It was tacos tonight, but I'm sure there are some left. Are you hungry?"

"Thanks, but no. I'm fine."

Nicole slowly shook her head. "I already asked that, didn't I?"

Rebecca shrugged. "I'm sure your day was as long as mine."

"It's not really that. It's ... oh, what the heck. Do you want to meet Ellie?"

"Ms. Eleanor Bethune-Peterson? She's here now?"

Nicole chuckled. "She'll never stand for that kind of formality, but yeah, her." Nicole paused, her expression becoming more serious. "I know you're exhausted and meeting her tomorrow or the day after is fine. But she came over to see some of the women and she's upstairs right now. If you feel up to it, you could say hi, maybe talk for a while?"

"Sure, I can do that ... as long as she's not offended by a yawn now and again. I'll head back to the office so we can talk there."

Nicole agreed and left to find her friend. Rebecca had no more than made herself comfortable when a woman appeared at the office door. She stood and came around the desk to introduce herself but never had the chance.

"Ellie Peterson," said the woman, as she closed the door behind her. She was tall and lean, looking much more like the prototypical rancher's wife to Rebecca than the widow of a billion-dollar business owner. "You can call me Ellie. And you must be the PI from St. Louis, Rebecca Marte?"

Rebecca's first thought was that this woman was a study in contradictions. Her hair was nearly white, but she was no fragile grandmother. There was an energy in her voice and vigor in her movements. Her face was lined and weathered, but her brown eyes sparkled with intensity and intelligence. She was dressed in a plain blue work shirt, boots, and jeans. But at the same time, she sported a wedding ring that would have cost more than Rebecca's car.

"I don't usually wear it around," said Bethune-Peterson, undoubtedly catching the direction of Rebecca's glance. "But somehow, me being married puts some of the shelter's guests more at ease. Can't say why because it seems like it should be the other way around."

"I'm not sure either," replied Rebecca. "And, yes, I'm the private investigator. Nicole speaks very highly of you."

"She's quite the young lady," said Bethune-Peterson. "Smart as a whip and as hard a worker as I've ever met. It's almost as if she's filling her days to overflowing to forget something in her past."

Bethune-Peterson studied Rebecca closely, possibly to see if she'd get a reaction. Rebecca, however, didn't oblige, but the sequence was enough for her to conclude one thing—Bethune-Peterson was perceptive. She shouldn't underestimate this woman.

After a moment, Bethune-Peterson continued. "Nicole would have come over and done the introductions, but I asked her to stay on the other side so you and I could talk. You see, there's something I need to tell you."

"Sure. What would that be?"

"I want you out of here."

Evening, Tucker Redd's Apartment, Denver, CO

Tucker Redd's phone rang. He hesitated, knowing that few people had this number and not wanting to talk to one of them in particular. But the reprieve from not answering would be short-lived. If it was who he thought, the man would keep calling until he gave up and answered. Or worse, he'd come to visit. "Hello."

"I thought I told you to get a cell phone," Whitten said without preamble.

Redd stared at the receiver a moment before realizing that if he had bought a cell phone, he would have given the number to his boss. He could lie, but then, Whitten would ask for a number he didn't have. "Sorry, Mr. Whitten. I just haven't had the time."

In fact, Redd hadn't bought a phone because they were expensive, and he wasn't sure he could afford one on what Whitten paid him. To pick up a second job, however, meant he'd lose this one. He didn't know how Whitten would find out, but he would. He seemed to know everything.

"Quit making excuses. Sooner or later, I'm going to need to talk to you, you won't be at home, and there'll be hell to pay. Got it?"

"Yes, sir."

"Anyway, that nosy broad, Veles, got back in town a few days ago. I want you to find out where she was and who she saw."

"Maybe she was just on vacation," said Redd, regretting his comment before the sound of his voice faded from his ears.

"How the hell do you come up with this crap? If she was on vacation, then get me the pictures. And if you're lucky, she was spending her time on a nude beach. You'd like that, wouldn't you?"

Redd wasn't sure what to say. He'd seen Veles, and she was attractive. But ogling pictures of her didn't seem right, although he doubted Whitten would agree. Before he could decide what to say, Whitten spoke.

"Look, moron, she wasn't on vacation. She went somewhere to hire a private investigator. That much of your job I've already done for you. You just need to find out who he is."

"I don't know, Mr. Whitten. That sounds pretty tough. And since I'm keeping a low profile, like you said, I don't even know anyone to ask."

"Well, someone a helluva lot smarter than whoever you asked about the age of that kid. His statement to the police was supposed to give Peterson a criminal record, not just a black eye. But no. He's an adult, leaving Peterson to swing in the wind for another ten months. No wonder he killed himself. If you hadn't screwed things up so royally, he might be in prison, but at least, he'd be alive."

"You don't really think that, do you?" asked Redd. He'd done some bad things in his life, but nothing that had cost someone their life.

"Hell, yes, I do. His blood is on your hands, and if you don't start getting results, this won't be the last time. Now, find out who Veles hired."

"Sure, but ...." Redd could hardly believe he was going to ask this, but he had no idea how to trace Veles's movements. He was supposed to be a bodyguard, not a detective. "Do you know someone I could ask?"

"Jeez, Redd, I must be crazy to ask you to do anything that involves a brain. Forget it. And forget the thousand dollars I was going to pay you for the job. I have other ways of finding out. Now, get the damn phone because when I discover what she's up to, I'm going to be calling with something you're qualified to do."

Whitten hung up.

Redd sat and stared at the phone a minute, then muttered, "Like hell you were going to pay me a thousand bucks."

Evening, Jen's Place

"You want me to leave?" said Rebecca, repeating Bethune-Peterson's words because she had trouble believing she had heard right. She paused long enough to let the woman correct any misimpression, but she remained quiet. She only stared, her eyes cold.

Rebecca raised a hand toward an empty chair, then walked back to the other side of the desk and sat. "May I ask why?"

Bethune-Peterson was still standing, but with Rebecca's question, she sighed and took a seat.

"Something's troubling Nicole, something from her past. She hasn't ever said what it is, but she was making progress toward putting it behind her. She was, anyway, until she had to defend herself from that lowlife, Kyle Logan. But even after that setback, she seemed to be improving until one day a few weeks ago. I was over here and we were just talking. Then, completely out of the blue, she blurted your name like it was the big reveal in some mystery movie. I wouldn't have thought much about it except after that she became obsessed with the idea that my husband had been driven to his death by his old partners."

"And you don't think that's possible?" asked Rebecca.

"Don't be ridiculous. The sooner she forgets this nonsense, the better. And the best way for her to forget is for you to get out of town."

"She'd just find another PI and you'll be right back in this situation," said Rebecca. She knew this wasn't true, but Bethune-Peterson didn't. And besides, she wasn't going to be driven off by this woman.

"I doubt that, but I'll deal with the next problem when it comes," replied Bethune-Peterson, her glare still in full force.

Rebecca pondered her options. Leaving things alone wasn't one of them. Without Bethune-Peterson's cooperation, discovering her late husband's thoughts and actions leading up to his death would be difficult, if not impossible. But perhaps she could justify her involvement without betraying her client's trust. "You're right. In Nicole's eyes, I'm uniquely qualified for this case. But for the same reason that she won't discuss why that's true, neither will I. I will, however, pursue this investigation to the best of my ability."

Rebecca wasn't finished with her reasons for taking the case, but Bethune-Peterson had already heard enough. "I may not be the richest woman in the area, but I have money. And I may not be the most politically influential, but I have friends in government. And if that's your final word, I'll see to it that your stay in Lone Tree is a living nightmare. You'll be stopped every time you drive off this property. They'll get to know your face in traffic court. Your simplest requests for help from the local police will mysteriously vanish. You'll be searching all over town for any merchant willing to take your money. Need I say more?"

As intimidation goes, Rebecca thought Bethune-Peterson needed a lot more practice. Perhaps she could pull off some of these threats in Lone Tree and maybe even in the neighboring towns. But the fact that she'd be running afoul of numerous state and federal laws meant the pressure couldn't last; that was assuming she got anyone to go along with her in the first place. Rebecca, however, needed the woman's cooperation, so pointing out all the fallacies in her scare tactic wasn't going to help. She had to find a different approach.

"You're right about Nicole wanting me to run the investigation. But you're wrong in thinking that I'm the reason she wants to go forward with it, that I'm filling her head with nonsense, as you put it. She had misgivings about your husband's death the day you visited her in the hospital after the incident with Logan."

Even that small detail caught Bethune-Peterson off guard as her glare faltered for a moment.

"As for the day she blurted my name, that was because she finally saw a way to pursue the case. And last, as for the investigation being a waste of time, I think that's entirely possible. But so does she."

Bethune-Peterson's transformation from anger to doubt became complete as she raised a hand to her throat, her eyes sweeping around the room as if in search of an answer.

Rebecca, however, needed the woman convinced, not confused. So, when her gaze returned to her face, she said, "Ask her if I didn't try to talk her out of investigating your husband's death. She'll confirm my reservation ... and hers. And if you succeed in running me off ... well, the only thing that will accomplish is that she'll take the case on herself. Do you want to live with the consequences of that?"

Bethune-Peterson dropped her hand, stood, and paced to a wall. She remained there a moment, her back to Rebecca. Finally, she turned around. "Nicole can be stubborn. You're probably right; she'd probably go ahead without you if she had no other choice."

Bethune-Peterson rubbed her chin for a moment. "I suppose if you're as good as Nicole thinks, this is the fastest way to get it over with. But I swear, if I find out you're leading her on with innuendoes and false promises, I'll come after you with everything I have. Nicole protects her guests like they were her own family, hardly ever thinking of herself. I'm going to do the same for her because whether she knows it or not, she needs protection. Protection from the likes of you."

"I'd expect nothing less from a friend."

Bethune-Peterson released a long breath, then gave a single emphatic nod. "OK, let's get this over with." She sat back down.

Rebecca thought about saying she was tired from the long drive because she was. Thirteen hours in her car had left her thoughts in a fog, her body buzzing to the tune of the car's engine and its tires on the pavement. She could request a meeting for tomorrow. But if Bethune-Peterson slept on even this slight concession, it might disappear in the morning. Better to push forward. Rebecca pulled a notebook out of her roller bag and leafed to the page she wanted.

"First, let me offer you my condolences on your loss."

Although Bethune-Peterson said, "Thanks," her tone would have fit had she been reciting her A, B, Cs. But whether she felt such civilities were hollow in general or only when delivered by a PI she didn't fully trust, Rebecca couldn't say.

"As you mentioned, Nicole feels that your husband's partners drove him from his position in HomeRight. She mentioned two primary detractors, two individuals who regularly found faults in his ideas and plans." Rebecca checked her notes. "A Mr. Daniel Milgrom and a Mr. James Whitten."

Bethune-Peterson seemed unfazed by the names; she didn't even blink, although that was probably because she knew who Nicole suspected.

"I'm sure that everyone who reported to Randy took issue with his ideas at some point in time," replied Bethune-Peterson. Perhaps realizing that this wasn't really the cooperation she'd promised, she sighed again, then said, "And, yes, Dan and Whitten rather consistently found fault with Randy's ideas toward the end of his time in charge. For Dan Milgrom, his opposition only started a few years ago and the change weighed heavily on my late husband's mind. Before that, they had pretty much seen eye-to-eye on nearly everything. Whitten's disapproval, on the other hand, was long-term, but not unexpected. Randy liked ... no, that's not quite the right word. My husband saw value in Whitten provoking debate so that the team could find weaknesses in their business plans, even if his comments could sting from time to time."

The change in Milgrom's behavior was consistent with what Nicole had told her, but Bethune-Peterson's impression of Whitten—that he was just doing his job as devil's advocate—was much more positive than her client's. But was the woman being forthcoming? Rebecca could hardly miss the difference in the way Bethune-Peterson addressed the two men. Milgrom, as the former ally of her husband, was Dan, while she referred to Whitten by his last name. Did she have a more deep-seated issue with the current CEO and president? And if so, why was she minimizing his possible role in bringing her husband down? She decided, however, to wrap up her questions about Milgrom first.

"Tell me a little about the relationship between Mr. Milgrom and your husband."

"I retired from HomeRight about five years ago," said Bethune-Peterson. "And slowed down a little before that. But earlier, I saw Dan and Randy working together every day. Dan was not only a supporter in the early days but a confidant as well. In many ways, the two of them started and ran HomeRight as a team."

"Along with you, according to Nicole," Rebecca added.

"Yes, back then, it was the three of us."

The woman's gaze became far away for a moment, then she said, "It was about two years ago when things started changing. I wasn't going to staff meetings at HomeRight, of course. But I ended up in the middle of one of their rows anyway. The four of us—Dan Milgrom, his wife Miranda, Randy, and I—had gone to dinner. We'd hardly finished ordering when Dan and Randy started angrily whispering about something. I think it was about some deposits Randy had forgotten to approve. Anyway, I changed seats with Dan. Miranda and I were hoping that if the men were side by side, the argument wouldn't disturb the other diners. It didn't work. They kept getting louder. And even when they tried to quiet down, it seemed like the tone of the conversation carried even when the words didn't. Everyone was staring at us. Miranda and I were about to suggest that we try this another evening when Dan got up and pulled her to her feet. She asked what was going on, but he didn't say a word. He just led her to the door and they left. That was the last time Randy and I saw them socially, although Miranda and I still get together sometimes."

"In your opinion, were Mr. Milgrom's complaints appropriate to the issue?"

"Well, yes and no. Randy was just rubber-stamping the deposits, mostly so he'd have a feel for cash flow. He'd do that at home sometimes, and when he did, he'd only glance at them for a moment. But at the same time, missing those deposits put the company in a very bad light. And in retrospect, this mistake was the beginning of the end, and maybe Dan saw that coming. Or maybe there was more going on at work that I didn't know about."

Rebecca knew of at least two other things that had occurred about the same time as the missing deposits, and it wasn't clear to her why Bethune-Peterson was ignoring them. She'd check on that issue, but first, she wanted to get a few more details.

"That night at the restaurant, did Mr. Milgrom show any concern about your husband's state of mind? Or perhaps, his forgetfulness?"

"There wasn't a shred of compassion in his tone ... and none in the words I caught," replied Bethune-Peterson. "And frankly, that wasn't like the Dan that I knew. He'd changed, but at the time, I had no idea why."

"You used the phrase, 'at the time,' which implies that you understand the reasons for his actions now. Is that true?"

"It is," replied Bethune-Peterson. "I was completely baffled at first, but later, it all came together." She paused, her head cocking to one side. "But you know what? I think it would be better if you finished your questions first. Maybe with some background, you'll see that I'm right, and you can close up shop and go home."

It wasn't the first time that Rebecca had questioned someone who thought they had all the answers but wanted to make her work for them. As to why people did that, one possibility was that they were lying, and they were using this tactic to "sell" their fiction. After all, what could be more convincing to the target of a falsehood than finding support for it themselves? That assumed, of course, that the dupe didn't realize they had been subtly guided to the conclusion they'd reached. The use of this tactic, however, wasn't proof Bethune-Peterson was intentionally telling a lie; she might fully believe the version of events she was trying to sell. So, as is the case with most tells, an instance of it is consistent with being deceitful, but not proof of it.

With her questions about the scene at the restaurant completed, Rebecca turned her attention back to the two incidents that had occurred about the same time as the disappearing deposits. "OK. Let's go on. Nicole mentioned that a local newspaper somehow got a copy of an old marketing concept report that Mr. Peterson wrote, and he apparently got some pretty bad press from it."

Rebecca had read the column as part of her homework on the case, and "bad press" was an understatement.

The writer had roasted Peterson, calling his report "Neanderthal thinking." And if that wasn't enough, in the first paragraph, the writer apologized to Neanderthals, saying that perhaps he was doing them a disservice with the comparison.

Bethune-Peterson, however, just waved a hand in the air as if shooing away an annoying insect.

"That may have made an impression on Nicole, but it was largely inconsequential. HomeRight was soon making the front pages of the business section of the papers on a rather consistent basis because of poor financial performance. And that started with the cash flow issue. Randy's naivety in the early days wasn't anything that started or furthered HomeRight's downturn. And besides, my husband was the one who kept that story alive. He often used that document in new-hire orientations to show the progress the company had made."

"But apparently the copy that the papers had was missing the date. No one could tell that these ideas were part of the past rather than current plans," replied Rebecca.

"You're assuming that it originally had a date. Back in those days, it was mostly Randy, and he didn't know if the company had a future or not. He jotted down a few concepts, then sent them to a friend at another company. Fortunately, the man was a good enough friend to be truthful, and he told Randy the concepts were already five years out of date. It was those kinds of experiences that led him to hire Dan Milgrom. Randy could visualize and communicate, but Dan knew marketing and was an expert on financial controls."

"So, you're saying the marketing concept document never had a date on it?" asked Rebecca.

"I'm saying, I don't know, but it's possible."

"Do you have a copy?"

"No, but you can probably get one from almost anyone at HomeRight."

Was Bethune-Peterson correct in considering the press's critique "inconsequential" for the company, and therefore, easily forgotten by her husband? Perhaps. After all, dissecting the policies of a business was what financial columnists did. Maybe the story wasn't that much more damning than a thousand others. Not being an avid reader of the business pages, Rebecca wasn't sure.

But for Bethune-Peterson to recall so little about a document that was often referenced at work and that had gotten slammed in the papers seemed odd. There was, however, a simple explanation—the document didn't support the version of reality that she favored. Long before one of her FBI training classes had given a name to the phenomenon, calling it "confirmation bias," Rebecca had held the belief that people hear what they want to hear and largely ignored or discounted the rest. Basically, Bethune-Peterson recalled little about the document because, to her, it was just so much background noise. At least, that was one possibility.

"OK. I'll see if I can get a copy elsewhere. Nicole also mentioned a story about a young man your husband allegedly propositioned. Charges were never brought because he was of age, but the damage had already been done. Any idea where that story came from?"

"The same place as the story about the woman in Omaha who gave birth to a goat, I suppose." Bethune-Peterson looked to the ceiling and slowly shook her head. She looked back down at Rebecca.

"If you're literally asking, do I know the source of the story, I do. He was staying at Jen's Place, although I don't recall meeting him. But the bottom line is, that story was more painful personally than any effect it had on business. I found it incredibly distasteful as well as patently false."

Bethune-Peterson looked away a moment as if reliving that pain. After a moment, she returned her gaze to Rebecca. "Look, I love Nicole like a daughter, but you have to remember—she's an engineer turned shelter director. She has no background in business. No investor's going to care about some trashy tabloid gossip, even if it does make the business news. Nicole's heart is in the right place, but her interpretation of the facts is ... well, for want of a better term, misguided. You need to look at the company's financial performance because that's why my husband was voted out. Not rumors and reports from ancient history."

If this was Bethune-Peterson's way of subtly guiding her toward her version of events, Rebecca didn't want to see a hard sell. Look to the numbers and ignore the rest. Why? Wasn't it all part of a dark cloud that had gathered over her husband in those days before he took his life? But in any case, Bethune-Peterson's feelings were clear.

"Actually, I did take a look at HomeRight's performance in the months before the vote of no confidence from the board," said Rebecca. "And they were in a financial tailspin. So, tell me, was your husband preparing for the worst? Did he, for example, have a succession plan at work in case this trend continued?"

"He did. Dan Milgrom was first in line, with leadership falling to Whitten if Dan wasn't available."

"Had your husband announced his intentions to retire any time in the months before he was removed from his position at HomeRight?"

"What the hell has that got to do with anything?" snapped Bethune-Peterson.

The woman's question and the edge in her tone caught Rebecca by surprise. Wasn't the reason for the question obvious? Apparently, it wasn't to her. "It's just that if your husband's retirement was imminent, Mr. Milgrom would have no reason to defame your husband in order to take his job."

"Yeah, I suppose," she admitted with some reluctance. "But we know Dan wasn't trying to ruin Randy. He resigned soon after Randy was voted out, so he didn't take the job even when it was his. And unless Whitten was going to get both Randy and Dan removed from the company, he had no reason to make false claims, either."

She had ample confirmation that Milgrom had resigned after Peterson's ouster but before his death—Nicole, the papers, and now, Bethune-Peterson. That sequence certainly introduced some doubt about Milgrom's motivation to criminally defame Peterson, although the possibility that he and Whitten were cooperating was still viable. Milgrom would help push Peterson out and then sit back and collect under-the-table checks from Whitten for the rest of his life.

Bethune-Peterson also wanted to exclude Whitten from suspicion because he wasn't next in line after Peterson. But all it would take was Milgrom mentioning his intention to follow his boss out the door, and suddenly, Whitten had the reason he needed. Rebecca made a note to follow up on this possibility later since Bethune-Peterson wasn't the right person to ask anyway.

"So, tell me," said Rebecca, "couldn't Mr. Milgrom or Mr. Whitten have faked these financial problems?"

"Absolutely not," replied Bethune-Peterson. "We're a publicly traded company. No one could get away with something like that."

"Perhaps not forever," replied Rebecca. "But over the shorter term, the timing of revenue and expenses can be adjusted, right? If nothing else, net operating losses can be carried forward."

Bethune-Peterson stared for a moment, her jaw set. "I think you're out of your league, Ms. Marte. Unless the FBI trained you on white-collar crime, I doubt you know more about accounting than what's necessary to balance a checkbook."

Rebecca figured that Bethune-Peterson had looked into her background—that action fit with the woman's resistance to her involvement—and her reference to the FBI proved it. But that didn't change the facts, which in this case meant Bethune-Peterson was due an admission.

"You're right. I don't have the skill to 'follow the money' if the path has been hidden. But given your belief that the company's financial performance is the key to understanding everything that happened, I thought you might have gotten an expert to examine the books, see if anything was amiss that might have weighed heavily on your husband's mind."

Bethune-Peterson's face turned red. "I don't know why you insist on getting into the weeds. All you have to do is look at the general financial trends, not some minor operating loss carried over from last year."

At some point, Bethune-Peterson had retrieved a handkerchief from a pocket, and now, she was wringing it so viciously that Rebecca thought the fabric might tear. But after a moment, the woman mastered her emotions.

"Look, I've had a long day," she said, relinquishing her stranglehold on the handkerchief. "And if you drove in today from St. Louis, so have you. How about we call it a night, and we can finish this up in a day or two?"

They had gone far enough into the interview that Rebecca figured Bethune-Peterson wouldn't back out now. And though she knew she was far from sleep—the constant concentration of driving had become a useless nervous energy in her body and mind—she also knew her focus wasn't good. How many nuances had she missed in Bethune-Peterson's words? How often had she overlooked a nonverbal cue that spoke louder than what she had said?

"I think that's a good idea. Could we make it Tuesday afternoon?" Rebecca hoped to meet the rest of the principles—the Milgroms and Whitten—on Monday if that was possible.

Bethune-Peterson paused a moment. "Tuesday afternoon would be fine, but it'll need to be later, say around 4 o'clock."

"OK. I guess we're done."

"Before we adjourn," said Bethune-Peterson, "I'm going to give you the facts. Maybe if you have time to sleep on them, you'll see we have nothing left to talk about."

"OK, let's hear them," replied Rebecca.

"I'm going to make your job really, really easy." She paused. "It pains me to say this about my partner in life for nearly forty years, but Dan and Whitten were right. Randy was dragging the company down. He'd become forgetful and careless. He even forgot our last ever anniversary together, and that wasn't like him." Her voice cracked as she offered the only personal reference she'd given since the start of the talk.

Rebecca gave her a moment.

"Basically, the rock on which HomeRight had been built was crumbling. Dan did what he had to for the company and the shareholders, and now he's suffering for being honest and conscientious. And while Whitten filled the vacuum left by my husband, he didn't orchestrate anything. He had no reason to, he had no way to, and frankly, he lacked the charisma to convince anyone to help him. So, do the job Nicole hired you to do, and I'll go along with the charade. But frankly, you can start writing your final report tonight because nothing's going to change these facts."

Late Evening, The Milgrom Residence, Lone Tree, CO

"Honey, James Whitten is on the phone," called Miranda to her husband.

Milgrom got up from his armchair near the fireplace in his study and moved to the desk. He had a smartphone, but since retirement, he had often let the battery run down. And why not? It wasn't like anyone was going to call him with an emergency when he was out. And besides, Miranda always had hers if they went anywhere.

"Got it," he called to his wife as he picked up. "Evening, James. To what do I owe the pleasure of this call?"

"Just wanted to see how you were doing," Whitten replied. "Hope your AC is up for the challenge, since it's been what? Nearly a week with temperatures pushing a hundred?"

"'Bout that," replied Milgrom.

He'd worked with James Whitten for over fifteen years, and he couldn't recall once in that time when the man had talked about the weather. Now, every phone call seemed to start with the latest forecast, a lament about the conditions they had to endure, or on very rare occasions, something positive in the outlook. But at least he called. Few others from the office ever did. Milgrom tuned into the man's monologue long enough to hear the words "La Niña," and he knew the meteorological part of the chat wasn't over yet.

After a while, Whitten said, "We started the rollout of the new à la carte menu for agent-designed warranties today."

This was the part of these calls that Milgrom loved, and he could hear the anticipation in his voice as he asked, "How'd it go?"

"Like a charm. Even though ninety percent of the final document is still standard verbiage, it looks like the real estate agent working with the seller had inventoried every system and appliance in the house and provided a tailored level of protection. And you'll never guess what coverage has increased the most in our early returns compared to our baseline policies."

"Some form of supplemental coverage for the roof?" replied Milgrom, knowing that Colorado weather could be tough on roofs and covering the deductible on the insurance could get expensive.

"Close, but that came in third. It was a re-keying service."

"No kidding," said Milgrom. "Locksmiths are expensive and getting one to change every door to work with the same key would cost a pretty penny, but I never would have thought that."

"Me either. It's still small potatoes compared to warranties on refrigerators and ranges, but a lot more of the agents are picking it up, probably because of the impression it creates. An agent that's getting to that level of detail obviously has your best interests at heart."

Or at least it would look that way, thought Milgrom. "Well, I suppose it wouldn't be a bad thing to have if you bought a house with enough external doors."

Whitten continued for a few more minutes, extolling the virtues of letting the agents and sellers design the policies rather than trying to carry all the variations people might want. And since there was a small surcharge for using this capability, they were selling the same protections at slightly higher rates. It was a win for HomeRight, whatever the agent and seller decided.

After a while, Whitten asked, "So, what's new with you?"

"Same ol', same ol'," Milgrom replied. But when Whitten remained silent, he began searching his memory for anything newsworthy. The problem was, every topic that came to mind—his allergies; his lawn, which seemed to get browner every day; his car, which was in for repairs to the radiator—seemed too close to the weather. If he wasn't careful, he'd end up in another climatological digression.

Just when he was about to give up and mention his dying yard, Whitten said, "I ran into Eleanor the other day. She seemed pretty upbeat compared to a couple of months ago."

"Really. I saw her Saturday, and she seemed about the same as always to me. Crotchety and stubborn as ever."

"You saw her yesterday? Or did you mean eight days ago?"

Damn it, he'd done it again. When he wasn't going to work and trying to cram the rest of his life into a weekend, it was easy to lose track of the days of the week. "Sorry, I guess it was Friday. Anyway, you say she was doing better?" he asked, sure he hadn't noticed any change in her disposition. But then, if he couldn't tell Friday from Saturday, maybe he had missed something.

"Seemed that way to me. I wondered if she'd finally gotten onboard with the private investigator that someone wanted to bring in to look at Randy's death."

"You mean, Nicole Veles. She's the one that wanted to bring in the PI," said Milgrom, wondering why the name had escaped Whitten. He had known it before. "But I think that Ellie getting onboard with it is pretty unlikely. She thought the whole thing was ridiculous from the start."

"So, nothing new on that front?"

"Well, actually, there is. The PI's in town, and he's coming by here tomorrow morning, although if anything, that might make Ellie less happy. She'll start worrying that Veles is wasting her money."

"Hey, I know several guys that are PIs. Maybe I know him. What's his name?"

"I'm not sure. Miranda took the message, but you wouldn't know him anyway. He's from St. Louis."

"Can you get Miranda back on the phone? You've really got my curiosity up."

Miranda didn't care for Whitten. Well, he hadn't thought much of the man either, although now it seemed like he was trying to make amends. But to call his wife back to talk to a man she didn't like and provide the name of a PI he couldn't possibly know wouldn't go over well.

"Sorry, but she said good night when she gave me the call. I'll ask tomorrow," he said, knowing he had no intention of doing so. Whitten would never remember to bring it up again, and he'd keep his wife happy.

"Sure. Let me know what she says. Say, the ball team really took it on the chin yesterday. What was the final? Twelve to three, or something like that?"

Sports was the third of their three standard topics—weather, work, sports—so the call was near its end. "Twelve to four, I think it was. But at least they worked a triple play. I'd never seen one of those before."

Too soon for Milgrom, the call was over. He was starting to look forward to them. He was starting to think that maybe Whitten wasn't such a bad guy after all. But whenever he had that thought, he also recalled the old saying, "A leopard never changes its spots." And in all the years he'd known James Whitten, he'd never seen the man do anything that didn't benefit him personally.

Late Evening, Jen's Place

Rebecca had only been going through the motions for the last half-hour.

She had thanked Bethune-Peterson for her time and showed her out. She'd unpacked her work files and found places for them in drawers and file cabinets. She had paced the room and checked the view at each window. But now, as she sat at her desk, her elbows on its top and her head resting between nested fingers, she knew she had accomplished nothing. She doubted she could even recall where she'd stored anything with her mind so full of some of Bethune-Peterson's final words—the rock on which HomeRight was built was crumbling.

Back in St. Louis, Nicole had offered evidence of foul play leading up to Peterson's suicide—damaging business reports with mysteriously missing dates, malicious rumors about his sexual orientation, a long-trusted ally who had inexplicably become a vicious detractor. And though Rebecca had questioned whether bullying someone in the boardroom to the point of committing suicide was possible, her client's concerns had created a shadow of doubt in Rebecca's mind about the innocence of the situation.

That shadow, however, had faded considerably under the million-lumen spotlight of Bethune-Peterson's commonsense interpretation of events. Yes, she had picked up on a ploy that might indicate Bethune-Peterson was being less than completely forthcoming. But now, she wondered if the woman was only steering her toward a version of reality that she truly believed.

In that reality, her husband had become absent-minded, and his carelessness was hurting the company. Rumors of his sexual orientation and a naïve marketing concept report had little relevance to her beliefs because they didn't directly affect the bottom line. With the business starting to flounder, Milgrom had stepped in only to suffer the pangs of guilt for doing so. And Whitten was just doing what he had always done—intellectually sparring with the late president and CEO for the betterment of their products and services. And though she was admittedly tired from the long drive, Rebecca had picked up on nothing else that suggested she was lying. True, there was still ground to cover, but nothing in the woman's story seemed amiss.

And if there was truth behind Bethune-Peterson's beliefs, then her client's concerns about the man's suicide were the product of a vulnerable mind. Nicole had lived too long in a fictional world created by her kidnappers solely to keep her alone and helpless. No wonder she found evil in the events surrounding Peterson's death. But Rebecca had decided before she left St. Louis to leave that possibility unexplored until she had exhausted all other options. So, once again, she pushed the idea to the back of her mind to focus on the case at hand.

Although Rebecca didn't regret the impromptu meeting with Bethune-Peterson—it had secured at least some begrudging cooperation—she wanted to be better prepared for their next talk. And motives for a wife to rid herself of a husband were the place to start. Perhaps the widow had designs on someone else and wanted a divorce, but her husband wouldn't agree? Or he concurred, but a pre-nuptial agreement would have left her penniless and that wasn't acceptable? Or he had been the reason she couldn't pursue the lifestyle she desired, and it was finally time to rid herself of his penny-pinching and staid ways? But when she examined the image of this fast and loose woman she'd formed in her mind's eye, she had to admit that Bethune-Peterson didn't fit it particularly well.

The means for her to create the black cloud that hung over her husband, however, were a bit more straightforward. She could have gotten the young man staying at Jen's Place to play the role of victim in a sexual encounter, then paid him and his mother to disappear. And she probably could have found a way to delete the deposit emails and to create some of her husband's erratic behavior at work. But even so, would that explain all the financial havoc at HomeRight? Had her late husband lost his touch that completely and that suddenly? If not, then someone inside HomeRight was creating that impression.

As the past Chief Operating Officer, James Whitten was certainly a candidate. So, if he was the inside man helping Bethune-Peterson, how had she secured his cooperation? If it wasn't lust, which seemed even less characteristic of the practical, gruff Bethune-Peterson the more Rebecca considered it, then it might be love or money. Love would leave a trail she could follow—sightings at intimate dinners at out-of-the-way locations, separate trips that just happened to align on the calendar, trinkets that she cherished that hadn't come from her husband. And though Whitten was already wealthy, she wasn't about to ignore cash as the tool Bethune-Peterson had used to gain his assistance. In some, having money just created the desire for more. She'd have to find out what the widow stood to gain financially from her husband's death.

When she turned her thoughts to Milgrom as Bethune-Peterson's co-conspirator, she found that all of the same questions applied. And then, of course, the inside man who was helping Bethune-Peterson might be someone she had yet to hear about. Just because Nicole suspected Whitten or Milgrom, there were several hundred more employees at the company that might have found a way to cook the books.

Rebecca got no farther in her internal planning session, however, as someone knocked on the door. Instinctively, her hand went into the second right-hand desk drawer, her fingers brushing the cool metal of her firearm. Though she'd placed it there without thought, it was exactly where it would be in St. Louis

... if she was working under an elevated level of threat. But that wasn't the case here. In fact, there was no known threat—not yet anyway—so she made a mental note to move it to a safer location until there was.

"Come in," Rebecca called.

The door opened and Nicole stepped in carrying a folder of paper that must have been four inches thick. "Ellie stopped by on her way out. She seemed to think things were on track."

"I'd agree. We didn't get finished, so we're getting back together Tuesday afternoon. But at least now, we understand our positions." Rebecca hadn't intended for her statement to be so close to reality, but Nicole didn't seem to notice. "I believe you said Daniel Milgrom and his wife would probably meet with me to discuss the case?"

"Yes, and I confirmed it with Miranda yesterday. They're expecting my call to schedule a time."

"I should make that call," replied Rebecca. "I need to mention a few expectations for the interviews. You don't happen to have their number, do you?"

Nicole pulled a phone from her pocket, hit a few keys, and read off the number, her smile fading slightly as she did. "My calendar is almost as open as yours, so just about any time Monday or Tuesday should work fine," she said.

Now Rebecca understood the shift in her client's mood. "Sorry, Nicole, but I thought we covered this in St. Louis. I need to do the interviews alone."

"I remember, but I was going to do the introductions and figured there'd be no problem if I sat quietly and watched."

"It sounds like you've already done the introductions." Nicole's face dropped even more. Why couldn't she have a client who just wanted to pay the fee and forget about the case until the reports started rolling in? Of course, if their positions were reversed, Rebecca knew she'd feel the same way that Nicole did.

"If you have time after managing the shelter and covering your part-time biomedical engineering work ...."

"I've taken a temporary leave from HealthVie."

Rebecca mostly suppressed a laugh. "You can take leave from part-time work?"

"You can if you're good enough," Nicole replied with a grin.

"OK," said Rebecca. "Then, if you feel comfortable with this, you can help me get all the police reports related to the case. Ms. Bethune-Peterson probably has a set you can copy."

"You mean these reports?" Nicole asked, holding out the file folder. "It's got everything the police gave Ellie. She didn't want them around, so I saved them from the trash. I thought they might come in handy."

"They will," replied Rebecca. "Anything interesting in them?"

Nicole grinned again. "Knew I'd look, huh?" She paused a moment, her eyes narrowing. "I guess there was one thing that surprised me. The gun that Mr. Peterson used in the suicide was fired twice. The first bullet grazed his scalp above the ear before lodging in the wall behind where he was seated. The idea is that he flinched with the first shot, so the slug glanced off his head. Then, the second shot finished the job."

"You don't sound convinced," said Rebecca, knowing she had some reservations about this scenario herself.

"It's just that I can't imagine taking a second shot with all the blood and pain caused by the first."

"Scalp wounds often bleed freely, but they may not be that painful," replied Rebecca. "So, it's possible it happened just the way they said."

"But there's another possibility?"

"Technically, there are dozens. For example, perhaps an unknown assailant snuck into the room, grabbed Peterson's gun and pressed it to his temple, and killed him with the first shot. Then, he or she placed the gun in Peterson's hand and fired the second shot so it grazed his head before becoming lodged in the wall. That way ...."

"That way, Peterson's fingerprints end up on the gun," volunteered Nicole.

"And the gunshot residue ends up on his hands," added Rebecca. "And even though he was dead before the second shot, the wounds happened very close in time and location. Even the best medical examiner would struggle to put them in sequence."

Rebecca figured there was little chance she'd get a positive response to her next question, but she needed to ask anyway. "So, since you've already finished getting the reports, do you want to take a few days off?"

"No, I'd like to help," Nicole replied, although her expression when Rebecca asked—a stunned look of disappointment—spoke more than those five words.

"OK, then how about working on some deep background on Daniel Milgrom—friends, pastimes, things like that. If he's active on social media, that can be a goldmine. And you can probably get a thumbnail of his social life from his wife. You OK with that?"

"Absolutely. I don't know Miranda nearly as well as Ellie, although she's always inviting me over for coffee. I'll just take her up on the offer. So, what's after that?"

"We compile and compare our findings in a day or two. Then, we go from there."

Rebecca felt somewhat guilty because Nicole's assignment was largely make-work. The information itself was potentially valuable, but she didn't know if she could trust Nicole's filtering of it. Would she return with a single social media post from Milgrom that mentioned Whitten and declare she had proof of a conspiracy? Or would she become so focused on bullying and suicide that she missed things like changes in Milgrom's affluence? Basically, most of her work would need to be checked. But then, two sets of eyes were almost always better than one. And besides, if the smile on Nicole's face was any indication, the involvement made her client happy.

"You've never mentioned a backdoor to James Whitten's life via his wife. Any chance that approach could work for us again?"

"None," replied Nicole. "The rumors run from 'it's a loveless marriage' to 'they have a mutual infidelity pact.' And frankly, I don't know anyone who runs in his wife's social circles." Nicole paused to shake her head slowly. "I don't even remember her name off the top of my head."

"OK. Just your gut feel on this, but do you think there's any chance Whitten would meet with me?"

Rebecca half expected Nicole to break out laughing, but she didn't. Rather, she seemed to be appraising her with the same sort of look she might have used to select a cut of meat for a barbeque. After a moment, she said, "If you send him a snapshot of you in those shorts and T-shirt, he'll go for a meeting."

"So, the infidelity pact wasn't a joke."

"All I can say is that he's often seen around town with attractive women who aren't his wife. She, on the other hand, seems to travel almost constantly."

"OK. I'll see about getting a meeting with him, preferably without resorting to a photo. Unless you have questions, the buzz in my head is finally going away and I'm bushed. When's breakfast around here?"

"Five-thirty to seven," replied Nicole. "We like to get an early start. And by the way, thanks for giving me something to do, even if it is trivial stuff."

"Don't say that," Rebecca snapped.

It was a harsh response, and Nicole looked shocked, but Rebecca had no intention of retracting it. She'd lost one partner on the job and had nearly lost Doc, and they were both fully aware of the threat. Nicole, on the other hand, was preparing herself for boredom, not the possibility of danger.

"Unless you've already decided there's nothing suspicious in Mr. Peterson's death, we are investigating a potential crime. Complacency in any form is your enemy."

Nicole blinked several times, the rest of her expression shifting slowly from startled to thoughtful. "Thanks," she said with a single nod. "Other than what I see on TV or in the movies, I don't know anything about what you do. I appreciate the warning."

"Just follow my lead and communicate all of your concerns, even if it's just a vague feeling. You do that and you'll be fine," said Rebecca. She received a determined nod from her client in reply.

"OK. I'm going to try to set up a meeting with the Milgroms tomorrow morning and one with Whitten later in the day. I'll let you know. After that, I've got a little light reading to do." She held a hand out toward the stack of papers Nicole had brought her. "Shall we plan on getting back together Tuesday afternoon before I meet with Ms. Bethune–Peterson?"

"Sure," replied Nicole. "Although I'm not sure I'll have a chance to talk to Miranda before that."

"No, you probably won't. If Milgrom has much of a social media presence at all, going through it will take some time, but that's fine. You can talk to Ms. Milgrom later."

"OK."

Nicole left the office with a look of determination on her face. Rebecca's feelings, however, weren't a match. Hers ran more toward resignation with a touch of foreboding. She either had to formalize these *ad hoc* associations with clients like Nicole to include standard training and insurance to cover the inevitable mishaps or she had to stop allowing them. And since she had no intention of doing the former, it had to be the latter.

"Just one last time," she said to the empty room.

MONDAY, AUGUST 29

Morning, The Milgrom Residence

Rebecca sipped the last of her coffee from a paper cup. The steam from the brew had long since dissipated in the warm, calm air of the morning, but the caffeine would still do its job.

She glanced at the home of Daniel and Miranda Milgrom through the side window of her car. It was a large one-story ranch with a set of windows fronted by a long porch on the right, the front door in the middle, and a triple-car garage on the left. If the garages had been a porch with a wooden railing and two stone columns holding up the roof or the porch had been three garage doors, the house would have been perfectly symmetrical. As it was, there was still a pleasing balance to the house's façade.

Clearly, it was a nice home. It wasn't, however, the palatial mansion she would have expected for someone who was being paid for his silence. Of course, the turnover in HomeRight's leadership was relatively recent. Perhaps Milgrom was waiting until an increase in his affluence was less suspicious. Or if ascending to the company's top spot had been his plan—a ploy that was then cut short by an attack of conscience—this is exactly where he'd be living. The same old place he had owned for the last twelve years, a fact Rebecca had established online.

Rebecca glanced at her phone. When she'd called at 8 o'clock to make an appointment to see the Milgroms, Miranda had said, "Come on over." It was like she was expecting the call, which in a way, she was. They'd settled on 9 o'clock. And because scheduling this first meeting had gone so quickly, Rebecca had decided to press her luck. She followed up with a call to Whitten who, once she got through to the man, amazingly used the exact same words: "Come on over." She suggested 1 o'clock, so as not to rush the Milgrom interview. He said he had a meeting then and countered with an offer of lunch. Rebecca, however, wanted to keep socializing and business separate. He accepted her second suggestion of 11. She just had to make sure she kept the Milgrom interview moving.

The only problem with having the two interviews on one morning—and Rebecca considered this minor and, most likely, ridiculous—was that she had dressed for the reputedly lascivious Whitten. She was showing considerable leg, a tactic that could sometimes distract men from their well-practiced lies. The downside, however, was that her look might also affect Dan Milgrom. All she needed were notes from an interview where her legs seemed the main point of the discussion. Of course, when she put that concern into words, she had to laugh at herself. Surely, Milgrom wasn't sidetracked that easily.

Rebecca glanced at her phone again. It was time. She picked up her notebook from the passenger seat and exited the car. A woman must have been watching from a window because, before Rebecca was halfway up the sidewalk, she came outside. She was a short stout woman with snowy white hair. She shaded her eyes from the morning sun with one hand while she gathered a sweater around her waist with the other, even though it was already warm.

"Ms. Milgrom?"

"It's Miranda, dear," replied the woman. "And you must be Rebecca Marte, that PI from St. Louis that Nicole told us about. You're even more attractive than she said. Twenty years ago, I probably wouldn't have let you in the house—no reason to show Danny what he can't have. But I reckon we're too old to go out and look for greener pastures now."

"Nice to meet you, Miranda. And I promise I'll be on my best behavior around your husband."

That drew a chuckle from the older woman, who now took the opportunity to launch into an extended monologue on the neighborhood. Clearly, Rebecca's challenge in interviewing her would be getting a word in edgewise. When Nicole was trying to fill in details on her husband, on the other hand, the woman's talkativeness would probably be a plus.

While Ms. Milgrom talked, she'd taken Rebecca by the elbow and was guiding her up the steps to the front porch. It struck Rebecca as a quaint custom from a kinder and gentler time, but inappropriate, at least in appearance. Shouldn't she be steadying the older woman? Or was that what the gesture was for?

"Rebecca?"

"Oh, yes, sorry. I was just admiring your home." Only then did Rebecca realize that she was standing on the threshold of an open front door and could see little of the house. Ms. Milgrom, however, didn't seem to notice the inconsistency.

"What, this old place? It's too big. I told Danny we need to downsize. There's way too much for me to clean every week. Now, how do you take your coffee?"

Had the topic of coffee come up? Had she accidentally nodded when it did? "Oh, no coffee for me, thanks. I just finished my second cup from Jen's Place and two's my limit."

"Ah, Jen's Place," said Ms. Milgrom as she closed the front door behind them, her eyes seemingly focused in the distance for an instant. "What a godsend for the community. And that Nicole Veles. She certainly keeps busy, although I don't know her well. So, if you're not having coffee, Danny's here in the study."

Ms. Milgrom stepped through a set of double doors that were probably nine feet tall into a cozy room, complete with a large desk, bookcases that lined the walls, and a seating of four overstuffed armchairs in front of a blazing fire. To Rebecca, the room didn't need the extra heat, but the ambience it created was worthy of a Norman Rockwell painting.

"Who's this?" asked a man seated in one of the armchairs.

"It's the private investigator I told you about."

"You didn't say she was a woman."

"It wasn't relevant." Ms. Milgrom's words made Rebecca smile inwardly. She doubted there were many males, if any, who would have considered gender irrelevant to the job of a private investigator.

"So, I understand you want to talk about Randy Peterson and HomeRight," said the man.

"Danny, where are your manners. Get up and introduce yourself," said Ms. Milgrom, her tone probably the same as she had used on her children when they misbehaved.

"Dan Milgrom. Sorry, but I won't get up to shake your hand. My knees have been a bit achy the last couple of days. Have a seat," he said, holding a hand out toward one of the armchairs in front of the fire. "Miranda, where's this poor woman's coffee?"

"She didn't want any. She's all coffeed up from Jen's Place."

"No offense to Ms. Veles or the woman who does her cooking, but it can't compare with what Miranda makes. Didn't you tell her?"

"Funny, but a sales pitch for my coffee isn't part of my standard greeting to a private investigator."

"Well, maybe it should be."

Rebecca was starting to feel like a spectator at a tennis match as her head swiveled to catch the verbal volleys between the pair. But despite the brusqueness of their comments, there was also an unmistakable undertone of caring. Was a bickering older couple who were still in love a stereotype? Rebecca wasn't sure, but in any case, the description seemed to fit.

"It's nice to meet you, Mr. Milgrom," Rebecca said as she took a seat. "I know it's a difficult time with the loss of your old business partner and friend, and I appreciate you taking the time to talk with me."

"No problem," he said. His forehead wrinkled. "Is this what professional private investigators wear to interview suspects?"

"Danny," said Ms. Milgrom, leaving her castigation at one word.

Rebecca didn't think Mr. Milgrom was necessarily affected by her look, but he'd obviously noticed, and even that much was negative. And if Whitten wasn't distracted, she'd made the wrong call all the way around.

"A lunch date later," she replied, using a readily available half-truth. "And besides, you aren't a suspect. I'm just trying to get some background."

"I'm still not sure why you want to talk about Randy Peterson," said Ms. Milgrom as she, too, sat down. "Is there something suspicious in his death?"

"No, not that I know of." Sometimes when Rebecca said that, it wasn't true, but not in this case. If she had to make a guess, the bullying at work might be a minor contributing factor in Peterson's suicide, but it being unrelated was probably even more likely. "My client just wants a better understanding of the situation surrounding his death."

"A better understanding?" said Mr. Milgrom. "What does that mean?"

That wasn't good. Most people didn't question those kinds of generalities, even if they were—as this one was—largely devoid of substance. Mr. Milgrom was astute, which came as no surprise to Rebecca given the position he had risen to at HomeRight. And yet it was surprising if he was as confused about his past behavior as Nicole believed.

"And your client?" he said. "That's Nicole Veles, right? I'm not sure why she cares."

"Danny, you know why," his wife countered, her scolding tone returning. "She and Ellie are close and she's concerned for her friend."

The mister looked at the missus and shrugged. Rebecca, on the other hand, took Ms. Milgrom's rejoinder as an opportunity to move the discussion away from questions of clients and their objectives. They could waste hours on those topics if Rebecca didn't re-direct them.

"I'd like to start with some background on the company. Its rise has been impressive with gross income exceeding a billion dollars in three of the last five years."

"If you two are going to talk business, is it alright if I excuse myself?" asked Ms. Milgrom. "I don't really keep up with the goings on at HomeRight."

Apparently, Nicole was correct; Ms. Milgrom wasn't that involved with the company. "Sure, but I may have some questions for you later. Will you be around?"

"I'll be here all day, dear. Just give a holler." Rebecca agreed and Ms. Milgrom left the two of them to their discussion.

"So, let me guess," said Milgrom. "Of those five years you mentioned, your real interest is the two outliers. What happened in years three and four when receipts dropped nearly twenty percent and profits followed the same downward spiral?"

Rebecca could see no reason to deny his conjecture, even though she had planned to ease into this topic after a few questions. "That's true. Was there anything going on here in Colorado that might explain the downturn at HomeRight?"

"If you'd taken even a cursory glance at the state's housing market at the time, you'd know that business should have been booming. But something tells me that you've already done that."

"I did," replied Rebecca, his comment further reinforcing her thoughts about his mental capabilities. "But the press can never provide the insight someone in the industry can. Other than the general health of the housing market, which was good, was there anything going on that might have produced the drop in cash flow?"

"Randy Peterson was going on," said Milgrom, then released a long breath. "You've heard about him forgetting to approve the deposits for nearly a month, right?"

"I did. Ms. Bethune-Peterson thought that her husband checking the deposits was just a formality, something to give him a feel for the company's health."

Milgrom nodded. "Yeah. His review was basically a holdover from the old days. As the company's finances got more complex, he'd delegated most of the responsibility. The final review of the deposits was one of the few that he'd kept and, yes, he thought of it as a way to keep his finger on the pulse of the business. Anyway, the incident where he forgot to approve the deposits seemed like the beginning of the end. Things just plain went to heck after that."

"But no problems before that?" asked Rebecca.

Milgrom paused. "I've thought about that a lot, and I don't believe so." He rubbed the back of his neck with a hand. "I was out on sick leave most of October two years ago and the deposit blunder occurred in late November ... or maybe early December. But if anything happened when I was gone, I didn't hear about it."

"If you don't mind me asking, what was the reason for the medical leave?" The chances he'd been treated for something like a brain injury were slight, but a medical issue like that might explain his sudden change in behavior.

"I don't mind," he replied, "although there's no connection between it and HomeRight's transition from well-oiled machine to sinking ship. It was a heart attack."

It wasn't the first time Rebecca had thought that this transition, as Milgrom called it, was quite abrupt. And although she didn't want to dwell on this issue too long—eventually, her expectations would influence his memory—one related question felt safe enough.

But before she could ask, Milgrom said, "The incident with the deposits was totally out of the blue. That's what made it so staggering. And I wasn't the only one who was floored. I talked to the VPs after the meeting, and they all said the same."

"Did you speak with James Whitten about it, too?"

"I did. I expected him to say something like, 'The old man's sure showing his age.' But that day, he was more flabbergasted than any of us. He kept shaking his head and saying, 'What the hell just happened?' He must have said that five times. I remember because I never really liked people swearing at work. Course nowadays, you can't go to the movies without hearing a four-letter word every thirty seconds."

Rebecca mentally corrected her earlier thought. The Milgroms were from a kinder, gentler, and less profane time. "You mentioned that overlooking the deposits seemed to be the start of the problems that Mr. Peterson was having. Do you recall what came next?"

Milgrom looked around the room as if seeking the answer. "Next?" he said slowly. "I'm not sure I can put them in chronological order."

"That's OK. Just some of the things that came up over the next few weeks."

Milgrom searched the room again with his eyes. "Randy's slipups were all over the place. He'd forget to sign a directive or issue it two or three times. A report with some of his early marketing concepts got leaked outside the company making him look completely inept. I think that one might have happened before the deposits. But anyway, it was things like that."

"That marketing report?" said Rebecca. "Do you happen to know if it had a date on it when it was written?" Although the report having a date that had been removed seemed a minor detail, it would help establish premeditation if someone had gone to the trouble to remove the date to make Peterson look bad.

"Tough to say," replied Milgrom. "We've used that report to give people a feel for the company's roots—and a bit of comic relief, I suppose. But when they get a copy, I don't believe there is any date showing. It's probably long been covered up by the headers we've used over the years. One year, it'll say, 'We're lucky to still be in business.' The next, it might be something like, 'From the humblest of beginnings.' But obviously, whatever the paper received didn't include one of those banners or a date, or they would have known it was ancient history and not operational."

Without the copy of the report that the newspaper had received, this line of questioning was becoming a dead end. No one seemed to know if the original was dated, and even if it was, the date could have been covered up by any of the numerous headers that had been added later. It would be her luck that the one header that didn't imply the report was water under the bridge was the one the media had gotten.

"I suppose it ...," started Rebecca.

Milgrom interrupted her. "You probably think some of the mistakes I mentioned are minor ... and they are. But when it becomes a pattern, it got on my nerves and made me angry."

Actually, Rebecca was thinking that anger was an odd reaction to his boss's mistakes. Concern, doubt, and even confusion seemed more likely. But after some consideration, she conceded that the emotional and physical toll of continually correcting his old friend would wear on the man.

"When Mr. Peterson mentioned the same directive two or three times, was he forgetting he'd already issued that policy? Or was he repeating himself so people would remember the change?"

Again, the man's gaze swept the room, only this time, the path was more erratic as his eyes jerked left and right. "I don't know," he said as he rubbed a hand through his hair. "Maybe both ... at different times."

"So, you weren't necessarily following up with him on all of these issues?"

Milgrom whipped his head around, surprising Rebecca with a glare. Then, he closed his eyes and released a long sigh.

"Yeah, I followed up with him," he said so softly that Rebecca leaned forward in her chair to hear. "Sometimes he'd admit he'd forgotten. But mostly, Randy made excuses till I couldn't take it anymore. He could make me so angry."

Little of this interview was going the way Rebecca had expected after talking to Nicole and Bethune-Peterson. Nicole had painted Milgrom as a confused man, and yet now, he seemed completely lucid. Sure, he couldn't recall the exact chronology of Peterson's mistakes, but since over a year had passed, she would have been more suspicious if he could recite them in order. And from the description that Bethune-Peterson had provided, she expected Milgrom to refer to Peterson as his brother of another mother, not the source of his ire. And asking him about their working relationship only produced exasperation. She needed a different tack if she was to discover how he felt now about his earlier actions.

"I'd like to get a little background on HomeRight. Maybe talk a little about when you and Randolph Peterson were just getting started."

"Sure, if you think it would help," replied Milgrom. He obviously liked the change in topic as a smile crept onto his face.

Within three minutes of starting that conversation, one thing was apparent to Rebecca—Milgrom wasn't confused about the early days. He knew dates and figures. He knew systems and capabilities. And where she'd found the corresponding information online, his recollections were spot on. But most of all, he remembered his good friend, a man who he'd stood beside for years as they built the company.

Recalling the glory days, however, was one thing. His role in forcing his old friend out of his company—and the emotional turmoil it would create—might be something entirely different. She just needed an opening to explore what had happened two years ago to change everything. And then Milgrom provided that opening without even being asked.

"I remember when Randy picked up some survey that was supposed to tell you if you were the persuasive type," Milgrom said, putting air quotes around the last two words. "It was probably supposed to tell you if you'd be any good at picking up girls at bars, but he thought it had some interesting marketing ideas. So, he wrote them up with some other thoughts and sent them out for comment. I'd say that was a big mistake because he got blasted, but it led to my hiring. So, I guess that cloud had a silver lining ... at least for me."

"For the company, too, as I understand it. So, is this the same marketing concept document that got leaked to the press? The document that made him look so inept?"

"Inept?" repeated Milgrom, perhaps recalling he had just used the same word. He held out two empty hands, then shrugged. "You have to remember, laughs between friends are one thing. The public laughing at you is another." He frowned.

Rebecca waited. She wasn't disappointed with the results as after a moment, Milgrom filled the silence.

"I suppose one friend laughing at another is worse, isn't it?" Milgrom said, his gaze dropping to his lap. "Sometimes, I could pass off Randy's missteps as minor, not worth mentioning. But at other times, I felt trapped into taking a stand. If I didn't expose his fantasies, he'd take us all down. Starting a couple of years ago, it seemed like acrimony at work was always the solution. I couldn't seem to stop myself from ranting if he so much as forgot to cross a T."

"You're saying your criticisms of Mr. Peterson were out of proportion to his mistakes?"

"Sometimes." He paused. "Mostly, I suppose. When he was alive, I never called him to apologize for being so judgmental, such a jerk, and now, I'll never have the chance. Of course, I still don't know what I'd say. It all seemed so strange, so out of the blue."

And with that statement, the story that Rebecca had expected after her talks with Nicole and Bethune-Peterson had fallen into place. Milgrom and Peterson had been close, but then he had turned on his old friend for reasons he couldn't explain.

Now the question was, how much of that description was true? If Milgrom had conspired with Whitten to remove Peterson or if he had tried to do it on his own, his self-proclaimed confusion could be nothing more than a smokescreen. He wouldn't want to admit to mental clarity because that would be confessing an intent to displace his boss. So, when Peterson turns his Glock on himself after Milgrom has carried out his smear campaign, his death might be considered manslaughter. The death wasn't premeditated, but Milgrom's actions that produced it were.

If Milgrom wouldn't admit to consciously organizing a psychological assault on the former president and CEO, perhaps he'd implicate someone else as a way to further deflect blame. "In your opinion, how much did Mr. Whitten's criticisms contribute to the board removing Randolph Peterson?"

"Not a darn bit," he replied with a bit of a smirk. "Whitten was always second-guessing Randy and the board knew that." His expression became more serious. "My criticisms, on the other hand, weren't common, and for that reason, they caught the board's attention. But more to the point, the problems I uncovered almost undoubtedly put Randy on the brink. I've even wondered if they were the final nudge that put him over the edge."

If Rebecca hadn't already been seated, her knees might have buckled under her. Milgrom had just wondered aloud if he had driven Peterson to take his own life. Didn't he see his possible culpability if that was true? Or did he have reason to discount it already? "You said you've thought about the effect of your business concerns on Mr. Peterson. Have you come to any conclusion?"

"Left to my own devices, I'd probably still be wondering, but the police answered it for me. Early on, I think they suspected I'd gone after Randy to steal his job. My rants about his work performance were so damning that he took his life. But later, they dropped the idea."

The police had already considered Nicole's theory that Peterson had been bullied to the point of suicide and had rejected it? Depending on how they came to that conclusion, this case could be over by this afternoon. "Do you happen to know why the police dropped this idea?"

Milgrom tipped his head to one side in what seemed a half-shrug. "I couldn't just ask why I wasn't a suspect any longer because they'd never said I was one. But even by the second time I met with the detectives, I knew I wasn't being considered in Randy's death. So, I asked one of them if there was evidence of foul play. He started off saying he couldn't talk about an active investigation, but he ended up giving me a pretty complete account of why they didn't think so. First, the suicide note is authentic. You know Ms. Bethune-Peterson, right?"

"Yes, we've met," replied Rebecca.

"Although it was typed, Eleanor verified his signature and she confirmed he wrote it—it had the words he used, the way he phrased things. I haven't seen it, but apparently, he apologizes to Eleanor and talks about how devastating it was to lose his company. He takes responsibility ...." Milgrom paused to swallow some of the pain that had risen to his throat. "He takes responsibility for his mistakes, and he lays the blame for his ouster at the feet of the board. He felt they should have given him more time."

Rebecca had read the suicide note the night before, and she recognized the parts Milgrom had mentioned—Peterson's apology, the admission of his mistakes, and his anger toward the board. All of that matched. But what she still found unusual was that his denunciation of the board sounded like unfinished business. When he placed the cause of his downfall in the hands of a half-dozen men and women, why had he felt so powerless to change their opinion? Why would he see death as his only option rather than fighting them? But then, perhaps trying to find reason in the writings of a suicidal man was wasted effort.

Rebecca glanced at her notebook, certain she had completed the questions she had time to ask but doublechecking anyway. Now assured, she said, "That's everything I have for now. Is there anything you'd like to ask or add?"

The last question was her standard for ending an interview and seldom did the interviewee have more. But this talk had been nothing if not unexpected.

"I do," said Milgrom after a moment of hesitation. "I'm being followed."

Apparently, the pattern of anomalies was continuing. "The same person? On multiple occasions?"

Any hope that she'd misunderstood vanished when he nodded and said, "Yes. Male. White. Maybe six and a half feet tall. Big guy, solid build. I don't go many places these days, but I've seen him in the parking lots at the grocery store and the country club. And twice, he's been across and down the street a little way."

"Do you think you could identify him from a picture if we went to the police station?"

"Not a chance," said Milgrom. "He's never been closer than maybe forty or fifty yards. But a guy that big sticks out. And he's always dressed the same— blue work shirt, jeans, and a tan baseball cap pulled low. The time at the country club, there were several people around, so I started walking toward him. For a big man, he's very agile. He jumped over a wooden fence that's about four feet tall and started jogging down the road. And he's obviously smart enough to park off the grounds or they'd have the number on his plates."

"Do your knees feel up to walking to the front of your home?"

Milgrom gave a single soft snort. "My knees are fine. You were an unknown and I didn't feel like welcoming someone into my home who might turn out to be the enemy. Sorry, but I wanted to check you out first."

He stood and started toward the front door with Rebecca needing to hurry to catch up.

"So, I passed?"

"With flying colors. If there's more to Randy's death than meets the eye, Eleanor deserves to know it. And you could be the person to find it. I wasn't going to mention that I couldn't explain my attacks on Randy. I've told a few people that and the conversation has never gone well. But you eased me into that admission with a walk down memory lane. That was well played."

They had reached the front door and Rebecca opened it and stepped out on the porch. "Thanks, but in all fairness, I was told what to look for."

"It was still well done."

Rebecca nodded. "Thanks. So, where did you see this man?"

Milgrom pointed to a house across and down the street. "He was just standing on the sidewalk looking in my direction. The first time, I didn't think much about it. But the second time was after I'd seen him at the grocery store, so I went in and called the police. He was gone by the time I came back out."

"Do you know the owners of that house?"

"Jeff and Lacy Stockmeyer, but if you're wondering if they have a video doorbell, they don't. I asked. And since they both work, no one was home when he was here. As for the grocery store, I'm not sure if they have surveillance in their parking lot or not." He mentioned the name of a local chain and the date he'd seen the stalker there.

"OK, I'll check it out," replied Rebecca. "But don't expect too much. Most businesses don't keep their recordings from a parking lot for more than a day or two. If they don't get any complaints, they just record over them. And that's assuming they have a camera to start with." Rebecca pulled a business card from a pocket. "Here's my contact information."

Milgrom studied it a moment. "St. Louis, huh? Miranda mentioned you were from out of town."

"That's my permanent office, but I'm licensed in Colorado." She started to reach for her identification.

"That's OK. I'm sure you are or Eleanor would have tossed you out on your rear. She's quite protective when it comes to her friends, and your client falls in that category."

So, I've seen, thought Rebecca. "Is there anything else I should know?"

"Not that I can think of," replied Milgrom.

"In that case, thank you so much for your time and your help. I'll set something up later with your wife, but please thank her for the time she's already spent with me."

"I will. Stop by and have coffee with her sometime. She'd enjoy that."

Rebecca said she'd try and started walking to her car, wondering what it was with the Milgroms and coffee? But that minor mystery didn't linger in her thoughts for long because she had a much more pressing issue crowding it out—what role, if any, did Dan Milgrom play in the death of Randolph Peterson?

Perhaps he was the sole perpetrator, starting his defamation campaign to make room for himself at the top of HomeRight? Then, when he saw firsthand the toll it was taking, he relented and retired, only to watch as the corrosive process he'd started continued to eat away at the former CEO until he took his own life?

Or had he and Whitten been working together from the start? Once Peterson was removed, Whitten would run the company and they'd share the spoils. Most likely, they wouldn't have expected their bullying campaign to culminate in a 9mm slug to the brain, but when it did, they decided to lay low for a while.

Then, there was the possibility that he was working with Bethune-Peterson. Since Rebecca had started to doubt a romantic connection between the two—he seemed too close to his missus and Bethune-Peterson didn't seem the coquettish type—there was still the motivation of money.

Or finally, was Milgrom only doing his job, correcting the mistakes of a man who was faltering in his leadership of HomeRight? This, of course, was the "official" and Bethune-Peterson's version of events, and in all ways, it made the most sense and required the fewest assumptions.

Rebecca slid behind the wheel of her car and started the engine, hoping the meeting with Whitten would prove more informative. She needed some type of break in the case.

Morning, HomeRight Headquarters, Denver, CO

Coming down a side street to an intersection with a major north-south thoroughfare, Rebecca wondered if she had misread the address for HomeRight's headquarters. The building should be just to the south of the intersection, except all that sat there was a two-story, beige building with black trim. Only its mirrored windows distinguished it from the many small businesses she had been passing. But when she turned south and then east again into the building's parking lot, she realized her error. She'd only seen one end of the structure; the building itself stretched the entire length of the block.

Business was apparently good, and Rebecca had to drive down a couple of lanes of parking before she found a spot in the far southeast corner of the lot. She walked the half-block back to the main entrance, where she found the building's receptionist. "I'm Rebecca Marte. I'm here to see Mr. Whitten."

Surely, it was only her imagination, but after the woman's short appraisal, Rebecca thought she heard her say, "Of course you are." But then, more loudly, she said, "I'll let his office know you are here. Please, have a seat."

Rebecca had been placing bets in her mind. Would Whitten be all business or in the mood for games? If the latter, she could see herself sitting here until almost noon. Then, he'd hurry out, apologize profusely, and suggest that he make it up to her by buying lunch. And with that kind of investment of his time, he'd probably offer to let her even the balance sheet with dinner. According to her mental calculations, it was almost an even bet between a professional discussion and his attempt to turn it tawdry.

"Ms. Marte?"

Rebecca looked up to find a grandmotherly type in a dress that seemed a size or two too big peering over her glasses. "Yes. I'm Rebecca Marte."

"Mr. Whitten is ready to see you now. If you'll follow me."

Professionalism had apparently won ... for this initial step anyway. The woman led the way to a single elevator that was tucked away behind the receptionist's station. After inserting a key, the doors opened and they rode to the second floor. When the doors opened again, Rebecca would have thought she was in a different building if she hadn't known better.

Open-plan homes with visibility between the living and kitchen areas had been in vogue for some time—and Rebecca assumed they still were—but open-plan offices? If they were the norm, it was news to her. But in any case, that was exactly what this part of the second floor looked like. A large wooden desk sat in the middle of an open space with two small groupings of chairs and a coffee table on either side near the walls. The nameplate on the desk said "R. Klammer, Office Administrator." A glass wall separated this area from a large office. A man she recognized as James Whitten from online photographs was sitting at a much larger version of the OA's desk.

Rebecca thought it would take her a long time to get used to working in this overly coordinated fishbowl.

Whitten looked up from his work, smiled, and waved at Rebecca to enter. She glanced at her escort, who smiled in return and said, "Please, go on in."

As Rebecca did, Whitten came around his desk and extended a hand. "Ms. Marte. It's a pleasure to meet you. I'm James Whitten."

As he stepped forward, Whitten's gaze traveled from her face down her body and then back up to her chest. It was a reaction Rebecca had anticipated. Of course, he could just be making sure he was guiding his open hand to hers, but she knew better; he probably would prefer that he missed. Hopefully, what she would learn in the next hour would be worth the leer.

"Please, have a seat."

"Thank you, Mr. Whitten. First, let me offer my condolences on the death of Mr. Peterson. I understand you worked with him for many years."

"Not as long as some in the company, but yes, we worked together for a little over twelve years. And I appreciate your sentiments. HomeRight will never be able to replace the incredible talent of Randy Peterson. He was one of a kind."

Rebecca was tempted to ask, "If he was such a talent, then why didn't you ever have anything good to say about his ideas?" Seeing Randolph Peterson through his wife's and Milgrom's eyes, she'd come to like the man even if she had never met him. So, her retort would feel good, if only for a moment. But the comeback was sophomoric and counterproductive. Instead, as she had done with Milgrom, she started her interview with the early days of HomeRight.

Whitten's walk down memory lane was brief compared to Milgrom's, but then, retirement allowed for more leisurely discussions and Whitten wouldn't want to appear as anything other than the busy executive. On the whole, his recollections were both similar and quite distinct from what Rebecca had heard previously. His account was similar to Milgrom's in the collegiality he described that existed at the top of the organization. But while Milgrom was much of the glue that bonded the group, Whitten unapologetically described his role as making sure cohesion didn't become complacency. He even cited—if he was to be believed—Peterson's own words: "In a world filled with yes-men, it's great that I can count on you for a reality check." Basically, in Whitten's view, he, Peterson, and Milgrom were the three musketeers of the home warranty business, each with a crucial function necessary for the company to prosper. Interestingly, he didn't include Bethune-Peterson as one of the cornerstones of the company even in its infancy.

The image he drew as he spoke was believable, although, to Rebecca, it sounded too much like the opening lines of a used car salesman—a little too slick and a little too light on substance. But as president and CEO, he was undoubtedly called on to describe the growth of HomeRight frequently. That could explain the well-practiced verbiage and tone. The whole feel of the talk began to change, however, as the discussion approached the beginning of the end for Randolph Peterson.

"So, about this time," said Rebecca, "Mr. Peterson forgot to approve three weeks of deposits and the company experienced something of an artificial cashflow problem."

She decided on the word "artificial" because it seemed accurate—the company wasn't actually experiencing a downturn yet—but at the same time, it was somewhat confrontational. Rather than being put on the defensive, however, Whitten seemed transported to that time and place by her comment as his eyes focused somewhere in the distance.

"Yes, that's one meeting I'll never forget," Whitten said slowly, his head tipped slightly to one side. "It was completely unlike Randy to forget something as important as approving those deposits. In fact, to this day, I have trouble understanding how those emails ended up in his trash rather than being forwarded. It's not like dragging something to the trash and hitting forward on an email are that easy to confuse." He slowly shook his head.

Either he had Oscar-winning talent or he was genuinely astonished by the error. He also had a point—it was difficult to see how Peterson could have confused those two actions. But perhaps he hadn't. "Who besides Mr. Peterson could have accessed those emails?"

Whitten looked at Rebecca almost like he'd forgotten she was there. "Now, that's a good question. When they were on the company server, his office administrator, Gloria Shaw, could. And Dan Milgrom and myself, of course. But he had forwarded them as unencrypted emails to his personal account, and from there, I don't believe anyone in the company could get to them."

"Your gross receipts can be unencrypted?" Rebecca didn't think anyone had mentioned that fact previously. And though it didn't contradict anything she recalled Nicole or Bethune-Peterson telling her, it made Peterson's mistake seem less like a conspiracy against him and more like a common slipup. He'd simply done some inbox cleaning and had grabbed too many messages for the trash.

Whitten smiled. "Welcome to my world. Yes, he could do that. Randy and I had several pointed discussions on the matter, but he felt that because gross receipts would be reported quarterly anyway, there was no need to encrypt them. Never mind the fact that if they were intercepted, someone could adjust their investment with every fluctuation in our business. It would be insider trading on steroids. But that's no more. It's just one of the many ways I've improved our processes in the last year."

"Sounds like a reasonable precaution," Rebecca replied while thinking, don't break your arm patting yourself on the back. True, she had come into this interview expecting some arrogance, but what she had witnessed so far wasn't that much. Still, she couldn't shake the feeling that there was a lot more of it just below the surface. "So, when Mr. Peterson forwarded those emails to his personal account, they would disappear from the company server?"

Whitten smiled again, although this one seemed driven by resignation rather than humor. "Forwarding may not be the right term even though I'm the one who used it. I believe the application that our Information

Technology department gave him opened a secure connection to the company server. He'd drag the messages to his company computer, which removes them from the company system. Then, he'd email them to himself. Or something pretty close to that."

Whitten released a long breath, perhaps unhappy that he'd admitted to any gap in his understanding of how things worked at HomeRight. Her surmise was at least partially confirmed when he added, "I was a lot more familiar with that app when we were using it, but we scrapped it almost a year ago. Even so, I could probably find someone in the IT department who could give you a better description, if you'd like one."

"Thanks, but I've seen software like that before. If it becomes an issue, I'll ask for that contact later. And if possible, I'd like to talk to Gloria Shaw."

"Gloria didn't introduce herself?" There was a slight bite in his tone. "She's the person who escorted you from the front desk."

"She probably did," replied Rebecca. "And I missed it." Rebecca wasn't sure that deflecting the blame for what was basically a minor lapse in etiquette was necessary, but it felt right. "Anyway, if she's walking me back downstairs, that should be enough time for us to talk."

This development, however, raised another question. If the woman she had met, Shaw, had been Peterson's OA, where was R. Klammer? And why was Shaw standing in for him or her? "I'd also like to talk to your OA if that would be all right?"

Whitten's eyes narrowed for an instant as he leaned to peer through the glass wall. When he sat back, he said, "My OA, Robin Klammer, is out for a few days. Not feeling well. But we'll see what we can do when she comes back in."

"Thanks," replied Rebecca. Her earlier claim to have missed Shaw's introduction now seemed justified. Whitten obviously didn't like any obstacles to his plans, and Gloria Shaw was starting to look like one. Hopefully, she wouldn't catch too much flak for Rebecca's actions because she needed to keep probing.

"Must be something serious," she said. Whitten looked confused. "If you already know that your OA will be out for a while, it must be something serious."

"Not life-threatening, but yes. She'll need some time to recover."

If Whitten had told Klammer to go home because he didn't want them to meet, Rebecca might well have arranged for her to get a few more days off. She had no problem with that. "So, the missing deposits came as quite a shock," Rebecca said, using a somewhat abrupt transition back to two-year-ago history.

Whitten handled it smoothly. "They did. Actually, two things shook my faith in Randy at that time. The problem with the deposits was one. The other was an evaluation of some of his marketing ideas. Everyone from the man on the street to tenured professors at the university was laughing at HomeRight when that story came out."

"But weren't those ideas from when the company was just starting? Would anyone care?"

Whitten shrugged. "They were out-of-date, but like they say, 'You can't put the genie back in the bottle'. Investor confidence had been shaken, and no one cared that later stories tried to explain it away."

It seemed like a good time to try to push Whitten from his comfort zone. "So, HomeRight set the record straight and had the paper print a retraction?" She knew she hadn't found anything like that in her searches online.

Whitten paused, exaggerating a look of concentration. "You know, I'm not sure. That wasn't my responsibility. Maybe Randy forgot to do that, too."

"A task like that would fall to the president and CEO of the company?" asked Rebecca. "I would think something like that would be the responsibility of a Communications or Public Relations department."

Whitten grasped the cuff on one of his shirt sleeves and gave it a tug. "As I said, I wasn't in that loop. Maybe he told them to do something about it, but they dropped the ball. Or maybe they did as he directed. I'm not sure."

"Did you ever find out who leaked that report to the media?"

"You know how the media is. They're not going to give up a source," replied Whitten.

"Really. I wouldn't think they'd put up much of a fuss when the story was hardly newsworthy to begin with."

Rebecca wouldn't have needed any training on interviewing methods to know that she'd produced a crack in the man's cool façade; Whitten was turning red. Close to his boiling point was fine, but past it would be a mistake that would end this interview prematurely. So, she reduced the heat some.

"Then again, I suppose the paper wouldn't want to set that precedent," she said. "Identify the leak to HomeRight, and pretty soon, everyone would want the same treatment."

It seemed to take him a moment to realize that she had just taken his side. But eventually, he said, "Exactly."

And now, to turn the heat back up a bit, she said, "So, it doesn't sound like the company did much damage control on either of the newspaper's mistakes."

"What do you mean?"

"Well, even though these were the two events that"—she checked her notes—"that shook your faith in Mr. Peterson, the response from the company didn't get your attention. It's not even clear that HomeRight explained the artificial cash flow issue to its employees, much less the general public. So, it seems like both matters were handled somewhat casually."

A muscle started working in Whitten's jaw. "I don't think you understand the complexity of running a company as large and diverse as HomeRight. No, I don't know all the details of what we did or didn't do about either of these matters. The cornerstone of efficient management is the delegation of responsibilities, and mine were elsewhere. So, you pointing a finger at me because of HomeRight's response would be like me blaming you for a botched FBI raid."

Two days ago, she had been an unknown entity in Lone Tree. Now, it seemed like everyone knew her business and background. "Point taken," she replied, again letting some of the heat bleed out of the talk. It was time for a different approach as well.

"There were some stories questioning Mr. Peterson's sexual orientation that came out in the papers about the same time. That incident didn't have the same or even more impact on your trust in Mr. Peterson as an ancient marketing report?"

"It was pretty damaging, too."

"But not one of the two events that really concerned you? Those were ...."

"Yes, I remember what I said," replied Whitten curtly. He paused a moment. "But I'm not really sure what you're asking. You want me to rate them on a ten-point scale?" He didn't wait for a reply. "The report was a ten. Propositioning that kid was only a nine. OK?"

Rebecca was hoping there was a reason, conscious or unconscious, that had led Whitten to single out two of Peterson's missteps over all others. But if he was aware of the reason, he wasn't saying. Of course, he could have seen them as pivotal simply because they were first. Although, when she thought about it, their actual sequence wasn't as important as the order Whitten had learned of them.

"So, were the slipups on the deposits and the marketing report the first indications that Mr. Peterson was having problems running the company?"

Whitten pulled on an ear for a moment. "I suppose the deposits were the first indication where we had clearcut data, but I'd suspected we had a problem before that. We kept losing our high-end real estate users. It took several weeks to track that back to the source—an automated re-enrollment feature that Randy had come up with. That happens, but the problem was that even though the ratings on it were abysmal, he wasn't authorizing any changes to it. Now, we believe that his mismanagement was a cry for help, even though he wouldn't take it when offered."

Whitten apparently liked the cry-for-help explanation for his boss's death; he'd used it in the formal company statement. Rebecca, on the other hand, thought it drivel. She'd heard nothing in any of the interviews that suggested Peterson was making mistakes to call attention to some personal plight, real or imagined. Rather, according to everyone else she had spoken with, he was still trying to come up with explanations for these problems.

Rebecca was working on a follow-up question when Whitten said, "I should also mention that the marketing report slipup caught my attention because we didn't do a good job protecting company proprietary information. We take information security quite seriously. In fact, we were one of the first in our industry in Colorado to have an information security management system that is ISO certified. That's the International Organization for Standardization. Our system documents all of our proprietary information, where it's stored, who has access, and maintains a calendar for the de-classification or destruction of the documents. HomeRight is very proud of that fact."

If Whitten was trying to cover up something, he would have been better served if he hadn't made this last comment. It was a classic tell. People trying to pass off a lie as truth often engage in a long soliloquy with lots of "pontification." But as with any indication of dishonesty, this one wasn't perfect. Maybe he was truly proud of their accomplishment and took every occasion to say so.

"OK, but I didn't think the report was proprietary."

"Well ... not in the formal sense. But it's not the kind of thing you want in the papers."

That admission further increased the likelihood he was lying, but toward what end? Rebecca couldn't come up with any reason these two events were uniquely significant in his mind.

"In addition to ...." Rebecca's question, however, was interrupted by a knock at the office door. Whitten leaned slightly to look past Rebecca, releasing a glare that would cause most to flee. But as Rebecca turned, she found Gloria Shaw holding her ground ... well, except for one slight flinch.

"Sorry to interrupt, Mr. Whitten, but there's a man on the phone. He said it was vital you talk to him now."

"What man?" Whitten snapped.

"He wouldn't say. He only said the man you met with late last Friday evening and that you would know."

"Hang up on him." Shaw turned to leave. "Gloria!" She turned back. "On second thought, I'll take it in my private office." Shaw turned and left.

Private office, wondered Rebecca. Did that mean she was in his public office? That description certainly fit the surroundings.

"Please excuse me," said Whitten. "This will only take a minute." He walked to what appeared to be the back wall of the space they were in, stood there for a moment, and then a panel slid open. Whitten stepped inside and the door closed.

She looked around the fishbowl, wondering if this is what animals feel like in the zoo—all alone, yet on public display? She glanced at Shaw, who had turned her chair slightly from the desk. She held out two empty hands, keeping them low and the gesture mostly hidden.

Rebecca gave a slight smile and nod in response. Shaw apparently got the "I understand" message and turned back to her work.

Morning, Whitten's Private Office

"What the hell is wrong with you?" Whitten yelled into the phone as he paced around the desk in his private office. He'd spent a considerable amount of money soundproofing the room, a precaution that was now paying for itself. Unfortunately, he hadn't padded the floor because, in his blind rage, he accidentally knocked the base of the phone off the edge of the desk.

"What was that?" asked the man on the other end of the line.

"Shut the hell up," Whitten snapped. "I'll call you back on my cell, so start thinking very carefully about what you want to say to me." He disconnected. While the room was soundproof, the company line wasn't listener-proof. He'd almost bet that Shaw was listening even as he hung up.

When Whitten called back on his cell, the man answered with, "After what you did to me, I should be the one yelling."

"Oh, something bad happened to you?" Whitten replied, not trying to hide the mockery in his tone.

"Don't play ...." The man paused, most likely recalling Whitten's reaction the last time he had used this line. "You know very well what happened. I got mugged walking to the parking garage last Friday night and spent the rest of the night in the ER. It'll be a month before I can take a deep breath."

"Oh, dear," replied Whitten. "Well, you've called the right person. I know several people in the Department of Public Safety."

"Can we cut the crap? I just called to say that I'm not taking it anymore. Let's just say I've taken steps to make sure that never happens again."

"Let me guess," said Whitten slowly. "You finally sprang for one of those pricey parking spots in your building ... although even that garage is awfully dark and deserted at night. And, wait, it's coming to me. You also bought a gun. So, I'll be watching the telly for the story about you blowing off your right big toe. I just love those dumb and dumber segments."

The silence on the other end of the line told Whitten he'd guessed right, most likely on both counts. He could picture the man on the line searching his surroundings, wondering if there was a camera hidden somewhere. But this game with him was getting old, and Whitten needed to get back to the lovely but infuriating PI sitting in his outer office.

"OK, let's get this over with. What is it this time?" asked Whitten.

"Veles has become obsessed. You know she hired a private investigator and I bet you know he met with Milgrom. But I bet you didn't know that Veles called my office."

That was news, and worth the interruption, but Whitten wasn't going to admit it. "What did she want?" There was no response for a moment, so he said, "It was nothing, right?"

"Are you literally going to wait until she brings the cops in to arrest me?"

"Are you literally going to answer me or do you need another visit from my associate to loosen your tongue?" replied Whitten.

It was still several seconds before the man answered. "This time, it was just the routine stuff—hours, address, my specialties. But I tell you, she's gonna keep her PI digging into my business until he finds something."

The PI is looking into Milgrom's friends and associates, thought Whitten. There's nothing unusual about that, although it was strange that a PI would let the client make those contacts. And that being the case, this call was more about the guy on the other end panicking than any real threat. It was time to placate him with some minutia. Small people, he thought, live for trivia.

"You should know, the private investigator isn't a 'he.' It's a woman. And she's sitting in my outer office right now."

"A woman?"

"Didn't Milgrom tell you?" he asked, knowing that he, too, hadn't known until this morning. He waited a moment, giving the man on the phone some time to fret about what else he didn't know. "Yes, she's not only female but quite the looker, too. Great legs, decent rack. But since I might talk in my sleep, I suppose she's off-limits. Well, unless it's just one last romp for her."

"You're sick."

"You would know, but I still hold all the cards … yours included," said Whitten. "Now, if you've given me all your news, I have work to do."

"And just what is it you think you can do to the PI to get her off our backs?"

Whitten paused as he hadn't really planned his next steps. But in that moment, he knew. "You don't cut off the arm when the enemy's head is showing."

"What the hell does that mean?"

"You're a smart guy. You figure it out." And with that, Whitten disconnected.

Morning, HomeRight Headquarters

Rebecca almost didn't hear the soft whoosh of the panel opening as Whitten reappeared. "Sorry for the interruption, Ms. Marte."

"Nothing wrong, I hope."

"Oh, no. Just some follow-up on some elective surgery I had done. Nothing that affects … you know, my vitality."

And there it was, thought Rebecca. A thinly veiled reference to his manhood. And the fact that he had made the comment eased her suspicions slightly. If he was even vaguely entertaining the idea of getting her in bed, then he wasn't worried about what she might learn in the throes of passion. But then again, he might have had the same thought, meaning his comment was designed to misdirect, not inform.

For an instant, Rebecca considered leading him further down the seduction path, wondering just how far he would go before he would back down because of the risk—assuming there was something to risk. But then, he was probably willing to go a lot further than she was; she was already feeling a little queasy at the mere thought. "Sounds like you know a doctor who not only makes house calls but on a Friday night, too."

Whitten seemed confused for a moment, then said, "Yeah, he's an old friend."

The slight hitch in his reply caught her attention. Had he forgotten already that Shaw had identified the caller as the man he had seen "late last Friday night"? Was the pause just to give him time to think?

"And your friend was OK doing the surgery himself? I thought doctors didn't like operating on people they knew?"

Damn, why had she added the clarification? It just gave him more time to form a lie, if that was what he was doing.

"He just provided the referral. I contacted him Friday because I had a question about the procedure, so he did a little checking. The call today was my answer. Anyway ...."

"Then, it was a good thing you didn't have Ms. Shaw hang up on him. You sounded somewhat displeased, and you would have missed your answer."

"I don't like being interrupted," Whitten replied curtly.

"Oh, I'm sorry. I didn't mean to interrupt."

"I meant the call, not you." His face turned red again. He made a production of checking his watch. "I know I mentioned giving you another fifteen minutes, but unless you have some pressing questions, I should start preparing for a lunch meeting."

He'd suggested that they meet over lunch just this morning, but now, he had a meeting at that time? But no sooner had she realized the contradiction than he must have done the same. "Yeah, I filled the lunch slot on my calendar almost immediately after you passed on it. But then, it's much better to be busy than the opposite."

"Absolutely," said Rebecca. "I think the rest of my questions can wait for a later time." Actually, she had asked all of the questions that were likely to elicit new information. If she asked about the other errors Peterson had made at work—the missing signatures, the loss of users, the repeated policy announcements, and the like—he would just confirm them, probably with the observation they were cries for help. So, to end the interview, she turned to her standard final question. "Is there anything you'd like to ask or add?"

For the second time that day, the line that usually elicited nothing produced a response. "I do have one question," replied Whitten. "Can you tell me what Ms. Veles hopes to learn about Randy's suicide? It just seems like a very expensive gesture by someone who's only a friend of his wife."

"Sorry, but I'm afraid the ...."

Whitten waved a hand. "I understand. Confidentiality and all." Apparently, he didn't mind interrupting others.

"Exactly," she replied, although her thought was that he'd given up awfully quickly. Why drop the name of her client when he knew she wouldn't respond?

Whitten reached forward and pressed something on his desk. "Gloria, you can show Ms. Marte out now." This time, he didn't stand, didn't offer his hand, didn't study her body as she stood to leave. Rather, he simply said, "It was nice to meet you, Ms. Marte. I hope you enjoy your short stay in Colorado." He turned his attention to the computer on his desk.

Whitten's question and his abrupt dismissal of her seemed a message, and if so, at least part of it was "I'm keeping an eye on you." Rebecca's client wasn't a secret, but neither was it front-page news. At a minimum, he was paying attention to the rumors; at the other end of the scale, he was taking steps to learn everything she and Nicole were doing.

And while the second part of the message was even more speculative, she felt like he was saying, "I win." He'd let her into his inner sanctum. He allowed her to ask all her questions. And though he'd become irritated a few times, he'd given her nothing substantial in return. And now he was showing her the door, letting her go back to stumbling around in the dark because she would never find his secrets.

His opinion, however, was arrogance speaking because he wasn't a particularly good liar. People don't hang up on old friends who are doing them a personal favor. But lying about what? Could it be as simple as a medical procedure he didn't want to discuss? Maybe something that did affect his "vitality"? Or perhaps the caller wasn't even a doctor? Maybe the call had nothing to do with the case?

Yes, Rebecca admitted to herself, she might simply be reading too much into his actions. But if it was a message, she could send one of her own. "Thank you for your time, and I'm sure I'll enjoy my visit. In fact, I've enjoyed the first couple of days so much, I may just stay." Translation: You haven't won; the game is just getting started.

Whitten looked up from the computer but had no opportunity to form a reply as Shaw entered the office.

"Ms. Marte, if you're ready, I can show you out."

"Yes, thanks." Rebecca walked out without a backward glance, although she could feel Whitten's stare burning into her back. When the office door closed behind them, Rebecca turned to her escort as they started for the elevator. "Thanks for showing me around. Good that you could fill in for Ms. Klammer while she's out ill."

"Robin's sick?" asked Shaw, turning her frowning face to look at Rebecca as they walked.

"Apparently. Mr. Whitten thought it could be a few more days."

"Really? He just asked me to stand in this morning. I'm sure if it's longer term, they'll let me know."

Rebecca paused a moment before changing the subject. "I understand you were Mr. Peterson's long-time assistant?"

"I was." Shaw didn't turn this time, but even from the side, Rebecca could tell she was smiling. "I worked for him for fifteen years. It's tough for me to think of this place as HomeRight with him gone and Mr. Milgrom retired."

The women had reached the elevator and Shaw inserted the key to call it.

"Yes, it's tough losing a long-time colleague," said Rebecca. "My partner died a couple of years ago, and I still look around the office like he should be there. And I suppose it's even worse when someone's mental state is deteriorating like Mr. Peterson's was, and no one steps in to help him."

"That's a bunch of claptrap," Shaw snapped, then looked around as if to make sure no one had heard her. Rebecca had expected a reaction, but not necessarily one mixed with so much raw emotion. If there was more to learn about Peterson's death, she hoped the results would be worth the pain she would have to cause Shaw to uncover it.

Shaw sighed deeply, then continued more quietly. "Sorry, but most of what people say about Mr. Peterson isn't true, or it wasn't that important. Like forgetting to sign a promotion memo. That's not worth mentioning, much less pointing it out to the board."

The elevator arrived and the women stepped inside.

"I don't know anything about HomeRight's business, but I keep hearing about these deposits he forgot to have processed and this young man he supposedly propositioned. Those sound more serious."

Rebecca glanced sideways at the woman, finding her wringing her hands, eyes forward.

"Yes," Shaw said slowly. "The slipup with the deposits was as bad as it is baffling. To this day, I have no idea how he could have opened those emails and then just delete them. It makes no sense. But the attacks on his … I guess we say sexual orientation these days? Anyway, those are definitely bunk."

The elevator doors opened on the first floor, and the women stepped off and started for the front of the building.

"Well, Ms. Bethune-Peterson thought no one took those rumors about his sexual orientation seriously anyway."

Shaw stopped in her tracks and turned toward Rebecca. "She said that?"

"Not those exact words, but yes."

Shaw started walking again, her steps as slow as the shake of her head. She glanced around the lobby.

"Not everyone brushed that news off as rubbish," said Shaw softly. "Two of the board members believe that gay unions are the devil's work. That rumor alone probably secured their votes against Mr. Peterson." She slowly shook her head again. "But I shouldn't be discussing office gossip."

"That's OK," said Rebecca. "It won't go any farther than me, although the personal beliefs of these two board members sound more like fact than gossip."

"They're not shy about making their feelings known."

"Would Ms. Bethune-Peterson know their stance?"

"I don't see how she wouldn't."

Shaw clearly knew much more about the events at HomeRight and the circumstances of Peterson's death than they could discuss walking through the lobby. "Would you like to have lunch sometime?"

They had reached the front door of the building and Shaw turned toward her. "I eat at my desk. Mr. Whitten doesn't like people to leave for lunch. And I usually watch one or more of the grandkids on the weekends and take them out to lunch."

"Then, maybe dinner?"

A slight smile came to Shaw's features. "My husband died six years ago and other than burgers and chicken nuggets on the weekends, I don't get out much. I'd love to. How about tomorrow evening?"

"That would be great. Since I know nothing of the area, you can pick the place and text me. I eat everything."

"Funny, I would have guessed you eat nothing as skinny as you are. End of my day is 5:30. Say, 6 for dinner? I'll meet you at the restaurant."

"Perfect." Rebecca handed Shaw a business card. "The address is my office in St. Louis, but the rest of the contact information is correct if you need to change the plan."

"Not likely," replied Shaw as the smile grew.

Rebecca returned the look, turned, and left.

Her contented expression, however, stayed behind. Despite the considerable difference in their ages, she liked the simple forthrightness of Shaw, which made asking her to revisit some of her darkest days at HomeRight all the more difficult. It would be an unpleasant reminisce for her, but again, Rebecca hoped the outcome would justify the pain.

TUESDAY, AUGUST 30

Afternoon, Jen's Place

Rebecca watched in amused fascination as Nicole carried a laptop and at least two-dozen pages of paper into her office. "Is there going to be a test afterward?"

"Depends on how much yawning I see," Nicole replied with a smirk. "Besides, you have to expect data if you're going to work with an engineer."

"You and Doc with all your data." Rebecca regretted her words even as they left her mouth. She and Nicole had only spoken a moment about Dr. Sam Price back in St. Louis, but it was enough for her to know that Nicole's memories of her one-time fiancé were vile, even if they were based on lies. Would she find the comparison demeaning?

"It's OK," replied Nicole.

"I'm that easy to read?"

Nicole smiled. "Not at all ... although I should say yes and let you wonder about it for a day or two. It's just that when we were in St. Louis, I told you he makes my skin crawl, so I figured you might be a little uneasy bringing him up. But it's no different than if you said Jack the Ripper and I both share an interest in human anatomy."

"Ouch!" said Rebecca. "That's an unflattering comparison, to say the least." She hesitated, considering her question for a moment. "You don't really think that Doc is like Jack the Ripper, do you?"

"No, Jack only killed prostitutes. Doc doesn't discriminate."

As an attempt to relief tension with humor, Rebecca thought this example particularly strained. Even Nicole was having difficulty pretending that her mood had lightened.

Perhaps realizing her joke wasn't going to help, Nicole said, "It's tough to draw the line between fact and fantasy in the history of late 1880s London. Some of what was in the papers about Jack the Ripper back then is now believed to have been written by journalists trying to increase the circulation of their papers. My memories of Doc, however, are mostly fantasy, if what my friends and family say is true. And I believe it is."

"I can't speak to all of Doc's history," said Rebecca, "but I did see him turn his back on his life and career in St. Louis to look for you. He was only about a half-day away when you escaped. I would think that would ease some of the pain caused by the kidnappers."

Nicole tipped her head back and looked at the ceiling for a moment. When her gaze came back down to Rebecca's face, she said, "Do you like snakes?"

"They're OK," replied Rebecca.

"How about spiders?"

"Oh, no," she replied with an exaggerated shiver and a well-practiced grimace. "And what are these big ones I see racing around the sidewalks here in Colorado?"

"Wolf spiders. They don't spin webs. Instead, they hunt down insects using their speed. And since they help manage the bug population without creating a mess, you should really appreciate them. You know, take a wolf spider to lunch and all that."

"OK, point made," Rebecca said, rolling her eyes for effect. "You can't tell me these spiders are the good guys any more than I can tell you that Doc is. Too bad it doesn't work that way."

"Yeah, too bad. But enough about some guy I used to know," said Nicole. "What did you learn from your interviews yesterday? Who's still on the suspect list?"

"Everyone," replied Rebecca.

"Surely, not me. Or Ellie."

"Yes, even you. Maybe you kill for the thrill of it and then bring in a PI when the police don't pay enough attention."

"Well, at least you didn't say I did it for the money. Mr. Peterson's charities didn't extend to Jen's Place, so if I was going to kill anyone, it would have to be Ellie."

Rebecca couldn't help but smile at the comment. "Good to know, 'cause it's tough to get paid when you have to turn your client in to the police at the end of an investigation. Besides, between you and Ms. Eleanor Bethune-Peterson as the serial emotional abuser that drove Mr. Peterson to his death, my money would be on her."

"Whoa. Hold on a second," said Nicole, her face flushing. "You can't possibly believe that Ellie killed her own husband. She lost her lifelong best friend."

"It's a stone that has to be turned."

Nicole's response was to cross her arms over her chest.

"Look, I'm not saying that's what happened," said Rebecca. "But I am saying, if there was financial gain from his removal from leadership, it's a factor that we can't afford to overlook."

"OK," Nicole said after a considerable delay. "But I'm telling you, you're wrong. First, there was no life insurance policy. Ellie always says that buying life insurance is just paying someone else to put away the money you should be saving. So, they paid themselves rather than insurance companies."

Rebecca nodded, having heard this idea before. It was, however, more easily implemented by people who had money to start with.

"Second," continued Nicole, "when the board voted Mr. Peterson out and he declined the figurehead position, they authorized a severance package. Reportedly, it was just under a million dollars, but he donated it to charity with Ellie's blessing. It took a while for the paperwork to clear, which probably explains why you didn't find that fact when you were reading up on the case. The bottom line is, Ellie doesn't need any more money."

Rebecca knew that how much money someone "needs" is highly subjective. Billionaires could want more, while those less wealthy could be happy with a few thousand in the bank. Hopefully, finishing up the interview with Bethune-Peterson would shed more light on her appetites.

When Rebecca looked back at her client, it was clear she wasn't happy that Bethune-Peterson was still a suspect. But her frown was slowly morphing into her look of determination, a look that Rebecca was coming to know well. It seemed she had accepted the investigation of her friend as necessary, if not pleasant.

"So, on to yesterday's meetings?" asked Nicole.

Rebecca agreed and spent the next fifteen minutes covering her meetings with Milgrom and Whitten. When she was finished, Nicole said, "So, it looks like Mr. Peterson's long-time OA, Gloria Shaw, might be quite a help. That's good because Fred Reese, the man on the HomeRight board, isn't going to be any. He feels like he's prohibited from saying anything by the board's rules. So, my gut feeling was wrong and that's a dead end."

"But still, good that you checked him out," said Rebecca. "And I agree about Ms. Shaw. We're meeting for dinner tonight after I finish my interview with Ms. Bethune-Peterson this afternoon." Rebecca's gaze went back to all the papers Nicole had brought in with her. "So, are all those pages filled with the phrase, 'Reese is a dead end,' repeated over and over."

Nicole grinned. "No, they're sociograms, which are graphs of the relationships among people. In this case, I included connections to events and places, as well."

"From social media?" asked Rebecca.

"Mostly, with some additions from Ellie and Miranda. Like this link," she said, pointing to one line on the graphics. "Whitten and Milgrom had a connection to the Aurora Reservoir because

HomeRight sponsored a fishing trip there for their employees. That was about eighteen months ago. Whitten caught the biggest tiger muskie and he must have posted that picture on a half-dozen different social media sites. But I wouldn't have even known that Dan Milgrom went if Miranda hadn't told me."

In a different setting, that might have prompted Rebecca to say something like, "That's because he didn't catch anything." But what Nicole was doing pushed that quip from her head. "I thought you were doing background on Dan Milgrom, not the lot of them. You need to back off on Whitten, in particular. He already knows you're my client, probably from Milgrom. But if he finds out you're checking up on him directly ... well, he won't be any too happy about it. And it seems like he could be vindictive."

"I thought about that," replied Nicole. "And if he checks up on who has searched his public pages, he won't find me. I logged on with some friends' credentials—women who are spread out across the country. I asked them to set up a temporary password for me, then to change it as soon as I was finished. They should be safe enough."

"You have some great friends," replied Rebecca. "Even if the risk is almost nil."

"When you're one of only a handful of women in a biomedical engineering program, you get close. They are my friends from graduate school. Thank goodness I still remember them. Anyway, here's a sociogram for Peterson. I color-coded the links according to how important I thought they might be to the case. It's black for no obvious relevance, with yellow, orange, or red in order of increasing levels of importance."

Rebecca took the graph and looked it over. "Hmm, these seem like they could be great for all the SODDI theories." When she saw the confused look on her client's face, she added, "Some-Other-Dude-Did-It theories. Maybe someone held a grudge against Peterson, got him removed from HomeRight, and his death was unexpected. Or his growing forgetfulness was natural and this person saw it as a way to get the ultimate revenge and staged his suicide. Mind you, I haven't seen anything to suggest something like that, but we need to keep the possibility in mind. And these might help." She paused a moment, realizing what was missing. "I don't see anything but black and yellow links. Nothing warrants an orange or red one?"

"Nope," replied Nicole with a shake of her head. "Not on this page or any of the others, and I've almost got all the data entered."

"That's unfortunate," said Rebecca absentmindedly as she skimmed a few graphs. "So, when the link between Peterson and this grocery store is yellow and has Whitten written on it, that means they both shop at the same place?"

"Not exactly," Nicole said slowly. "Maybe I should have represented it a different way, but in this case, it means they both used the food delivery service at this store. What I really need is the name of the person who selects, packs, and delivers those orders because he or she could have been tampering with Peterson's food before he received it."

"Or they use the same delivery service, but it's different people all the time."

"True," admitted Nicole, her gaze dropping to the page in her hands. "They probably have several different people doing the shopping. And there's probably not a lot of continuity in the job."

Sure, there were limitations in the graphs, but given her request, Nicole was being too hard on herself. "I can see dozens of possible leads coming out of these," said Rebecca, hoping to spin the tone to something more positive. "And you have ones for Whitten and Milgrom, too?"

"I do," said Nicole, a little vigor returning to her voice. "Multiple ones for each of them actually. I have eight on Whitten, for example."

"Eight?" After a moment considering the number, Rebecca said, "Well, I suppose when you try to summarize a busy man's life in a graph, it's going to take a few pages. Do you happen to know the number of yellow links in total?"

"Eighty-seven so far."

"And how far back do these graphs go?"

"As best I could tell, they cover the last three years or so. But from context, I'd guess that some of the older posts have been deleted or archived."

"So, let's go through all eighty-seven yellow ones," said Rebecca, eliciting a resolute nod from her counterpart.

At the end of an hour, most of the links were still yellow, but they had elevated twenty-six of them to orange. Rebecca now thought of orange as meaning that they needed more information rather than an increase in suspicion, *per se*. A common link between Whitten, Milgrom, and an individual named Rose Kline was a good example. The shared connection would mean little if she was the principal of the school where both of these men's grandchildren were students. But if she, for example, had a record for dealing hallucinogenic drugs, how these men knew her might make for some informative reading.

Although Rebecca still saw these graphs as extremely useful, the review helped her further refine her understanding of them. For example, even if Rose Kline had a record for dealing illegal drugs, a link between her and one of the men was probably more suspicious than a link to both Whitten and Milgrom. Why would both of them need to meet with her to make a drug buy to pollute Peterson's mind? But on the other hand, Rebecca felt like she was getting exactly what she'd requested—deep background on the relationships and habits of Milgrom, with Nicole taking the initiative to put Whitten and Peterson under the same microscope.

When they'd finished the review, Rebecca pushed back from the desk and took a long look at the woman sitting across from her. When Nicole looked up, Rebecca said, "You can hardly watch a crime show on TV or in the movies without seeing an evidence board, and most investigators create their own versions, me included. But your sociograms are great. And you did all this in the last day and a half?"

"I probably spent a half-day deciding what to do, finding an application that did it, and coming up with a coding scheme. After that, it went pretty fast."

"A coding scheme?" asked Rebecca.

"Yeah. The software is online, and maybe I'm being paranoid, but entering real names and places online seemed a little risky. If one of them got wind of what I'm doing, I'm sure he could buy his way to the bottom of it. So, I came up with my own version that takes the data from coded spreadsheets."

"That's not paranoid," replied Rebecca. "In fact, that's a good common-sense precaution since you can obviously handle the task this way."

Nicole grinned at the compliment. "So, this is the kind of thing you do? Checking into people's backgrounds online?"

"Deskwork is part of the job, but there's plenty of legwork, too," Rebecca said, wondering if she heard some defensiveness in her tone. She felt a little. That emotion, however, was wasted on Nicole, and she knew it. "Frankly, a hell of a lot of it is exactly like this," she added with a laugh. "It's tough to spot something suspicious without knowing what's routine, and people's online lives can be a great help in defining what's common for them. And if some other dude did it, hopefully, he'll be in one of your graphs as well."

Nicole's grin wavered, then turned to a frown. "But if someone else is involved and he's in these pages somewhere, would he necessarily have had contact with more than one of these three people?"

It was a good insight, Rebecca knew, and not just because she had come to the same conclusion. "No, not necessarily, which is why I thought you could check out the orange links while I look into the connections Milgrom has to unidentified people on your graphs."

"Yeah, looking closely at Mr. Milgrom's connections makes sense," said Nicole. "Ellie always said it was the change in loyalties that bothered her husband the most, which is just another way of saying that it was the change in Milgrom. Whitten never had any loyalties. So, I can see you looking at Milgrom's connections first."

"Exactly. So, with my second visit with Ms. Bethune-Peterson this afternoon, a first with Ms. Shaw tonight, and a tentative meeting with Ms. Milgrom tomorrow morning, maybe we can get back together tomorrow afternoon?"

"How about tomorrow night after dinner?" Nicole asked. "I have a couple of other commitments in the afternoon."

"Works for me."

Rebecca watched as Nicole packed up her laptop, thinking how this was working out better than she had ever dreamt it would. Nicole was doggedly loyal to her friend but accepted that Bethune-Peterson should be in the suspect pool—to the extent they had a pool. She was extremely hardworking and organized. And she was obviously quite bright, something that came as no surprise given her previous career. It was easy to see why Doc had become infatuated with her, even without considering the physical attraction he had undoubtedly felt.

"Nicole?" The woman looked up from her packing. "Back in St. Louis, you wanted to tell me something about the night Kyle Logan died."

Nicole stopped what she was doing and sat up straight. "I thought it might help us work together. And if you hesitated because you thought I wanted to unburden my conscience, that's not it. I don't regret what happened, although it haunts my nights."

"No, I cut you off because what you tell me isn't protected under the law. It's not privileged information like a conversation between a lawyer and client. So, if you got away with a crime, you should keep it to yourself."

Nicole nodded, her lips drawn in a tight line. "I'd guess it's something of a gray area legally … or maybe not. I'm no expert. But as far as this case goes, it's just one more factor that you should be considering in what I tell you but can't because you don't know. I want to correct that."

"OK, let's hear it."

Nicole finished closing her laptop case, pushed back from the desk, and leaned back in her chair as her eyes seemed to focus on a time and place months ago and miles away.

NINE MONTHS EARLIER, THURSDAY, DECEMBER 9

After Midnight, Mountain Brews Bar and Grill, Denver, CO

Nicole looked out over the nearly deserted parking lot of the bar and grill, its neon lights divvying up the otherwise gray gravel into patches of pale red, green, and blue. It was Thursday, making her wonder how they were staying in business if this was the typical weekday crowd. But, as Linda had mentioned to her when she was at Jen's Place, Logan was doing his bit to keep them going; his battered pickup was one of only three vehicles in the parking lot.

If the signage on the building was any indication, they weren't making up for slow alcohol sales with fine dining. The only food that was shown was a hamburger—if indeed, that was what the grayish-brown blob represented. It was joined by a highball glass and a beer mug floating over a lopsided M that represented the mountains.

"Maybe that's a cloud?" Nicole muttered, her
breath fogging up the inside of her car's window.
Studying the flashing red neon sign to decide,
however, was making her nauseous, so she opened
the car door and stepped out into the cold evening air.

The sky was crystal clear. It was an occasional feature of her new life that she'd come to appreciate after wildfires up and down the West Coast had partially hidden the mountains during some of the previous summer.

Nicole heard the faint crunch of gravel behind her, and she spun around to find Kyle Logan.

"Now what have we got here?" he said.

Nicole took a breath, silently repeating the words she'd practiced dozens of times. It was to be a logical appeal, one that would make sense to anyone. His wife, Linda, had agreed to move from Jen's Place for her own protection. And for the same reason, Nicole didn't know where she was. She had nothing Logan wanted and so, she was going to propose they go their separate ways.

"If it isn't that nosy bitch who got me thrown in prison," he hissed. "It's time you paid me back for the five months you cost me."

Logan may have still wanted to get his wife back, but standing there in the middle of the night with no one around, that wasn't his objective. She had misread him and this was going to be a painful mistake, but hopefully, mostly for him. His left hand flashed forward, his knuckles digging into her cheek as he wound a fistful of her hair around his hand. He leaned in close, the reek of alcohol on his breath making her turn away. With his right hand, he grabbed her wrist and began to twist her arm.

With Logan's touch, however, the man and the cold quiet of the parking lot vanished in an explosion of white-hot rage. Adrenaline flooded Nicole's bloodstream, fueled by the months of pain, anger, and helplessness of captivity. The man before her vanished, his sneering face replaced by that of a kidnapper. Her heart thundered in her ears. Blood rushed to her arms and legs, preparing her body for fight or flight.

When she'd escaped the kidnappers, she swore that no one would ever cage her again. Then, she'd given substance to that promise with months of strength and self-defense training. Now, that training kicked in. Muscle memory, honed over countless repetitions of individual moves, transformed her hand into a weapon—a V formed by her thumb and fingers of her flattened, right hand. She had selected that particular strike rather than one using her fist or forearm because the hand was the easiest to slip under the chin.

This particular strike, however, was also the most dangerous—it could kill as easily as stun—so much of the training had focused on the precise amount of force required. She delivered that blow to Logan's neck as she had practiced ... or so she thought. But to her astonishment, rather than coughing and choking for an instant, Logan grabbed his neck as his lips moved in silence, his words failing to form with the lack of air. His eyes went impossibly wide, and he slowly crumpled to the ground. She had crushed his windpipe.

For several minutes, she checked for his pulse. There was none. He was dead. She had killed him.

Nicole looked around the parking lot. It was still empty. No one could verify her claim that he had attacked and she had been forced to defend herself. But even if there was a witness, she doubted it would make any difference. What was she doing in the middle of the night in the parking lot of a bar that Logan was known to frequent? The only reason anyone would accept was that she was there to end his harassment once and for all. She would be painted as the hunter, he the hunted.

Unbidden, the cold, clean air of the Colorado front range disappeared, replaced by bare walls and the stifling odor of chemicals, sweat, and stale food. It was the room where her kidnappers had held her. Nicole tore off her coat and threw it to the ground. Then, she sat next to the lifeless body of Kyle Logan and began to shiver.

Nicole wasn't sure how long it took the frigid night to return some semblance of rationality to her thoughts, but if only seconds, that was too long. She couldn't be caught; she'd die in prison. Quickly, she devised a plan. But every time she tried to consider its limitations dispassionately, her mind screamed at her, "They're coming to cage you forever. Move!"

Eventually, her body obeyed. Nicole stood and put on her coat, then dragged Logan to his pickup and leaned one of his shoulders against it. She quickly checked the cab, finding nothing suitable for her purposes. So, she removed his belt and wrapped it around his neck. Then, she wedged a knee against his back and pulled on the belt as hard as she could, mimicking a position that would keep her away from his flaying hands while she strangled him. She kept up the pressure until her arms began to quiver with fatigue.

It was a common myth, Nicole knew from school, that people would not bruise after death, but unfortunately, she didn't recall the exact conditions that allowed it to occur. She just hoped that her staged strangling would mask anything unique in her killing blow to his neck. She retrieved a pair of gloves from her coat pocket, put them on, wiped off the belt, and put it back on Logan. Tapping into the last of the adrenaline in her bloodstream, Nicole then half-dragged and half-lifted him into the passenger seat of his truck.

Nicole removed her coat, turned it inside out, and put it back on. She pulled a stocking cap from another pocket, tucked her hair underneath it, and pulled it low. If the bar had cameras on the lot, she and her car might be on the tape already, but there was nothing she could do about that now. If nothing else, however, she'd give the police a different look. Casually, she walked to her car, got in, and drove away.

She parked a couple of blocks away in a residential area, careful to avoid any commercial properties. If any of the residents had video doorbells, they might get a glimpse of her car or her returning to the bar. But if this ploy worked, the detectives would be looking elsewhere and the recordings would be overwritten before anyone saw them.

In a few minutes, Nicole was back at Logan's truck. She took the keys from his pocket, removed her stocking cap, and donned his baseball cap. Just the feel of it made her shudder, but she made herself keep it on. She climbed into the truck, turned the heat up all the way, and drove out of the lot.

First, she made the trip to Jen's Place. She knew exactly where her cameras were focused, and she drove through their field of view close enough that the truck would be recognized easily but too far away to identify anyone inside the darkened cab. To be sure the video wouldn't include her face, she pulled the bill of Logan's cap even lower.

The next stop was Logan's home. He'd want some privacy for what he had in mind for her, which meant the basement or the garage. Nicole couldn't bring herself to enter his house, so the garage would do. She pulled inside and closed the door. For a moment, she sat there shivering even though the temperature inside the truck's cab had to be close to 90 degrees.

Her trembling eased after a few minutes, though now she was weak and nauseated. She reached across Logan's body, opened the door, and shoved him out.

"Stupid, stupid, stupid," Nicole snarled at herself.

Logan had been dead for nearly an hour and whatever injuries he had sustained in the fall would be easily classified as postmortem. She couldn't change the timing of his cuts and bruises, but at least she could provide a plausible explanation for them. After a moment's search, she found what she needed—a tall stool with a low back. She selected a spot where Logan would have tortured her and pulled the chair there. She no longer had the strength to lift him onto it, so she tipped the chair over and laid him where he would have struck the floor when he fell.

She stood back to check her work, spotting the flaw in her plan almost instantly but not understanding its cause. There was a path in the dust of the garage floor and in places, it looked damp. She examined Logan. At some point, probably in the parking lot, his sphincter muscle had relaxed. She was leaving a trail of urine wherever she dragged him. The parking lot at the bar shouldn't be a problem; it probably saw use as a toilet in the wee hours of many mornings. But the damp spot on the truck seat and in the garage? Those could be problems.

Nicole knew what she needed to do, and yet, she hesitated. It took another quick visit to the prison cell of her mind to create the resolve she needed. She climbed into the passenger seat and tried to relax, but the smell was making it difficult. How had she missed this odor before? But then, desperation could play tricks on your senses.

It seemed to take forever, but finally, she felt a wet pool of warmth growing beneath her. She slid out of the door and onto the floor. There, she kicked and scooted her way across the floor to where Logan lay. Again, she stood to examine her work. No flaws this time, but the scene needed more—more pain, more violence. Unfortunately, she knew what that meant.

On the workbench, she found a short board, walked back to the place of her staged torture, and smashed it into her face. Regrettably, her instincts had slowed her hand at the last instant, so while the blow brought tears to her eyes, it hadn't brought blood to her nose. She tried again, this time successfully. She placed the bloody board in Logan's hands.

Nicole then returned to the truck, allowing the blood to flow between her fingers, down her shirt, and onto the seat. She put a bloody hand on the dash, the seat, and the door. She repeated her slide out of the truck and her crabwalk to Logan. When she stood this time, she nodded in satisfaction. From all indications, she'd put up a valiant fight at Jen's Place, but Logan now had her at his mercy inside his locked garage.

It was time for the final step in her plan and as abhorrent as the rest of this scheme had been, it would be far worse. To be convincing, she needed more than a bloody nose. She searched the garage for implements of torture, finding no shortage of them— utility knives, pliers of all shapes and sizes, a drill with an ample supply of bits and wire wheels, and electric saws with dozens of blades.

Nicole took a pair of pliers and clamped them on a finger until it broke the skin, then transferred the tool to Logan's hands. But while the act was painful, it didn't really look like much. Next, she picked up the drill and fitted it with a wide, flat blade of the type used to drill large holes in wood. But the thought of the time it would take and the pain she'd have to endure was more than she could stomach. Still, Logan could have threatened her with it, waving it in front of her face, so she replaced the pliers in Logan's hand with the drill. She placed the pliers next to the bloody board, his cache of implements of torture growing, but still woefully inadequate.

What she needed, she realized, was an act of self-harm that could be implemented in a moment of determination and finished nearly as fast, while leaving undeniable signs of physical harm. After a moment's reflection, a torture scenario started to take shape in her mind.

Nicole found a small wooden box and a rope. She fashioned a loop in the rope with a simple slip knot, threw one end over a ceiling joist, and tied the other to a heavy-duty vise bolted to the workbench. She placed the box below the makeshift noose. Logan and the toppled chair were next to the workbench where he would have sat after raising her off the box and tying the rope to the vise. He'd want a ringside seat to her struggles.

For Logan's sadistic entertainment, he wouldn't have tied her hands. He wouldn't have pushed her off the box. That might break her neck, and the end would be too fast, too humane. Rather, he'd let her use her arms to hold herself up for as long as her strength lasted. And if she tried to climb up to the rafter and free herself? He'd simply pull her back down or punch her in the stomach until her grip failed.

At some point, she would have tired and he would have lowered her to the ground so she wouldn't die too soon. Or maybe he would grow weary of the show and want to end it with a bullet to the brain and a shallow grave out on the high plains? But whatever the reason, he would let her down. That was his fatal mistake. Once on the floor, she would regain enough of her strength to sneak up from behind and strangle him. She found a piece of rope that was approximately the same width as his belt. She wrapped it around his neck, not tight enough to bruise, because that injury would be easily classified as postmortem, but tight enough to leave rope fibers on his skin.

She replayed the entire torture-and-escape scenario in her mind, looking for any loose ends. The individual acts seemed fine or at least as good as she could make them in the time she had. The setting, however, still needed work. The viciousness of their final death struggle would have left Logan's work area in shambles. So, she rubbed some of her blood on Logan's hand, leaned him against the workbench, and used his hand to leave bloody fingerprints and knock several of the tools to the ground. The stream of blood from her nose was starting to slow, so she blew it vigorously. That not only restarted the flow, but left splatters on the tools, the floor, and Logan. She added her bloody handprints to the workbench and scattered a few more tools around the area. Now, the scene was perfect.

Nicole climbed onto the box, slipped the noose over her head, and placed each hand between the rope and her neck. After a moment to steel herself, she stepped off the box. Her precautions, however, did nothing to ease the pain as the rough fibers of the rope cut into her flesh. She would have screamed had her throat been open. Instead, only the sound of a rasping groan reached her ears. Tears filled her eyes and though she tried to blink them back, she felt one roll down a cheek and sting when it reached the raw skin of her neck. She clenched her fists tightly around the rope and pulled with all her strength. The friction of the rough fibers, however, was too much and the noose stayed taut. Darkness began creeping into the corners of her vision.

As her foot felt for the box, her right hand slipped from under the noose, shot up to grasp the rope above her head, and pulled her up to reduce the tension. It was an instinctual response driven by pain and panic, and it ended her ordeal at about the same moment as her foot found support. Her self-torture was over, but she already knew that her reflexive reaction had produced more damage than it had saved.

Carefully, she removed the loop from her head. When she gingerly checked the right side of her neck, she gasped even though her touch had been as light as a butterfly's kiss. But as unpleasant as the rope burn was, it was minor compared to the pain that radiated from her chest to her scalp with every move. She must have strained or torn a muscle in her neck and now, even tiny sips of air produced stabbing agony.

She teetered on the top of the box, her hand tightening on the rope to keep her balance. She started shivering, the toll of the last hour's events now coming due. She looked down, screaming with the torment the sudden move produced. The pain had cleared her head and stopped the shaking. At least it had for now. Nicole carefully climbed down from the box, knowing that if she mastered the pain, then shock was the next enemy that would visit her.

But before she could address that problem, her scream came to mind. "Damn," she muttered to herself. The closest house to Logan's garage was probably fifty yards away, but he wouldn't want to take the chance they would be interrupted. He would have gagged her. How was she going to create that evidence now that she could hardly move?

She scanned the garage. Logan would have wanted something to stuff into her mouth, which would leave her saliva on the rag. Then, he might have secured it with tape or another piece of cloth. Tape was plentiful with duct and electrical tape hanging from hooks above the workbench. But a simple rag? She found nothing in a search that had to be completed quickly; darkness and fatigue were closing in on her rapidly.

Perhaps the tape alone would work. She raised her right hand, getting it to her chest before the pain became intolerable. The tape would have to stay on the hooks above the bench.

Not trusting herself to climb on the box again, she walked to the vise, pulled some of the rope back across the joist by keeping her hand low, and leaned over to grasp it in her mouth. Then, she pulled it taut with her left hand, hoping it would leave an imprint, perhaps even some bruising. But when she considered what she had done, she knew there were flaws in this planted evidence. If she had been gagged with a rope, where was it? And why was her saliva on the rope from which she had been hung? And why was the noose now about eight feet above the box when she was only five foot, six inches tall?

The time for staging her torture, however, was over. Her shivering had become uncontrollable even though the sensation of being cold had been pushed out of her mind by an ever-encroaching void. Her body was shutting down. She found her coat and phone, donning the former before she lay down on the floor. She put her feet up on the box to counter the shock, then dialed 9-1-1. The conversation was a blur, but she remembered saying, "I'm dying. Follow my signal." She left her phone on and dropped it on the ground.

Her last thought was, "God, I hope the battery lasts."

TUESDAY, AUGUST 30

Afternoon, Jen's Place

When Nicole finished the story of her fatal encounter with Kyle Logan, Rebecca took a couple of slow, silent laps of the office. She could feel Nicole's eyes on her back, but she wasn't sure how to respond. Finally, she said, "You're taking a chance by sharing that with me. You want to tell me why you did?"

"After I got back from St. Louis, I thought about not telling you," admitted Nicole. "You were very quick to pick up on ... well, on how my history might be coloring my beliefs. But not being willing to shake hands is quite a bit different than being mentally transported back to a time and place where I was at the mercy of my kidnappers. Maybe this information is unnecessary, but I don't think so. I can't very well expect you to weigh all the possibilities if I'm holding back on perhaps the most likely of them all."

Rebecca wasn't sure she agreed. After all, her investigation wouldn't cover Nicole's psyche; that exploration would have to fall to others with more appropriate training and backgrounds. But then again, it was difficult to know what bit of information might prove pivotal. Perhaps her client was right.

"So, you had a flashback that night in the bar's parking lot?"

"I did," replied Nicole slowly, her gaze dropping to the floor before she looked up again. "In all my hours of self-defense training, I was picturing some generic, unknown assailant. I should have realized that the first time someone grabbed me, I'd be right back at the mercy of my kidnappers."

Nicole paused a moment, her eyes starting to look moist. "My therapist said I have all the symptoms of post-traumatic stress disorder—the nightmares, the endless days when I feel nothing but emptiness." Through it all, Nicole had held her emotions in check ... until now. Her last admission proved too much and she squeezed her eyes closed. A tear escaped one anyway. She wiped it away with a fist clenched so tightly that her knuckles were white.

Somehow, Rebecca thought she understood. A void where Nicole's sense of self should have been was more than she could stand; it was perhaps more than anyone could take. Rebecca watched helplessly as the woman's chin began to quiver. Then, her body started to shake with suppressed sobs. She was afraid to console Nicole, afraid her touch might make her suffering worse.

After a few moments, Nicole regained enough composure to continue. "Sorry. My therapist told me that flashbacks might occur, but I didn't think so. I've never had anything like hallucinations. But ignoring that possibility was a huge mistake. The instant that Logan grabbed me, all the emotions of being violated came rushing back—the hatred, the fear, the helplessness. There's even this rancid odor that I associate with the kidnappers' compound, maybe from something they used to drug me. Anyway, when Logan's hand clamped down on my wrist, I would have sworn that I smelled it again."

Rebecca had guessed that counseling was part of the protocol for returning to normalcy after a kidnapping, but this was the first time Nicole had mentioned it. She wondered if the sessions were continuing in Colorado, but the topic seem much too personal to broach.

"After Logan, I started adding a lot more visualization to my self-defense training, which is something most of the trainers wanted to do anyway," said Nicole. "So now, in my mind, I picture the kidnappers when I'm smashing a nose with the heel of my hand. I also picked up a male therapist when I moved here, which lets us do some roleplaying."

And there was her answer, though it raised another less intimate question in Rebecca's mind. "You do hand-to-hand roleplays with your therapist?"

"Sort of ... I suppose," she said slowly. "If I show him exactly what to do, he'll try, but he's pathetic. And because he's mid-50s, bald, and overweight, I get to work on my visualization skills even more." Nicole drew back, her eyes widening fractionally. "Would you be interested in working out with me over the next couple of weeks? I could use a partner, both to keep in shape and to prepare myself mentally. And frankly, it would be a lot easier picturing you as an attacker."

"Thanks ... I guess," Rebecca replied, laying on the sarcasm to, hopefully, reduce some of the tension that still filled the room. But in fact, she found the idea intriguing. Two weeks away from her gym back in St.

Louis wouldn't do her conditioning any good. And in her line of work, practicing self-defense was never a wasted effort. She'd just have to remember to protect herself at all times, although that was standard guidance for this type of training anyway.

"I'm better now," said Nicole, almost as if she had read Rebecca's thoughts about self-protection. "I still have nightmares and days where I feel nothing but empty, but I'm not nearly as jumpy as I was. And I've had nothing like a waking flashback since that night. I can control my demons."

"I'm not sure any of us can control them completely, but the fact that you're working on them is what's important. You have some place where we could work out?"

"The basement. It's all set up as a gym with mats, weights, a punching bag, the whole nine yards." Nicole paused, her brow wrinkling. "I don't have anything like a firing range, although I can recommend some places if you want to practice. But otherwise, the guns at Jen's Place stay locked up in our safe."

"Good policy. And I have an addition to your collection." Rebecca pulled her sidearm out of the desk, opened the action to confirm it was unloaded, and handed it to Nicole. "If things get tense, I'll need it back."

"Of course."

"As for working out, I'm interested. Tomorrow morning, say half-hour after breakfast?"

"Perfect," replied Nicole. But then, as if to belie that statement, she frowned. "An hour ago, when we started talking about Kyle Logan, I said my actions that night probably fell in a gray area of the law. Seeking him out when I had a protective order to keep him away makes me look guilty, although I could play the surprised-to-see-you card he kept using. And even though killing him was an accident, covering it up afterward has to be a problem that would require some fancy, legal two-steps to explain. Or do you think it's obvious that I took the law into my own hands?"

That was a tough question. "Sitting here in my office—sorry, I mean in the Jen's Place office—it would be easy to say you should have simply called the police from the bar's parking lot. There are a lot of reasons why you could have been there and, in point of fact, wanting to defuse the situation is a good one. Then, he attacked you, giving you the right to protect yourself. But it's also easy to see why you weren't thinking that way. And you never know what a jury might believe."

Rebecca paused, weighing the alternatives, but failing to find a clear winner. "Maybe the best way to leave this question is to say, it's good you don't need to test the legal waters."

"Fair enough," replied Nicole. "Well, I'm heading back to my room to start on my twenty-six unknowns. I can probably eliminate half of them tonight with a little more digging online and finish the rest tomorrow morning with a few phone calls or visits."

Calls or visits? Rebecca was on the verge of saying, "No way you should be talking to these people." And yet, Nicole seemed quite capable of handling herself ... as long as there were no more flashbacks. There was also the issue that she couldn't really stop Nicole if she decided to go it alone. And since making Doc handle an issue by himself had nearly gotten him killed, she didn't want to repeat that mistake.

"If you contact anyone, you need to be extremely careful," Rebecca said finally. "Keep the talks in the context of public information as much as possible. So, if Rose Kline is a school principal, you could drop the name Milgrom only after exhausting all of the school's entrance requirements and most of their history."

"Rose Kline? A principal?" Nicole said with a laugh. "See, I had her pegged as a lady of the evening that Milgrom frequented, and Whitten was using her as leverage to get him to defame his boss. Guess we'll see."

"That we will," Rebecca said as she watched Nicole pick up her laptop and leave.

Late Afternoon, The Peterson Residence, Lone Tree, CO

Rebecca rolled down the window of her car, hoping the cooler air of the approaching evening would help tame her headache. She'd read up on altitude sickness before the trip and knew it was unlikely at elevations below 8,000 feet. And although Lone Tree was higher than the mile-high city of Denver, she was still 2,000 feet below that height. More likely, the pressure between her eyes was the result of everything else this case had thrown at her.

First, within minutes of completing her thirteen-plus hour drive to Colorado, she'd been required to justify her presence to the widow of the victim. True, she had been able to form an uneasy truce with Bethune-Peterson, so the pain wasn't from conflict. In fact, if the crotchety old woman had any effect, it was probably the opposite. Rebecca had found Bethune-Peterson's commonsense explanation of events completely consistent and generally persuasive. Unfortunately, however, they were close to the antithesis of the beliefs of her client, and that fact alone might account for the vise tightening on her head.

As for her meetings with the two individuals Nicole blamed for Peterson's depression and subsequent suicide, they, too, had given her no reason to accept Nicole's version of events. Dan Milgrom seemed a kindly old man who, if Bethune-Peterson was right, had saved HomeRight from a failing leader. It was the case that he now seemed puzzled by his vocal opposition to his old boss, but then, wouldn't anyone feel ashamed of attacks on a man who later killed himself? As for the mysterious stalker that only he had seen, coincidence, imagination, and even false memories were ready explanations.

As for Whitten, he was undoubtedly unsavory, but that wasn't a crime. He was arrogant and controlling, too, but there wasn't a law against that either. And none of those traits came anywhere close to explaining why or how he had turned the once-loyal Milgrom against his boss and lifelong friend. Simply put, he had no apparent way to drive Peterson to his death.

So, by process of elimination, Bethune-Peterson had become her primary suspect, albeit not a very strong one. The woman obviously had continuous, unfettered access to the victim. She also had the means. With her access to the company, she could have staged her husband's failings at work. Or alternatively, maybe she had dosed his food with something that made his behavior erratic. Then, a constant diet of emotional, and perhaps, physical abuse at home had been the final straw. In fact, if Rebecca had to choose between badgering from his subordinates at work or the abuse a wife could apply to her husband at home as the primary cause of a suicide, she would take the latter every time.

Bethune–Peterson's motive, however, was elusive. When Rebecca glanced at the Peterson residence, she had much the same reaction as she had at the home of the Milgroms—it was nice, but not lavish. If money had been Bethune–Peterson's motivation for ridding herself of the mister, she hadn't used it yet to move up the property ladder. There was also the possibility that the financial windfall she had expected had never materialized. Randolph Peterson had, as Nicole said, been offered a severance package of nearly a million dollars that he donated to charities. That fact was in the papers about six weeks after his removal from HomeRight and two weeks before his death. Bethune–Peterson could have thought she'd push him to the grave before he donated the money. And when the donation came sooner than expected, she couldn't stop the process she'd started.

Rebecca picked up her notebook from the passenger seat, left her car, and walked to the front door.

"I guess it was just a dream," said Bethune–Peterson when she answered the door. "I dreamed you dropped all this nonsense and went back home."

Rebecca was tempted to say, "And a nice day to you, too," but she didn't because ... well, because the questions she needed to ask the woman would be painful. But given that greeting, she decided to drop her customary apology before beginning. If the woman seemed anything other than condescending as the interview proceeded, she'd apologize later.

"I just have a few more questions," said Rebecca. "This shouldn't take long."

When they were seated in the living room, Bethune-Peterson said, "So, what else do you need from me?"

"We finished the questions about HomeRight and the actions of Mr. Daniel Milgrom and Mr. James Whitten. What I have left deal with the suicide and events immediately after."

Bethune-Peterson nodded once.

"First, I understand from the newspaper accounts that you discovered the body."

The woman released a long sigh. "That's right. And if you've read those stories, then you probably know I was away that morning for a planning meeting for a benefit. I came home a little before noon and found Randy dead at his desk in the study."

"Was there anyone else in the house while you were gone?"

"You mean like help?"

Rebecca nodded.

"No, there wasn't. We have services for cleaning, landscaping, and the pool, but this was a Thursday. They come in on Tuesdays."

"All of them?" asked Rebecca.

"Yes, so I can be around if there are questions."

So, she was at a planning meeting with lots of witnesses. He was home alone. If she had orchestrated this situation to give herself an alibi, it was a poor effort. The estimate of Peterson's time of death included both the time before she would have left for the meeting and the time she would have returned home.

"That morning, before you left, did your husband seem unusually distraught?"

Bethune-Peterson rubbed her forehead with a hand for a moment. When her hand came down, her gaze was steady, unblinking. "That's a question I've asked myself dozens of times. And the answer is, no, he didn't. But when you see someone every day, I think the small changes go unnoticed. It's only after a time when you stop to think that you may realize—things have changed. And when I did that with Randy, I knew he was deteriorating, slowly but steadily. He obviously passed some breaking point in the days leading up to his death, but I missed it. As to anything specific on that morning? No, I didn't notice anything unusual."

"Did your husband also feel like he was deteriorating? For example, did he seek medical attention for his condition?"

Bethune-Peterson paused. "Tough to say if he knew or not. Before the vote of no confidence by the board, he was angry a lot, but work can be frustrating even when you're very successful. And after his removal, I felt that he needed a few weeks to ... well, grieve for his lost company. But after three weeks, when all he was doing was sleeping, eating, and watching television, I started suggesting that he see our doctor. He did, eventually, and not surprisingly, our doctor referred him to a psychiatrist. But Randy died before that appointment was scheduled."

"But he agreed to see the doctor, the psychiatrist?"

"It took some persuading, but yes," Bethune-Peterson said. "I've thought about that, too. Why would he have agreed to go if he was just going to kill himself? Truth is, while I've used words like suggesting and persuading, I was nagging him. He probably just wanted to shut me up."

Rebecca couldn't quite decide if this admission meant anything or not. Certainly, a wife knowing she could drive her husband to empty promises wasn't unusual. But if she had been abusing him emotionally and it had gotten out of hand, would she have said this? She filed the question away to consider later.

"Unexpected deaths generate a lot of documents—police incident reports, autopsy reports, things like that. I'd like to make a copy of whatever you have if that's OK?"

"They gave me copies but I didn't keep any of it," said Bethune-Peterson. "I don't want that stuff around."

Rebecca knew this from Nicole, but she wanted to hear Bethune-Peterson say it anyway. People deal with grief in many different ways, but most of the victims Rebecca had seen kept the paperwork, even if they didn't look at it often ... or ever. For many, it provided reassurance that law enforcement had recorded everything and had followed up vigorously. But there were reasons why others didn't want any of it sitting in filing cabinets and desk drawers.

"Just too painful to keep around?" she asked.

"Maybe, in part," said Bethune-Peterson. "But mostly, it's just secondhand for what I already know.

I know when, where, and how Randy died. I know the reasons he gave in the suicide note. I know more than those pieces of paper could ever say. So, why hold on to them?"

Bethune-Peterson's confidence in her version of reality hadn't weakened since Sunday, not that Rebecca really expected it would. "You mentioned reading the suicide note?"

Bethune-Peterson nodded. "I read it."

"Did the police ask if you thought he wrote it?"

"A detective did, and I'll tell you what I told him — Randy wrote the note. It sounded like him, had the words he used. It even included one of his favorite sayings — that HomeRight had been founded on bedrock and the wind. He always talked about getting as many hard facts as he could, but how business decisions sometimes came down to taking a shot in the dark."

"I like that," said Rebecca, not needing to feign the sentiment. And while she couldn't vouch for the saying's accuracy in business, it was certainly true in investigations.

"So earlier, I said we'd finished all the questions about Mr. Milgrom's behavior, but I did have one follow-up," said Rebecca. "It came up when Nicole discussed the case with me and again when I talked to Mr. Milgrom. Apparently, when he thinks back to some of the contentious staff meetings, he's not sure why he opposed your husband's new policies or criticized his mistakes so strongly. Have you seen Mr. Milgrom acting disoriented or confused in any way?"

"No, not directly," replied Bethune-Peterson. "Most of what I know is from Miranda and she's mentioned that Dan can't ... well, justify his actions. But from what I hear, I'm not sure confusion is the right term. It sounds more like regret to me, and that makes perfect sense. Dan would have wanted to support Randy, but when he couldn't any longer, he did what was necessary. Then, after the fact, he felt guilty about it."

Another completely logical inference in a series from this woman. Of course, it didn't hurt that she was basically repeating the official version of events. Having come to the end of her questions, she said, "That's it for me, at least for today. Is there anything else you'd like to ask or add?"

Bethune-Peterson paused, slowly nodding her head. Finally, she said, "If you get your answers—proof that Dan or Whitten plotted against my husband or proof that it's all nonsense—will that help Nicole with whatever's troubling her? I hate to see her so ... uneasy all the time."

That wasn't a question Rebecca had considered, and at first blush, she didn't know quite what to make of it. It certainly painted a picture of a woman who couldn't have driven her husband of forty years to his grave if she had this much compassion for a woman she'd known less than two. But then, she had no way to know if her sympathy for Nicole was real. There were simply too many convicted criminals—serial killers seeming to top the list—who could feign compassion when their actions proved the opposite.

But even though she couldn't be sure what Bethune-Peterson was experiencing internally, the woman deserved an answer. "I'd like to think so. I'd like to think that resolving her questions about your husband's death might heal old wounds, but honestly, I just don't know."

Evening, The High Plains Rib House, Denver, CO

"I took you at your word," said Gloria Shaw as Rebecca approached the table in the High Plains Rib House. "A lot of women wouldn't care for this much meat, but if you eat anything?" She raised her eyebrows.

"I wasn't joking," replied Rebecca. She took a seat and picked up the menu. "I love barbeque. With the Texas toast slathered in garlic and butter, I have the grain group covered. The two tablespoons of slaw I'm going to order are my veggies. And tonight, before bed, I'll down a glass of milk to hold the heartburn at bay. See, all four basic food groups are covered without even considering the beer."

"Something tells me you've given your answer a lot of thought," replied Shaw.

"It comes from working around men so much. I got tired of having my lunches described as rabbit food. And besides, a meal somewhat heavy on protein once in a while isn't going to kill me. I just balance it out with a day or two of greens."

Rebecca sat back and looked over the top of her menu, finally realizing what was different in her dinner partner. "I noticed the change in your hair style when I walked in, but no glasses? And that outfit is very flattering." Shaw looked ten years younger than she had the day before.

"Well, not as flattering as ...." Shaw raised a hand toward Rebecca. "No one could miss all the guys drooling when you walked in, and it wasn't just the ribs on the plate in front of them. And as for the glasses, I don't really need them, but they complete my more matronly look for the office."

"Whitten?" Rebecca had promised herself she'd ease into the case, but somehow, the transition was too tempting. At least, she could give Shaw the option of delaying this part of the dinner conversation if she wanted. "Sorry, you'd probably like a break from work talk."

A young man appeared at the table and took their orders. After he left, Shaw said, "Since I was sitting in for Mr. Whitten's regular office assistant, I know why you met with him. And I'm OK with you looking into the events at HomeRight before Mr. Peterson was voted out. Actually, I'm better than OK; I'm all for it. As for Whitten being the reason for the transformation in my appearance, you already know the answer to that."

"Yeah, I suppose I do." Rebecca felt that women had made gains in the business world, but she also knew there were pockets of male chauvinism in every commercial industry and government sector. She'd experienced some of that herself. "Look, I appreciate you being so upfront with me, so I'll return the favor. Yes, I'm interested in what happened at HomeRight that led to the board's vote of no confidence. But I'm also interested in dinner with a pleasant new acquaintance."

"Thank you, and I'm sure we can do both. I'll just start by saying that I don't know exactly what happened at work other than the fact that a couple of years ago, the environment at the top turned abhorrent. Mr. Whitten was always something of an arrogant jerk, and Randy had no problems with that."

"Your boss let you call him by his first name?"

"Let me? More like insisted," said Shaw. "Mr. Whitten, on the other hand, would probably fire me if I called him Jimmy." She paused. "This is all confidential, isn't it? I'd be out on my fanny if anything like that last statement got back to him."

"Absolutely. I share summaries with my client, but they focus on implications rather than verbatim statements. So, the only way something like that would come out would be if it's required in a legal proceeding. And if that happens, Mr. Whitten will have bigger problems than worrying about you calling him Jimmy."

"Good," replied Shaw. "I'm not sure anyone besides his mom would get away with that nickname ... and maybe she wouldn't either. Anyway, Whitten was always a pain in the backside, but it seemed like his attacks became more vicious a couple of years ago. Dan Milgrom had been an ally, but at about the same time, he changed and joined in the name-calling and finger-pointing. On top of the venom from those two, there were setbacks in other areas of the business—declining revenues, unhappy clients, confusion among the troops. And finally, completely outside of work, a young man claims Randy practically raped him and then drops out of sight. I know, when it rains, it pours, but this was more like a year-long flash flood."

Rebecca had done enough research online to know Shaw wasn't exaggerating. It had been worse news after bad for months. And while Shaw wasn't a professional business analyst, she had fifteen years working for the head man at the company. She'd know the inside stories that went along with the numbers. "So, in your opinion, was Mr. Peterson losing his touch? Were his decisions becoming worse all of a sudden?"

"Wow. You're not easing into these questions, are you?"

Rebecca started to offer a different starting point for the chat, but Shaw raised a hand to stop her.

"Unfortunately, I've given that exact question a lot of thought. Too much, perhaps. But it seems to me that there were three real zingers right at the start: the young man who accused Randy of solicitation; the leaked marketing concepts report that was out-of-date; and the missing deposits. Only one of those was directly under Randy's control—the deposits—but that slipup really hurt the company." She paused a moment. "Well, I suppose his sexual urges are under his control, too, but that whole story's a bunch of bunk.

"Anyway, for a couple of months after those three things happened, a lot of Dan's and Whitten's complaints seemed pretty trivial. Then, for the final nine or ten months, it was a combination. Sometimes, it seemed like Dan and Whitten were making something out of nothing. At other times, Randy had clearly messed up. But after months of being berated by his subordinates and the papers, that's to be expected, isn't it?"

"I would think so," replied Rebecca. "Enough pressure will make anyone crack." And while she meant it, it wasn't just the mistakes that bothered her. It was the rapidity of their onset and their regularity. "I looked at the stock market forecasts from two years ago, and it seemed like HomeRight's projected returns got downgraded every month, just like clockwork. I know those projections are based on a company's reported data, things like gross sales and additions to backlog. So, my question is, were the books showing these consistent drops, month after month?"

"Unfortunately, yes," said Shaw as her gaze dropped to the table. When she looked up, she said, "As part of his previous job as COO, Mr. Whitten would prepare performance timelines, which were annotated with world, local, and business events that might aid in their interpretation. You wouldn't want to interpret a drop in cash flow at the start of the COVID pandemic the same as an equivalent drop when public health wasn't an issue.

"There is, of course, some art in picking these interpretive factors, and starting two years ago, it seemed like all the annotations involved a misstep by Randy in one way or another. He makes a mistake and soon after, HomeRight suffers financially. Then, as if the conclusion wasn't already apparent, in each staff meeting Whitten or Milgrom would say something like, 'Damn, Randy. Do you have to f-up every month?' Except they'd use the f-word. Reports to the board were similar except without the profanity."

"Nice," replied Rebecca, her tone dripping with sarcasm. But then, she had a thought. "Could Whitten have faked any of the data in those reports? He was COO, after all."

Their food arrived and after waiting for their server to leave, Shaw said, "By the end of the month, Whitten's reports and the revenues and expenses across the company would have to match or there would be all kinds of people to answer to—bankers, investors, the Securities and Exchange Commission. But exactly when losses are taken can be adjusted within certain legal limits. They can be nudged a few weeks or even months under the right circumstances. And larger, long-term losses can be carried forward for years. So, yes, he would have some latitude to ... well, not fudge the data, but adjust the time when the losses hit the books."

The implication was clear enough to Rebecca. If Whitten had been adjusting the time when losses were taken, he could create the appearance of cause and effect when there was none. Peterson messes up and soon after, the company suffers the consequences. And with enough repetitions of that pattern, it becomes a self-fulfilling prophecy. Investors hear that HomeRight had to revoke a personnel policy three days after instituting it, and they pull more of their money out. They don't care how or why the misstep occurred, or even if it has financial implications. To them, it's just another instance of a pattern they've already seen too often. One look at Shaw said that she, too, had realized what this latitude might mean.

"I might be able to find evidence that Whitten was adjusting the timing of these downturns," Shaw said. "It wouldn't be perfect because I'll have to work from lower-level data, but it should give us some idea."

"Let me try to find another way to get that information," replied Rebecca. "You digging around in two-year-old reports is going to raise too many red flags."

"And you trying to get those data from outside the company is never going to work," countered Shaw. "I can be discreet. Besides, Whitten thinks I'm too old to be a threat. I can say I thought the reports were the current year, and he'd buy it."

Was it something in the Colorado air? Shaw sounded just as confident as Nicole had been when she wanted to look into the backgrounds of their persons of interest. And while Nicole had shown some skill at keeping herself behind the scenes, Rebecca didn't know if Shaw had the same aptitude. To guess wrong would put her in danger. "I'm sorry, but it's just too risky. And besides, you've already given me a new lead on Mr. Whitten."

Shaw looked disappointed, but after a moment and a sigh, she said, "I suppose you're right. So, what else do you want to know?" She took a bite of her brisket and followed it with a sip of beer.

"Would you happen to know if Mr. Milgrom was first on the succession plan for president and CEO?"

"That's what I've heard, followed by Whitten. But only Human Resources would know for sure. And if you're wondering why Dan retired rather than stepping into the job, I can't say. But the rumor was that he didn't have the heart after helping to push Randy out."

That matched what Bethune-Peterson had told her, although all it confirmed was that they had both heard the same gossip. "Before, or perhaps even while the financial downturn was occurring, did Mr. Peterson talk much about retirement?" If he had, his words might have emboldened Milgrom to seek his ouster. Whitten might have taken an interest, too, if he believed he could get rid of Milgrom and clear his path to the top.

Shaw hesitated. "Maybe. It seemed like he was thinking about it a few years ago, but sometimes it was hard to tell if the idea came from him or Ellie. And she made no bones about her desire for him to retire. Once or twice a week, she'd bring in a travel brochure about where they might go, and the locations got more distant and more exotic as time went on. One time, she even mentioned the French Riviera, although I couldn't see the two of them there. Basically, I don't think she wanted to move. She loves Colorado. But I think she was afraid he'd be sneaking back into the office if they didn't get out of town."

"So, she was talking about spending their retirement together even after all their years of marriage?"

"Ah, there's a marriage cynic among us," Shaw said.

"Not really," replied Rebecca. "With people delaying marriage or deciding against it entirely while the divorce rate hangs around fifty percent, marriage is not the healthiest institution. And I understand that divorces of people over fifty are increasing. So, it's not my cynicism so much as the trends, and Mr. and Ms. Peterson would have been in the trendiest group."

Shaw laughed. "I think Ellie would be surprised to hear anyone call her trendy. Rock solid and stable, maybe. Crotchety, probably. But trendy?" She let loose with another chuckle.

"But Ms. Bethune–Peterson was looking forward to days of leisure, traveling and laying on the beach with her husband?"

"Absolutely," replied Shaw. "At first, Ellie and Randy ran the company together, with Dan Milgrom joining them after a year or so. But about five to ten years ago, she started slowing down. I don't think she lost interest in HomeRight as much as she knew it had outgrown her. She was just waiting for Randy to get on the same page."

At least in Shaw's opinion, Bethune-Peterson wanted to spend her golden years with her husband, not find some amorous young man for a May-December romance or strike out on her own with a windfall in her pocket. But then, something as obvious as parading a series of possible retirement locales in front of an OA might be a case of misdirection. "And you feel like Ms. Bethune-Peterson was the one who was mostly talking about retirement?"

"Like I said before, I thought he might be considering it. At least, I thought that until the business problems started. After that, he got stubborn. He said they were going to have to bury him with his desk." Her gaze dropped to the tabletop. "I guess that's sort of what happened, isn't it?" she managed to ask as her voice cracked.

Just this afternoon, Rebecca had denigrated the idea of using emotional responses at face value in an investigation; they were just too easy to fake. So, despite Shaw's pained expression and moist eyes, she would remain a person of interest. That's what logic and her training dictated. But that didn't mean that she felt no remorse in forcing Shaw to relive those days. Most likely, Shaw's memories were unpleasant, making Rebecca hope, once again, that what she was learning was worth the woman's pain.

After a period of silence during which Shaw took a couple more sips of her beer, Rebecca asked, "How about Mr. Milgrom? Did he ever talk about retirement?"

"Dan? No, not that I recall."

So, if Whitten had his eye on the top job all along, he either had some other way to push Milgrom aside or Milgrom's discussion of his future plans had happened outside Shaw's earshot. "OK. About the missing deposits. I understand that the information was on a company server first, and then Mr. Peterson would pull the reports off and email them to himself using his personal email account. Is that right?"

"That was the process," confirmed Shaw.

"Do we know for sure that Mr. Peterson actually downloaded and emailed those files?"

"We do," said Shaw. "Randy even admitted to finding the messages in the trash of his personal account."

Knowing that these files ended up in Peterson's trash wasn't proof he had downloaded, emailed, and deleted them—it only showed the final resting place of the files. Perhaps if she knew more about Peterson's habits, she could draw a firmer conclusion about what had happened. "Did Mr. Peterson ever bring his personal computer into work?"

"Oh, I seriously doubt that. Why would he?" Shaw asked.

"But he could access his personal email from his work computer, correct?"

"As far as I know, everyone in the company can do that, although it's not really encouraged during business hours. But if there's a personal problem important enough ...." She held out a hand in a there-you-go gesture to complete the thought.

"Did Mr. Peterson keep his office locked when he wasn't there?"

"Oh, absolutely."

If Whitten or Milgrom had deleted those emails, the list of things that had to have happened was getting long, and by extension, unlikely. At some point in time, Peterson had failed to lock his office, and someone had installed software that recorded keystrokes, had hidden a camera in his office focused on the keyboard, or had done something similar. In that way, they had gotten the login credentials for his personal email, assuming he had checked it at work because of some pressing personal issue. Then, this person recognized an opportunity to make the boss look bad when the deposits showed up in the account, and he or she deleted them. That was a lot of clandestine preparatory work just to smear Peterson with no guaranteed payoff ... although Peterson's username and password for his personal email might have come in handy for any number of other reasons.

But overall, it was much more likely that Bethune-Peterson had deleted those emails than anyone at HomeRight.

All of Rebecca's questions about who and how people accessed information were apparently troubling Shaw; she was frowning. "Maybe you're getting the wrong idea, what with Randy occasionally using his personal email for business. But that was just for public information ... or information that was soon to be public, anyway. For everything else, he was practically part of Security, reminding people to change their passwords or to mark company proprietary documents and handle them accordingly."

"That's good to know," said Rebecca, although for her purposes, it would have been better if he'd been more careless. She had planned to ask about the marketing report next but considered dropping it. Without having the copy that had been leaked to the press, there were just too many versions of it in circulation to draw any conclusions. But then, she'd only heard Milgrom talk about the various headers that might or might not have covered the date that might or might not have been included when the document was written. So, if for no other purpose, she should get corroboration of this story.

Shaw did verify it and even removed some of the uncertainty—the original document had been dated. But with as many iterations of the report as there were, Shaw couldn't say if all the headers implied the ideas were obsolete or not. As she was finishing her story, she released a single laugh and shook her head.

"What?" asked Rebecca.

"My favorite copy of that report—in fact, the one that I keep in my desk—is one with a header that says, 'In Your Dreams.' It was one of Randy's originals. And although I never heard his orientation talk, I can imagine him in the early days saying something like, 'These will be our marketing approaches ... in your dreams.' I suppose that doesn't necessarily mean the ideas are old, but they weren't anything we were counting on."

Rebecca smiled too, although her reason for doing so was different than her dinner companion's. She was smiling at herself for once thinking this document might be the smoking gun, or at least, one of them, to show premeditation. "Look at how our perp blocked out the date," she would say. "Clearly, he or she had planned the character assault that pushed Peterson over the brink."

So, the dead end she suspected before was now confirmed. Anyone could have leaked that document and possibly, without any changes. Similarly, just about anyone could have hired a young man to pretend to be Peterson's romantic quest. Getting him to disappear later implied this person had money, but with her current set of persons of interest, that didn't eliminate anyone. They were all loaded. Even Shaw, after being Peterson's right-hand woman for years, appeared quite comfortable financially, if the ring on her finger was any indication.

"Would you excuse me for a minute?" said Shaw.

"Everything OK?"

"I just need to use the lady's room." She started to stand, then sat back down. "You hear how alcohol hits you harder at altitude. I wouldn't know. I've always lived a mile high. But getting on in years? I swear all it takes is ...." She glanced at her beer. "A half glass and I'm feeling it." She stood with a smile and left.

Evening, Tucker Redd's Apartment

James Whitten paused on the third-floor landing to catch his breath. Although elegant at one time, the grandeur of this five-story building had long since faded, replaced by dingy efficiency apartments crammed into every square inch of space. And at this hour, every one of those rooms teamed with life—music floated from under one door, the voices of an arguing couple from another, a barking dog at a third.

"Damn the super," Whitten muttered, as he started up the last flight to Tucker Redd's apartment on the fourth floor, cursing the man because the elevator wasn't working. After a short walk down the hall, he knocked on Redd's door. "Couldn't afford the penthouse, huh?" he said when Redd answered.

"Mr. Whitten?"

"You were expecting someone else?"

"I wasn't expecting anyone," Redd said.

Whitten pushed past the man as he'd obviously forgotten his manners ... if he had any. "Well, get the elevator fixed and maybe someone would drop by."

"I don't ...." Redd stopped, shaking his head slowly.

"What?" demanded Whitten.

"I don't think there are any plans to fix it. It's been busted since I've been here."

Now it was Whitten's turn to shake his head. "Is this really the best you can do with what I pay you?" Redd looked down at his feet. "Oh, yes, that's right. You send most of your pay back to that useless wife of yours in Mississippi, don't you."

"She's a good woman and it's Alabama."

"Whatever." Whitten wasn't going to get into a debate with a man who probably thought a "good woman" was any female with a pulse. "Anyway, I bought you a gift." He held it out.

"A phone?" said Redd.

"I know you weren't going to get one." Redd started to say something, but Whitten held up a hand. He couldn't stand being lied to. "And just so you know, I can track this phone, so if it ends up in a pawn shop, you'll be walking back to your good woman in Mississippi."

"Yes, sir."

Good, thought Whitten. At least he wasn't going to say something like, "I'd never do anything like that."

"So, like I promised, I did your job for you. I found out what Nicole Veles has been up to ... and it wasn't laying on the beach with or without clothes. She was in St. Louis to hire a private investigator. Marte's the name."

"Must be good, if Veles went all the way there," said Redd.

"More likely, a drunk relative who can't get any other job," replied Whitten, figuring Redd didn't need to know Marte's background. The big man found enough excuses to avoid doing what he was told already. "Don't worry about the PI. You just need to convince Veles to back off. Stop her and the PI goes away."

"But Veles is a woman."

"You don't say," replied Whitten. He knew that Redd would balk at this assignment, so he had his persuasion ready. "Start up your new phone."

After a few moments of Redd turning it over and over in his hands, Whitten said, "Don't you even know how to turn on a phone? It's the button on the back. Then, enter 1-2-3-4 when it asks for your PIN."

After Redd finished, Whitten said, "You know the symbols for placing a call and a text message, right?" Redd nodded. "Good. Most of the rest of that stuff you'll never need, but you will need the one that looks like an arrowhead."

Redd frowned. "The one that says video?"

"Correct. Go ahead. Press it." Redd did. "Now, the file named fun and games."

After a moment, the video started. It was dark, but the moment Redd recognized the scene, Whitten knew. His eyes got as big as saucers.

"You .... You didn't go back to your car," Redd said.

"Figure that out all by yourself, Einstein?" said Whitten. "You know, that guy you beat up was plenty mad. He even went down to the police station and filed a report." That was a lie, but Redd wouldn't know that. "And now, all the police need is a name to fill in all the blanks. I'd hate to have to make an anonymous call."

"But can't I just talk to the PI?"

"You just don't understand, do you. If you're going to stop people butting into my business, we have to cut off the head. Veles will just hire someone else if we get Marte to back off. So, use your unique skills to convince Ms. Veles that she's not really interested in what happened to old man Peterson."

Evening, The High Plains Rib House

When Shaw returned to the table, Rebecca asked, "Are you going to be OK to drive home?"

"I doubt that the Uber driver will care if I don't walk a straight line to his car."

"I can give you a lift," replied Rebecca.

"Don't be silly. I live close. And besides, I get a senior discount."

"Well, if you change your mind ...." Rebecca paused long enough to know that Shaw had nothing else to say on the topic. "So, shall we drop all the talk of bullying and suicide, and move on to something more pleasant. Like, what would you recommend I do with my free time the next week or so."

"Oh, you want the scoop on the big Bingo tournament down at the rec hall? Why didn't you say so?"

Rebecca was working on a carefully worded affirmative reply—one that left plenty of escape clauses—when she noticed the amused look on Shaw's face. "You had me going for a minute."

"I play Bingo," replied Shaw flatly. "Well, once, when I was about twelve, I think. Look, unless you've had enough, I'd like to finish up talking about the case. After all, when you break it, I want to be able to tell people that you owe it all to me."

"I'm not sure there's anything to break, but if you're sure?"

Shaw nodded.

"OK, let's talk about Dan Milgrom for a minute. The change in his allegiance to Mr. Peterson sounds sudden and extreme … at least, to an outsider. Or am I making too much of it?"

"No, not at all," said Shaw. "You never know what's going on in someone's head, but it was almost like someone threw a switch. He'd been back at work for about a month and then out of the blue, he started getting on Randy for every little thing. And it wasn't just me who noticed. Everyone in the office was talking about it. He seemed so angry with Randy all the time."

"How did he treat you?" asked Rebecca.

"Same as always." Shaw paused a moment. "I suppose that's not completely accurate. My loyalties were with my boss, so Dan's constant haranguing produced a little friction between us. Nothing major. In fact, I'm not sure he felt anything, but I couldn't help but feel some resentment toward him in the beginning."

"But not so much later on?"

"I liked Dan. Still do. He was a tremendous asset to the company, and he's a really decent guy. And while I never liked how he delivered his criticisms—he could be really mean—he was consistent. So, like everyone else, I started to question my beliefs. Yeah, I hate to admit it, but by the end, I came around to the same opinion as everyone else. Randy was slipping. There just wasn't any other explanation. I wasn't even that surprised when the board voted him out. I'd been hearing the rumors for weeks. But when he killed himself?" She paused a moment, the pain of the memory returning as she closed her eyes. "Well, nothing could prepare me for that."

Rebecca wondered if she hadn't been trained and was being paid to be skeptical, would she have even questioned anything that had happened in the HomeRight conference and board rooms? She thought not. It sounded tense, but then, when you're running a billion-dollar business, isn't that expected? It was mainly the speed with which everything had changed that was troublesome. Peterson had suddenly lost his touch and Milgrom immediately pounced on him?

"I know you didn't work for him, but did you ever talk to Dan Milgrom about his arguments with your boss?"

"Well," said Shaw slowly, "not often. It wasn't my place. But the few times I mentioned something, Dan would shake his head and say his temper had gotten the better of him. Then, he'd tell me not to worry, that he'd make amends. But the next time they got together, the fireworks would start all over again. It was like he couldn't control himself."

"Did Mr. Milgrom have a temper?"

"No, not really." She paused, perhaps searching her memory. "In the twenty years I worked at HomeRight with fifteen of them reporting directly to Randy, I only saw Dan mad one other time. Somebody had hit his car and only left a blank piece of paper on his windshield. That was why everyone was floored when he tore into Randy. Or like me, they were at first. But Dan's one of those people who you can't stay mad at for long. He's just too nice for that."

"You mentioned that Mr. Milgrom had been out on medical leave a month or so before things got tense between the two men," said Rebecca. "Heart attack, I believe I've heard. And yet, it sounds like some of these staff meetings became shouting matches. That must have made things stressful."

"Oh, Lordy, yes," replied Shaw. "I used to cringe when he and Randy got into it. Dan would get so red in the face that I was surprised he didn't have another heart attack. But his doctor cleared him for work, and nothing ever happened."

"Did you ever see Mr. Milgrom react so strongly to anyone other than Mr. Peterson?"

She paused again, her head slowly shaking. "No, no one else. If you weren't in Randy's office for the staff meetings, you wouldn't know anything had changed.

Well, until you read the financial section of the paper, of course."

"How did Mr. Milgrom and Mr. Whitten get along?" Bethune-Peterson had said Whitten held no sway over Milgrom, so it would be interesting to see if Shaw agreed.

"Dan got along with Whitten about as well as anyone at HomeRight. Whitten can be charming. I've seen it when he's going after new business ... or some unsuspecting woman. But in general, he's self-centered, arrogant, and rude. And I don't mean just with the support staff. He'll publicly humiliate anyone he believes has messed up, including Randy. Dan, like I said, was much too decent to do anything like that."

"So, Mr. Milgrom would listen to Mr. Whitten's advice, maybe follow his suggestions? And vice versa?"

"Oh, no. I didn't mean that. If Whitten suggested something to Dan, he'd probably do the opposite. Whitten's advice tended to help one person—Whitten. As for advice flowing the other way? I doubt Dan ever wasted his breath. Look, I may have confused things by saying that those two ended up generally on the same page regarding Randy, but that's only because Dan had to do what had to be done. Before Randy started slipping, Dan and Whitten were more like oil and water."

"How about Mr. Peterson's inner circle?" asked Rebecca. "Did Mr. Whitten come down on them as well?"

"They were his favorite target. If some salesperson out in the field made a mistake, he probably wouldn't take the time to look him up. Instead, he'd publicly chastise his director at the next staff meeting. I suppose the positive spin on his behavior was that he was brutally frank, but he liked the 'brutal' part of that role a bit too much."

It was pretty easy for Rebecca to see why Shaw was laying low until she could retire. Whitten sounded like he could be spiteful if you got on his wrong side. "Mr. Whitten seems to have something of a wandering eye. He's married, right?"

Shaw winced. "Maybe I should stay clear of Mr. Whitten's personal life. After all, it's not like I've ever done anything socially with him ... or his wife."

"Fair enough. But what I've heard is that he's married in name only and that he and his wife go their separate ways by mutual agreement. Then, he uses that freedom to chase other women. Any reason I should go back to anyone I've spoken to for further clarification?"

Though the motion was slight and her voice nearly imperceptible, Rebecca saw a slight shake of the head and heard, "No reason that I know of."

It appeared that Whitten was a tyrant at work and a womanizer the rest of the time. Rebecca couldn't help but believe that if he had been the dead man rather than Peterson, there would be no shortage of suspects. "So, how about Dan Milgrom and his wife, Miranda? They seem close to me, but that's based on one brief meeting. Or maybe you haven't seen them socially either?"

"I guess it's a strange thing to say since we're all about the same age," Shaw said, apparently ignoring the option to avoid the question entirely. "But I think they're the cutest couple. Yeah, they seem like they can't agree on anything. Well, anything other than coffee. But if you watch them, you'll catch Miranda slipping her hand into

Dan's. Or he'll give her a kiss behind the ear when he thinks no one is watching." She made a funny shivering motion like she was experiencing that kiss.

"So, I suppose you want to know about Randy, too?" said Shaw. "Did he have, as you put it, a wandering eye?"

"You're a mind reader," replied Rebecca. Even though Whitten's wife didn't seem to be in town long enough for an affair and Milgrom's wife was close to him, other members of Peterson's inner circle could have been involved in his ill-fated defamation. All it would take was Peterson paying too much attention to a married woman, and the husband might set out on a mission to teach the philanderer a lesson. Or if the rumors of his sexual orientation were true—even though no one she had interviewed thought so— perhaps Peterson's attentions had turned to the husband of a jealous woman.

"No way he strayed," Shaw said matter-of-factly. "You probably know the saying, keep your friends close and your enemies closer?"

"Sure."

"Well, I think Ellie lived that advice. When I started working for Randy, I could catch a man's eye. That probably bothered her because it seemed like she went out of her way to be friendly toward me. But the funny thing is, we actually became pretty close. We still talk most weeks, and she's never said anything about his lack of faithfulness. And as for Randy, you can't work for someone as long as I worked for him without learning a lot about their lives. There were never mysterious calls to the office from a woman. He never needed a last-minute gift idea for anyone but Ellie. He never took long lunches or went on unnecessary business trips to romantic places. So, I can say with some certainty that neither of them was looking for other options."

"Is there any chance Ms. Bethune-Peterson was upset by the story about her husband's sexual orientation? If she loved him and thought it might be true, that kind of thing might be hard for her to accept."

"She didn't talk about that rumor much, but when she did, it was just to say the idea was ridiculous." Shaw raised a hand to her mouth to half cover a titter. "She once implied they were still too active in bed for anything like that to be true."

Even if Peterson was attracted to men, if Bethune-Peterson believed otherwise, the truth would make no difference.

Rebecca quickly went through her mental checklist, finding all the topics she'd wanted to discuss now covered. Unfortunately, little in the dinner conversation had suggested new leads or supported new conclusions. Whitten was unsavory but had been consistently that way before, during, and after Peterson's death. He might have shifted the timeline for business downturns and might have become more vicious in his attacks on Peterson two years ago, but both possibilities were only speculation. And even if he had done both, neither was criminal nor did they seem sufficient to drive someone to suicide.

Milgrom's attacks on Peterson and their viciousness were too consistently reported to be anything but true. But as to why they occurred, Shaw had no more of an idea than Milgrom himself. Of course, if he was hiding his agenda behind a façade of mental confusion, he wouldn't have given Shaw or anyone else a reason to doubt it.

And finally, if Nicole and Shaw were right, the tough-as-nails Bethune-Peterson had a major soft spot in her heart. She just wanted to retire with her husband in peace.

"Oh, my God!" Rebecca blurted before her last bite of baked beans reached her lips.

"What is it?" asked Shaw.

It was wild speculation, a random thought so unlikely that Rebecca wouldn't share it with anyone without something to support it. "Oh, sorry. It's not really that big of a deal. It just slipped my mind," said Rebecca as she worked out a plausible explanation for her outburst. "It's just that I forgot to leave Nicole a note saying I wouldn't be around Jen's Place for dinner."

Even for the best of reasons—and keeping Shaw safe was the best of the best—Rebecca hated holding out on her dinner companion. But the omission was infinitely better than getting Shaw involved in something that might get her hurt.

"Well, if she's got any kids in residence, they'll take care of the leftovers."

"One small boy, I believe," replied Rebecca. Shaw's comment had been delivered with a knowing wink, which gave Rebecca the perfect segue to small talk. "Your comment sounded like the voice of experience and you mentioned grandkids earlier. What are your children up to?"

And that's how Rebecca intended to end the evening with her dinner guest—nothing but mundane, completely safe small talk.

WEDNESDAY, AUGUST 31

Evening, Jen's Place

Sitting in his car for the last two hours, Tucker Redd had watched Jen's Place as the sky darkened and thunder rumbled in the distance. It had been a day typical of Colorado's monsoon season—a sunny, calm morning had given way to clouds and the threat of thunderstorms in the afternoon. The rain, however, hadn't materialized, unless the few drops on his windshield could be considered the storm. That, too, was typical. But Redd's mind wasn't on the weather.

When he'd moved to Colorado, he had been interested in finding work as a body guard. He had the physique for the job, and Whitten offered what seemed the perfect entry-level position. It was only part-time and barely paid him enough to help his wife, but there were bonuses when Whitten had "special assignments." In Whitten's case, that was code for strong-arm persuasion. And Redd wasn't above that kind of work. But when it involved a woman? He'd been raised to respect females, not beat them up.

A woman came out of the main house. Redd sat up and trained his binoculars on her. It was almost too dark to see, but she was blonde and too tall to be Veles. She walked across the porch and entered a second smaller door on the right. An inside light came on, then dimmed but didn't go out. He couldn't be sure, but it was probably the light from a second room on that side of the sprawling house.

Redd slouched back down in the car's seat. "Maybe just a stern warning?" he muttered into the night. But he knew better. If word got out that he'd only talked to Veles, Whitten would just find someone else. And the next guy might have no qualms about beating up a woman ... or worse. And knowing what Veles looked like from online pictures, "worse" might be the first choice of anyone who'd take the job. He'd just have to slap her around a few times if she ever came out of the house.

Redd decided he should call it a day. Unless Veles liked evening constitutionals, she was probably in for the evening. Tomorrow, she'd run some errands. He'd follow, and as soon as she was alone, he'd make her realize the foolishness of hiring a private investigator and the consequences of telling anyone about their meeting. Of course, her most likely destinations were busy public places—grocery stores, banks, shopping malls. He knew he needed a better plan, but nothing had come to mind. And Whitten's part in these schemes ended with demands for results; figuring out how to get them was beneath him.

Redd had just reached a hand into his pocket to fish out his keys when the porch light came on. He raised his binoculars as the door to the main house opened again. It was Veles. She walked across the porch and entered the door on the right without a knock. It was apparently unlocked, or at least, had been. He couldn't make out many details before Veles closed the door, although the remaining light did appear to come from a second room.

And since both rooms on that side had been dark, it was probably just the two of them inside.

Research wasn't Redd's forte, but even typing "Jen's Place" into a search engine was enough for him to learn about Kyle Logan's demise at Veles's hands. But even from the pictures online, it was clear that Logan was slight. And with nearly twice Colorado's legal limit of alcohol in his blood, Veles overcoming her attacker wasn't that surprising. And the blonde? Tall, but slender. Even together, he probably outweighed them by twenty pounds. Without a doubt, this was the opportunity he had sought. And if the blonde got in the way? Well, that was her problem.

Not wanting to don his balaclava and walk a hundred yards to Jen's place—it was August, not ski season—he started his car, waited until there was no traffic, and then drove to the end of the driveway with his lights off. He put on the mask and retrieved a short length of rope from under the passenger seat. He hadn't planned on using it when it was just Veles, but he might need the rope if her friend wasn't happy just to watch.

As he started down the drive, lights on each corner of the building came on. He stopped and shaded his eyes with a hand, the output from the lights uncomfortably bright to his dark-adapted eyes. After watching the windows for a moment, he decided that no one inside was paying attention. He started walking again.

When he reached the porch, he mounted the steps and walked to the door on the right. Quietly, he turned the knob. Foolish women, he thought, as it was still unlocked. He peered inside. There was a second room, light from its open door falling on the floor. He listened for several minutes, hearing the voices of two women from inside. Slowly, he crept along the edge of the room, knowing that the creaks and groans of floorboards were less likely near the walls. But less likely wasn't the same as impossible, and about halfway to the second door, a board protested under his weight. Fortunately—or unfortunately for them—one of the women had said something funny and the creak was lost in the sound of laughter.

He stepped into the open doorway to the second room. "Not a sound," he snarled. He didn't necessarily expect them to comply, given that the mask and rope made the purpose of his visit obvious, but the blonde, who was facing the door, just sat quietly and stared at him.

Veles turned, and while she might have gasped softly, what she said was, "In addition to the laws against trespassing and breaking and entering, you should know this facility is protected under Colorado's Domestic Violence program. Now, unless you want to spend the next twenty years behind bars, I suggest you turn around and walk away."

It wasn't the welcome Redd had expected and it took him a moment to process what he had heard. Clearly, he needed to establish control over the situation before the two of them became even more brazen. "Just shut the hell up. My business is with you, Veles. So, blondie, just stay seated behind the desk while me and her come to an understanding."

Rebecca shrugged. "I'd say, kick him in the balls before you throw him out on his ass, Nicole."

Redd flinched involuntarily, a hand going down reflexively to protect his private parts. Veles apparently thought his reaction funny as she snickered behind her hand.

"I don't know, Rebecca," said Nicole. "I'm no private investigator, but since he knows my name, I'd like to hear what he has to say."

Redd's eyes moved from Nicole's face to Rebecca's and back. "You can't be Marte. You're a woman." Whitten hadn't told him to expect a female private investigator, much less one who was so attractive. Maybe he figured it wasn't important.

"I think you're right, Nicole," said Rebecca. "Now, he's got my attention, too. So, let me guess. Since you know a little about both of us, I'm betting this is related to Mr. Randolph Peterson's suicide, right? Or was it a suicide? You have something you want to tell us?"

No harm, thought Redd, that she'd guessed the real reason for his visit; they were going to know sooner or later anyway. But he found the speed they were drawing these conclusions unnerving. Now, he saw no alternative to smacking them both around a little. Hopefully, they'd get the message because he didn't want Whitten sending him back to break some legs. "Let's just say I'm here to deliver some friendly advice. Keep your noses out of places they don't belong." He took a menacing step forward.

"No problem," said Nicole. "I'll spend tomorrow shopping. How about you, Rebecca?"

"I had the spa in mind."

"You're a couple of smart-mouthed bitches, aren't you?" replied Redd. He moved forward to reinforce his words with some pain.

But rather than retreating, Nicole took a step forward, planting her left foot firmly on the floor. Then, her right foot flashed up and landed on his chest in a blur of motion so fast he wasn't sure it had even happened. Certainty, however, came a split-second later when the pain and the emptiness of his lungs registered in his brain. Redd had stumbled backward with the force of the blow and was now bent over with his hands resting on his knees. It seemed incomprehensible to him that someone so slight could deliver a blow of such force, but he had his current state of discomfort and breathlessness as proof.

Redd had, of course, taken hits before, and he knew the game was far from over. He stood to his full height, even though it made the pain worse, and forced a grin of false bravado to his face. The blonde PI, Marte, had come from behind the desk and was watching. But strangely, she seemed to be looking at Veles more closely than at him. Maybe they had some type of coordinated attack they'd practiced and she was waiting for her cue. If so, he'd have to break it up before it started. And the easiest way to do that was to remove Veles from the equation.

He rushed forward, telegraphing a frontal assault. But just before he was within striking distance, he planted a foot and feinted to the left. He knew the move would steal energy from the straight right jab he had planned, but even half of one of his punches to her chin would put her out for the night.

But as his fist traveled forward, Veles spun, his punch only grazing her cheek. Then, too late, he realized her move wasn't only defensive. Rather, using the momentum of the turn, she slapped his right ear with the open palm of her hand. The pain, although not that bad, was mixed with a deafening sound and a disorienting percussion of air. He twisted blindly from the blow, wondering how he could possibly cover up when he no longer knew where she was.

When his head came back around, Veles was nowhere to be seen. But in her place stood the PI. The heel of her right hand flew directly toward the bridge of his nose. His mind screamed "block it," but his arm responded too slowly. Stars exploded in his vision. Tears came to his eyes. All he could really make out was the open door and he raced toward it. He ran through the reception room, out the front door, and into the dark without looking back.

Evening, Jen's Place

"He's getting away," yelled Nicole, glaring at the retreating figure of her would-be assailant. She started for the door at a jog.

"Wait."

Nicole stopped and turned around slowly.

"I don't think following him out into the night is such a good idea," said Rebecca. "You miss one of those big paws of his coming out of the darkness and you'll have more than a sore cheek to worry about. Now, let me take a look at that."

Rebecca stepped forward. Nicole raised an arm, intent on shielding herself from Rebecca's touch. But apparently, the PI realized her mistake and stopped her hand before it got there.

"My cheek's OK," said Nicole. "I just need a moment." She wasn't sure she agreed about letting the home invader escape, although the lack of light would be an equalizer. So, she relented, releasing a long sigh to relieve some of the tension she felt from being so close and yet, so far from a solution to her case. She turned her head so Rebecca could see her cheek better.

"You're going to have a bruise. Let me get some ice from the fridge. You needed another half-inch of fade before the counter."

"Yeah, his reach was a bit longer than I expected," replied Nicole, working to keep the frustration she felt out of her tone. But she failed to keep it out of her words. "It's just that the case would be over if we'd caught him."

Rebecca came back over carrying a few ice cubes wrapped in a microfiber cloth she used to clean her computer screen. "And when he refuses to say anything, what then? You're going to beat it out of him? Now, hold this on your face."

Nicole's temper flared, and for an instant, she thought about knocking the ice out of Rebecca's hand. But after a long moment, reason took control of her thoughts. The man was probably hired muscle, and if so, he wouldn't say anything ... just as Rebecca had said. She took the cold compress and pressed it against her cheek. "OK, I suppose you're right. It's just that I'd like to see him cooling his heels in jail for a good long time."

"And you will," said Rebecca. "So, let's call the police and make a report. Then, we can talk about what we learned from his visit."

"But aren't you going to finish what you were telling me before? Something about an idea you had during dinner with Gloria Shaw?"

"That can wait," said Rebecca. "Let's go over the interruption while it's still fresh in our minds."

"OK," said Nicole, although she wasn't sure they had learned anything from the intrusion. She pushed the question aside for now and called the police department's non-emergency number. After it was established that they were in no immediate danger, the police asked Rebecca to call on her phone so they could take their statements separately. When Rebecca started dialing, Nicole stepped into the reception area so that they'd each have some quiet.

As Nicole got into her statement, it seemed that the location of the attack—a shelter for victims of domestic violence—was both a help and a hindrance. It immediately got the attention of the female officer taking her statement, but she seemed somewhat fixated on the idea that the man must have been one of the women's husbands. While that was a logical guess, Nicole's theory—that the man was somehow involved in Peterson's death—only came up when she mentioned Rebecca having said as much during the attack. The officer didn't follow up, but perhaps that was for the best. She and Rebecca still had nothing solid to indicate foul play.

All of the information Nicole provided during the interview seemed pointless to her. The attacker was masked, so she couldn't describe him beyond general physical characteristics. He wore gloves so he'd left no fingerprints. His clothes were typical—jeans, tan cap, blue work shirt—except that the shirt had long sleeves. Perhaps he had some unusual tattoos hidden under that fabric? Or maybe he figured he might be out until dawn and the nights, even in August, could be cool. When the information was collected, it was apparent to Nicole how little they had. Putting out a bulletin on a six-foot-five- to six-foot-seven, 250- to 270-pound, brown-eyed white male in work clothes would be a waste of everyone's time. And the attacker's race was something of a guess, based on the small patches of skin showing at holes in the balaclava for his eyes and mouth.

But when Nicole mentioned that there would be blood on the man's shirt from a nosebleed, her hopes rose. She was quick to add, "And there are several drops here on the floor."

After verifying this last statement, the officer also seemed more hopeful. She put Nicole on hold. When she came back on the line, she said, "We're sending someone from our Criminal Investigations unit to your address. He'll meet someone from the Parker Crime Scene Unit and they'll take custody of the evidence."

"Someone from Parker?" Nicole asked wondering why a neighboring town would be involved.

"Correct. They handle crime scene investigations for all of Douglas, Arapahoe, Lincoln, and Elbert counties, so you're in good hands."

After that, the interview finished quickly, and when Nicole stepped back into the office, Rebecca was just finishing up hers. "There's a detective and crime scene investigator on the way," said Nicole.

"So, they told me. Now, shall we consider what we learned from this incident while we wait?"

Nicole started for one of the chairs across the desk from Rebecca. Her first thought was that she'd been through this already with the Lone Tree Police Department, and if there wasn't a match to the attacker's blood in the federal DNA database, they'd learned nothing. But she also knew that Rebecca wasn't prone to wasting time, so she gave the question some thought as she settled in.

"Well," she said slowly, "he must have been watching the house. He came in just minutes after I came over to see you. Maybe they can find tire tracks?"

"Maybe, but I doubt he parked anywhere there weren't hundreds of sets of tracks already. Let's queue up your alarm system video. We can answer the question of where he parked and make sure he was wearing his mask when he came within the range of the cameras."

"Use your laptop?" Nicole asked.

"It's on and logged into your network."

Nicole sat behind the desk, and in a matter of a few moments, she had the video playing. Since they knew the time of the thug's visit, it didn't take long to fast-forward to the scene they wanted. "And here he comes," said Nicole. "He's already wearing the mask and gloves, and there's no sign of a car. He must have parked out on the road. So, that's two strikes."

"Fortunately, there's no limit on strikes in an investigation. Now, run it up to the time he left."

Again, it only took a few minutes for Nicole to find the segment. She watched as the big man ran a serpentine path down the driveway until he was out of sight. "The zigging and zagging doesn't seem necessary since he was out of the house. The 'Make My Day' law wouldn't apply, would it?" she asked, mentioning a Colorado law that gave homeowners the right to use deadly force against an intruder that posed a physical danger. Her battered cheek would be proof that he was a threat.

"Probably not, since the danger was over, but he wouldn't want to count on your interpretation of the law. So, what else do we know?"

"More?" Nicole gave the question some thought. "The officer who took my statement thought the intruder must have come here to see one of the women upstairs. But that doesn't add up to me. He didn't say anything about anyone but you and me, he never mentioned the shelter, and he didn't even look in that direction."

"Seems like a reasonable assumption. So, if that's true, what follows?"

At first, nothing more came to mind, but then, Nicole saw the connection. "Well, if you're still wondering if this whole case is a figment of my overactive and somewhat damaged imagination, I'd say this incident is pretty strong evidence to the contrary. If he came to see us and not the women upstairs, then something made the people he works for nervous."

Rebecca nodded, handing the burden of deduction right back to Nicole with an extended hand.

"The attacker was probably looking for me rather than you," said Nicole after a moment. "He came in right after I did."

"Not only that, but he knew you by sight."

"That's right. And while he knew there was a PI here and your name, he wasn't expecting a woman," Nicole added. "Does that mean I'm the one that made them nervous?"

"Probably. Although if it was me, he might have gone after you so you'd drop the case. That stops both of us." Rebecca paused a moment. "You know, I've only been talking to the principles—Bethune-Peterson, Milgrom and his wife, and Whitten. This nervous party or parties would have to expect that I'd do those interviews, so I'm thinking, you've learned something that they don't want us to know. Or you're getting close to something."

"Great. If I only knew what that was," said Nicole.

"It often feels like you have nothing until the pieces come together. Anything else?"

"Not that I can think of."

"Me either. So, I suggest that I recap my meetings with Ms. Bethune-Peterson and Ms. Milgrom, and then we call it a day."

"OK, but what about dinner with Gloria Shaw? You said you had something of an insight during it."

"That'll get covered as I go along," replied Rebecca.

Nicole didn't quite understand the response. Before they had been so rudely interrupted, Rebecca had mentioned something like a "voila moment" she'd had over dinner. And now, it sounded like whatever she had come up with was closer to an afterthought than a breakthrough. But before she could say anything, she heard the crunch of car tires on the gravel driveway.

"Sounds like the cavalry has arrived," she said. "I'll let them in."

She passed through the reception area and opened the front door. As promised, there were two men outside, both in civilian clothes. "You're from the police?"

"Yes, I'm ...," the older of the two said as he held up a badge. But Nicole interrupted.

"So you don't have to repeat yourselves, come in. There are two of us." The older man nodded and they followed Nicole back into the office. Once inside, she turned to them. "I'm Nicole Veles. I run Jen's Place. And this is Ms. Rebecca Marte, a private investigator."

After the detective—Phillip Berra—and the Crime Scene Investigator—Brien Clarke—introduced themselves, Berra asked a few questions about the statements they had given. He apparently already had a copy of them on a tablet he was carrying. Clarke, on the other hand, busied himself by taking pictures, writing notes, and collecting blood samples.

"And neither of you have any idea who this intruder was?" asked Berra, as he and the two women stood around the desk. It was the third time he'd asked that, although in different forms.

If he was expecting a different answer, they disappointed him when she and Rebecca both said, "None" for the third time.

Clarke had finished documenting the scene and started toward the group. When he was close, he said, "Ouch. Your cheek is starting to swell a little, so keep that ice on it." He paused. "You gave this 250-pound gorilla a bloody nose?"

"She did," Nicole said, gesturing toward Rebecca. But Clarke's head was already turned in the PI's direction. In fact, when she thought about it, Clarke had been looking at Rebecca almost constantly when he wasn't working the scene. And when she glanced at Rebecca, she was returning the appraising gaze.

It made sense. Clarke was tall; she wouldn't be looking down into his eyes. He was dark-complected with longish black hair and brown eyes—the perfect complement to Rebecca's pale skin, blonde hair, and blue eyes. He wasn't a bodybuilder, but he had the muscle tone of someone who enjoyed the outdoors and weekend sports. And on the occasions when he looked at her cheek, she caught a slight grimace. Was he also sensitive? That seemed too much to ask of any man, but she could hope for a friend.

Clarke glanced at her and stepped closer for a better look at her cheek, but that was too much for Nicole. He had invaded her personal space. And although hers was probably five times the size of anyone else's, she couldn't help it. She took a step backward.

"The cheek will be fine," Nicole said, knowing this wasn't what was behind Clarke's questioning look. But she wasn't about to explain herself to this complete stranger.

"Do you think the attack tonight had anything to do with Kyle Logan?" asked Berra.

The question made Nicole realize that they probably had their own conclusions about her standoffishness already. She didn't recognize Berra as any of the detectives she had spoken to before, but if he knew of Kyle Logan, he would know what she had supposedly endured at his hands. And it wasn't much of an inferential leap to believe that Clarke would know as well. Theirs was a misimpression that she could not only live with but welcomed.

"The intruder didn't say anything about Logan," replied Nicole simply.

"It doesn't sound like he had much of anything to say, except keep your noses out of his business ... whatever that is. Although, I guess you thought it might be something to do with Randolph Peterson's death. Why'd you think that?"

"I'm the one who mentioned Randolph Peterson," volunteered Rebecca. "Since he knew my name and I'm here looking into his death, it seemed logical."

Berra frowned. "I suppose. But if you're looking into that death, I assume his board of directors is your leading suspect?"

The comment was more than a little impolite in Nicole's opinion and she wondered how Rebecca was going to respond. But perhaps Berra realized the rudeness, too, as he quickly went on.

"Other than the blood sample, I don't see that we have much to go on. We'll run it through our databases, of course, and see if we get a hit. And we'll increase our drive-bys. Otherwise, I'd just make sure you keep your doors and windows locked. The guy might come back to finish what he started."

Nicole considered saying, "I hope so," but she was still under the cloud of the Kyle Logan incident. She didn't want to appear to be looking for a fight or the police might decide that was her normal disposition and reopen the case. So, instead, she said, "Thanks for coming out to collect the blood sample." She nodded toward Clarke, implying her feelings toward Berra without words. "Let me walk you out."

Rebecca, however, surprised her by cornering Clarke for a moment, but then, followed everyone to the front door. There, Berra delivered his final admonition about doors and windows, after which Clarke added, "Wish it had been under better circumstances, but it was nice to meet you." He had started the statement looking at Nicole, but he had redirected his eyes to Rebecca for the ending.

When the door was closed, Nicole turned to Rebecca. "Sorry you had to apologize for my behavior to Mr. Clarke."

Rebecca looked puzzled for a moment, then smiled. "What apology? I asked him if he wanted to show me a good place for a drink since I'm new around here."

"In that case, I'm glad I made you stand out as the friendly one," she said with a grin.

"Thanks," said Rebecca. "I owe you one."

"So, how about a walk?" asked Nicole. "Muscles isn't going to make me a prisoner in my own home, and I could use the time to unwind a little more. We can finish up when we get back."

"OK."

"So, what did Mr. Brien Clarke have to say about a drink?" asked Nicole.

Late Evening, Jen's Place

The clouds that had threatened rain earlier had moved out onto the plains, leaving a beautiful moonlit evening for the women to enjoy. And despite the harrowing earlier events, they did enjoy it.

Nicole wanted to know every detail of Rebecca's talk with Brien Clarke, and since it lasted less than ten seconds, Rebecca recounted it verbatim: "I've only been here a couple of days, so if you'd like to show me a nice place for a drink, give me a call." She'd handed him a business card. And though Rebecca had read pleasure in his answer—"Sure, I'd like that"—she didn't mention it to Nicole. She'd been mistaken too often in the past to believe she could distinguish potential from deceit from a four-word reply.

After that, the women broke into small talk about their upbringings. Rebecca was struck by how their stories seemed mirror images. Her family had been well-to-do. Nicole's family wasn't poor, but both parents had worked to make ends meet. She had become somewhat wild, sampling boys and booze with the invincibility that youth presumed. Nicole, on the other hand, had been serious about everything—her studies, the opposite sex, her responsibilities toward her younger siblings. Rebecca had fallen into criminal justice in college after nearly flunking out in her freshman year. Her reasoning was, if she wasn't chasing criminals, she'd probably end up being one. Nicole, on the other hand, had always wanted to help people. And while most any engineering field benefited society, she couldn't ignore the promise of biomedical engineering.

When the conversation turned to more recent events, Rebecca shared a few stories about her time with the FBI, a couple of tales of deceitful married men—one of which overlapped with the FBI stories—and one about her mentor, turned partner, Gus, who had taught and protected her until his death. And while the bureaucracy of the Bureau hadn't been a good fit for her, its lessons made her current occupation possible.

Nicole, on the other hand, volunteered little about that period of her life, but rather, skipped forward to the days of moving to Colorado and taking over management of Jen's Place. The gap in her history was obvious, and it hit Rebecca how difficult it must be to have lost those years of firsts—her first apartment, her first job, her first dreams of a life with a man she had once loved. Now, those days were just myths built on lies.

When they returned to the ranch house, Rebecca knew that despite the differences in their life stories, or perhaps because of them, she felt a growing kinship with this woman. She just hoped that the outcome of the case wouldn't unravel the camaraderie because it certainly had the potential to do just that.

"You feel like some tea before we get back to work?" Rebecca asked as they entered the office.

"Sure," said Nicole. "You should have some decaf in there. I'll take that."

Rebecca busied herself at the coffee station and in a few minutes, was returning to the desk with two mugs. "Funny, but tea never keeps me up. So, the meeting with Ms. Milgrom first?"

After Nicole agreed, Rebecca covered the highlights. Unlike Bethune-Peterson, Miranda had never had much interest in the events at HomeRight, and apparently, Dan hadn't felt the need to burden his wife with business problems. So, during the year when he'd been one of Peterson's primary detractors, he'd said nothing about it at home. It was only after he had retired in November—the month after Peterson's ouster—that he admitted to his wife some unease in the role he had played. And he had described that role to his wife in much the same terms he had used with Rebecca just the day before. He recalled being incensed by Peterson's business decisions, but in retrospect, his vehemence seemed excessive in some cases and largely unfounded in others.

It was, however, significant in Rebecca's mind that his pattern of fervent verbal attacks followed by confusion hadn't followed the man into retirement. He didn't rail at the neighbors and later claim he didn't know why. Nor did he act that way toward anyone else, including his wife. After a time, Miranda decided that whatever had happened at the office was history not destined to be repeated.

Then, after Peterson committed suicide, Miranda said her husband's unease about his actions became self-loathing. She feared that he, too, might take his own life. So, she watched him closely. Eventually, his self-hate eased, leaving only his questions about his actions toward his old friend. Unfortunately, it was too late for him to get any answers.

When Rebecca paused for questions, Nicole said, "Not a question, but you mentioned the issue about how fast dementia might come on?" Rebecca nodded. "Apparently, some types—and the Creutzfeldt-Jakob form in particular—can come on quite fast. It seems to come out of nowhere and generally appears between the ages of 60 and 65. And Mr. Peterson had just turned 61."

"And I thought I might have to find an expert to get that information. I didn't know I was working with one."

"I'm not really an expert," Nicole said quietly as she looked away.

"Well, you could have fooled me," replied Rebecca. But rather than receiving a smirk or a shrug in reply, Nicole ... blushed? The woman's reaction stumped her, although her lack of familiarity with Nicole seemed a ready answer. True, she had heard Doc talk about Nicole for months, and she'd read about her in the papers for weeks, but they were still virtual strangers in terms of actual face-to-face interactions. The last few days had given rise to a feeling of connection, but that wasn't like years of sharing dreams and fears. And they had no common friends except for ....

But that couldn't be it, could it? Nicole detested Doc. She had said she wanted "... to stay as far from him as possible" when they spoke in St. Louis. And besides, he wouldn't know much, if anything, about dementia. How many times had he mentioned there was more than enough to learn about thought, learning, and memory when everything was working right. Disruptions in those faculties simply fell outside his area of study. And if she knew this, Nicole would, too.

Rebecca was about to change the subject—she didn't want to pry into anything too personal—when the other woman spoke. "I called Doc to ask him."

Fortunately, Rebecca had prepared herself for the unexpected. Otherwise, the sip of tea she had just taken might have ended up on her client. "Oh ... good," she replied, nothing more meaningful coming to mind.

"I know what you're thinking. Poor Nicole doesn't know what she wants. But it's more like, poor Nicole doesn't know what's real."

"Which is what I would expect anyone to wonder if they'd gone through what you have," replied Rebecca. "Any conclusions?"

Nicole slowly shook her head. "Not really. It's not like happy memories from the good ol' days that everyone says we had came flooding back. But it's not like I had to run to the bathroom to throw up, either. In fact, it was sort of nice, sort of peaceful." Nicole paused. "So, tell me you're OK with me doing that because ... well, because I feel guilty about it."

Rebecca stood, came around the desk, and sat in the chair next to her so she could look her client in the eye. If things had been different, she might have put her hands on the woman's shoulders, but that would distract Nicole more than help if she could stand the closeness at all. "You have absolutely nothing to feel guilty about. You're still testing the boundaries of your world. I know mine, and Doc's place in it is as a friend."

"Thanks," Nicole said. "It's just ...."

"What?" Rebecca asked when it became clear that Nicole wasn't going to finish the thought.

"It's just that I expected you and Doc to be a lot closer than you seem to be. In fact, back in St. Louis, I half expected you to put up a fight for him, not that I would have fought back."

"I don't think there's room for anyone else in his heart."

"Anyone else?" Nicole paused, looking confused. Then, she sat back, her eyes widening. "Oh ...."

Rebecca wasn't sure if this was a welcome realization for Nicole or the cause for panic, but it was nothing she could help with. She didn't even have any words of wisdom more profound than what she said. "Give it time. It'll work out."

Rebecca stood and started back toward her chair. She had one possibility left to discuss with her client, and she was concerned that Nicole would reject it outright. And if she didn't, the notion would still lead to a long and probably heated argument. But that was still much better than leaving the issue an open, festering wound in a promising but still fragile friendship.

But when Rebecca considered the digression that this hypothesis would cause, she decided it was more important to finish the other topics before she broached this one. "Would you mind summarizing your findings on the sociograms before I get to my final concern? If nothing else, twenty-six suspicious connections in your graphs have to take precedence over a possibility that's going to require a lot more work. How'd you make out?"

"Well, not so great, if the point is to catch the bad guy. Of the twenty-six, I left two at orange and the rest went back to black. That's twenty-four dead-ends and two connections that I still need to work on. I'll go through each one, see if you think I need to take a second look at anybody."

Nicole started shuffling pages, then looked up. "And by the way, Rose Kline is a physical therapist.

Whitten has a bad hip and Milgrom's problem is his knees."

Rebecca chuckled recalling their wild guesses of principal and prostitute.

As Nicole went through each link, it became clear to Rebecca that she had been very thorough. For each case, she provided a simple explanation that, while it didn't eliminate every shred of suspicion, reduced it substantially. After all, it was possible that a wandering stranger, who just happened to be a mad scientist with a sonic gun to disrupt thought, had taken a disliking for Peterson and used it on Milgrom. It just wasn't very likely, and Nicole had reduced twenty-four of their twenty-six cases to almost that level of improbability.

The twenty-fifth case, which was one of the links that had stayed orange, was more like unfinished business than anything else. So far, Nicole hadn't been able to trace the name, John Fredrick, to a specific individual in Whitten's and Milgrom's lives. Part of the problem was that there were a lot of John Fredricks, and Rebecca was leaning toward the possibility that they were talking about two different people. Whitten had mentioned Fredrick in a post about a convention in Denver; Milgrom had a picture of a John Fredrick at a class reunion. Rebecca even suggested dropping the inquiry, but Nicole wanted to pursue it another day or two.

Finally, they reached the last unchanged link. At first glance, Rebecca couldn't see why it hadn't been demoted to black ... or yellow at least. The common association was a surgeon, Dr. Nicholas Spencer—or Dr. Nick as he liked to be called. He had been a member of the same country club as Whitten for years and had performed Milgrom's heart surgery. But as to why he was suspicious, Rebecca didn't have any idea. Did Nicole think she had to justify her voluntary effort by keeping one long shot in play?

Whatever the case, this wasn't the first time a doctor had come up during the investigation, and her client should be aware of that. "When I was interviewing Whitten, he received a telephone call," said Rebecca. "At first, he seemed angered by the interruption, but he stepped out to take it. When he came back, he said the caller was a doctor and a friend who had been checking into the results from some procedure he'd had done."

"He's angered by a friend calling about a favor he's completed? That can't be right."

"My thought, too," replied Rebecca, "which made me wonder if the doctor story was to cover up something else or just a segue to a new topic. He followed it up with a not-so-subtle reference to his manhood."

"What a sleaze."

"True, but that doesn't explain why you kept this link orange."

"Well, there's an interesting story around Dr. Nick, if not an incriminating one. He's brilliant and, at least in his mind, something of a playboy. He's been married and divorced twice. And reading between the lines, 'took him to the cleaners' seems to be part of each settlement. So, he's not as well off as you might expect for a surgeon who fronts for the most advanced pacemaker on the market."

"Doctors promote specific devices?" asked Rebecca.

Nicole's face said "seriously?", but the words out of her mouth were, "Medical reps are always trying to get doctors to use their products. It's just good PR. But I doubt Dr. Nick was influenced by any trinkets they might offer. More likely, he wants to be the face of an incredibly advanced piece of technology. And the pacemaker he implants is exactly that."

"So, there are differences among pacemakers?"

Once again, Nicole seemed to be battling against saying "seriously", but again, she didn't. "There are differences, and some of them are pretty important. All of them send signals to your heart when heartrate gets too low, a condition known as bradycardia. The more advanced models, on the other hand, have sensors that detect movement and breathing, so they can increase heart rate to support physical exercise."

"OK," said Rebecca slowly, "but I'm still missing something. Are you saying that during open heart surgery, Dr. Nick not only implanted a pacemaker, but he also put electrodes in Milgrom's head to mess up his thinking? I kinda think someone would have noticed."

Nicole laughed. "Yeah, I can just hear someone in the operating room yelling, 'Hey, Dr. Nick. I think you missed his heart by a foot and a half.'" Nicole's expression turned more serious. "Actually, implanting a pacemaker only requires local anesthesia, not open-heart surgery, but I wasn't thinking about the procedure. What I was wondering was whether he could have spiked Milgrom's after-surgery medications with something that distorted reality. And before you say it, yes, I know that a drug that makes only one person, Randolph Peterson, a part of Milgrom's fantasy world is unheard of. But you have to start somewhere."

"So, you're thinking he might be working with someone at the local pharmacy?" asked Rebecca.

"Maybe, but not necessarily. He might have given Milgrom something he described as a free sample. So, I was hoping Miranda would remember if her husband took anything like that, anything that didn't come through regular channels. That would increase my suspicion of Dr. Nick at least some. But even better, if they still had a pill or two left in their medicine cabinet, the contents could be tested to make sure it's only antiplatelet medication or a beta blocker or whatever it said on the outside of the bottle."

"That doesn't sound very likely, but there's no harm in checking," replied Rebecca.

"I wanted to talk to Dr. Nick, too."

Rebecca could feel her back press into the chair almost as if the unexpected suggestion had pushed her into the padding. "You're not thinking of trying to trap him into an admission, are you? Without some training in interviewing methods, there's a good chance he'll figure out what you're doing, and that could be a disaster if he turns out to be an accomplice. Or worse yet, a murderer."

"I wouldn't be trying to get him to confess. I thought we'd just discuss the pacemaker first. Since I'm a biomedical engineer, he'll be concerned about disclosing something proprietary about the device, but I'm sure he has a spiel fit for the public. Then, I'll work around to the medications he recommends after surgery. Hopefully, there will be some inconsistency in how he describes his standard approach and what happened with Milgrom."

"OK," replied Rebecca. "Just make sure you stick within those boundaries. The first time you ask something like, did you ever give Dan Milgrom any free samples of heart medications, he'll know."

"Understood."

The word was the one Rebecca wanted to hear, but the look in Nicole's eye wasn't what she wanted to see. Suddenly, the woman seemed far away. "What are you thinking?"

Nicole shook her head as if she needed to dislodge an image. "Maybe I'm ignoring the possible effect of the pacemaker on Milgrom's behavior before I should."

"So, we're back to the pacemaker-to-brain connection that I couldn't see before?" asked Rebecca.

"Yeah, and frankly, neither can I. But I've always been amazed by how interconnected the systems of the human body are. Maybe it's not a butterfly flapping its wings in Peking to produce rain in Central Park, but even things like the bacteria in a person's gut can affect emotions like depression and anxiety."

Jeez, Nicole, are you serious? At least, those were the words Rebecca was thinking. But discouraging her, on the other hand, made little sense. What if she was on to something whether Rebecca could get her mind around it or not? And besides, would she even stop if Rebecca asked? Probably not unless she had a good reason, and "it's risky" wouldn't make the grade with Nicole. All that was left was to prepare her as best she could. A couple of days of working on her interviewing skills should help. "Have any thoughts about how you're going to approach Dr. Nick?"

"I was hoping you could help with that."

So, Rebecca quickly went through the basics. It wasn't even a crash course, but more of an outline to which she'd later add the details. She did, however, take a few moments to discuss the risk that Spencer posed. She knew Nicole could handle herself in a physical confrontation; she'd seen that with the intruder. But Spencer, if he was involved, was a different type of threat entirely. She suspected that the man's prestige and a clever line or two would keep Nicole off balance more reliably than any right hook.

But the hour was late and Rebecca wasn't certain her message had gotten through. At least, she had laid the groundwork. "So, when is this interview going to happen?"

"Ten o'clock tomorrow."

"Tomorrow? Ten o'clock? I can't possibly have you ready for an interview by then and I can't go along. That's the same time I'm meeting with Bethune-Peterson."

Nicole sat bolt upright, staring for a moment. "Why the hell are you meeting with Ellie again?" she demanded, her expression turning cold.

Unfortunately, Rebecca had just let the cat out of the bag and not at all in the way she had planned.

Late Evening, The Whitten Residence

James Whitten picked up his cell phone from the side table, then set it back down. Was it worth spoiling the mood his twenty-year-old Scotch had wrought over the last hour? Unfortunately, he decided the answer to that question was yes.

He'd already taken one panicked phone call this afternoon, and he was getting sick of placating a man he had once liked but now considered a weak, sniveling coward. Unfortunately, there might be several more of those sessions in his future because he hadn't given Tucker Redd a deadline for his visit to Veles. He needed to correct that. He decided to offer the big man $750 to change Veles's mind, but dock him $50 for every day the job wasn't done.

"That'll light a fire under his lazy butt," Whitten muttered to the empty room.

He picked up his phone and placed the call. Redd answered on the sixth ring.

"Hello, Mr. Whitten."

"You forget how to answer a phone?"

"No, I just ...."

"Forget it. You take care of Veles yet?"

"Well, ah .... You see, I was over there tonight."

"And you chickened out, didn't you? For a guy your size, you are the biggest, damn ...."

"I took care of it."

Whitten stared at his phone for a moment. "When?"

"A couple of hours ago."

"And you didn't think to call me?"

"You don't like to be disturbed at night, and since your problems are over, I thought it would wait till morning."

Whitten shook his head, a grin coming to his face. But then, it faded as fast as it had come. He'd heard too many lies in his life to swallow one more. "So, why all the hemming and hawing before?"

"Well, sir .... It's just that you didn't say anything about not leaving a mark on her like the other guy ... and well, I might have gotten carried away ... a little bit."

Whitten laughed. "I don't give a damn if her whole body is black and blue and she's missing a leg, as long as she backs off. So, what is it? A broken finger or two?"

"Nothing like that," said Redd. "And most of her punishment won't show. Sore ribs and stuff like that. But I smacked her across the cheek something good, and that's gonna show."

"Her punishment, huh?" said Whitten. "I like the way you put it. You know, this is one of the first jobs you've pulled off without a hitch of some sort, and you should profit from it. I was going to pay you $400, but I think it's worth another $50."

"$450?"

"That's right," replied Whitten, not sure if Redd's repetition was an attempt to open negotiations or just gratitude, but he didn't care. The job was done. "Not bad for what, fifteen minutes of work and great working conditions. I mean, slapping Veles around had to be fun." He disconnected.

Whitten put the phone down, picked up his glass, and walked to the bar to pour himself another two fingers of Scotch. "Someday you'll learn to settle on a price before the job. But until then, I'm $300 richer."

Late Evening, Jen's Place

"So, what's your excuse this time?" Nicole demanded loudly when Rebecca didn't answer immediately. She stood from her chair and started pacing around the room.

Rebecca had been through this moment several times before in her mind, but she'd never pictured Nicole this upset. She'd even considered introducing the idea with a disclaimer—while this possibility explains what we know about Mr. Peterson's death, it's far from proven. But then, that qualification could be applied to virtually every new hypothesis they discussed, and her client would know that. Nicole would accept the tentative nature of the scenario; what she would have trouble with was why Rebecca thought it worthy of further examination at all.

Rebecca, on the other hand, felt certain that there were secrets to be uncovered. Crimes? Perhaps not, but something was going on, and Bethune-Peterson had insight and probably involvement in it. She had felt that from their first meeting, from the first time Bethune-Peterson had tried to run her out of town. And now, the next few minutes would determine if the woman would get her way, and Rebecca would be leaving Colorado, case unsolved.

"I understand this is going to be difficult for you to hear, but give me ten minutes to make my case."

Nicole stopped pacing and, for a moment, just stared. Finally, she walked back to the chair, sat, and crossed her arms over her chest. "OK. You have ten minutes."

"Much of the information on which this possibility is based came from the meeting with Ms. Bethune-

Peterson and dinner with Ms. Shaw, but the pieces didn't come together until halfway through dinner. First, let me say that Shaw agrees with you. She feels like Bethune-Peterson was devoted to her husband."

Rebecca was almost expecting an I-told-you-so, but Nicole only held out an empty hand.

"In fact," continued Rebecca, "she was so devoted that she was bringing brochures about possible retirement locations to him almost weekly for a year."

"So? She can be a little pushy at times, but that's not a crime," said Nicole.

"That was at work," replied Rebecca slowly. "What do you think it was like at home?"

Nicole stared blankly for a moment, then her eyes narrowed. "You aren't suggesting that she sabotaged her own husband to get him to retire from HomeRight, are you? That's .... That's preposterous."

"It's not a common motive for defaming someone, but it fits what we know and what we can guess," replied Rebecca. "Bethune-Peterson had the opportunity, of course, since she was around her husband and his business all the time. As for means, it's easy to see how she could have found what she needed. For example, we know that Peterson emailed the deposits to himself on his personal account. It's not much of a stretch to think that she knew or discovered his log-in credentials. He might have even had them written down somewhere in his desk at home. It would be a lot harder for anyone at HomeRight to come by this information because he rarely used that account there and he kept his office locked when he stepped out."

"Perhaps, but harder and impossible aren't the same thing," said Nicole. Unless Rebecca was imagining it, she could swear the woman's jaw jutted out with her reply.

"True," replied Rebecca. "It's not impossible. As for the old marketing concept report, we know Peterson kept it around as a motivational tool. So, anyone, Bethune-Peterson included, could have leaked it to the media. But despite nearly everyone at HomeRight having a copy, she recalled very little about it. I found that odd."

"Why would she recall it?" demanded Nicole. "Maybe she didn't think it was as funny as everyone else. And certainly, she wouldn't have seen it as often as anyone who was involved with new hire orientations. It wasn't her prop; it was his."

"OK. Again, that's true." Nicole would either accept that the gap in Bethune-Peterson's memory was a cover-up—she hadn't leaked the report, she didn't even remember it—or she wouldn't. Whether Rebecca or others thought it was suspicious would make no difference. So, she moved on to the next concern. "Do you happen to know if Ms. Bethune-Peterson met the young man who claimed Peterson had propositioned him? You mentioned that he was staying at Jen's Place before that happened."

Nicole sat scowling for a moment, her head slowly shaking. But even before she spoke, Rebecca knew the gesture meant she didn't want to say rather than they hadn't met. "Probably," she said finally.

"So, it's possible she offered him money to make the claim and then disappear. Maybe his mother was in on it, too, but maybe not. It makes no difference."

"And how many hundreds of other people knew that boy? Ellie meeting him one time means nothing. And besides, what about all the mistakes Mr. Peterson was making at work? Knowing how to get into someone's email isn't going to make them issue the same policy memo three times."

"Ms. Bethune-Peterson could have manufactured those errors, too. She wasn't in the office full time, but she still dropped in several times a week. How hard would it be for her to make two additional copies of a policy memo and then drop them into company mail over the next week or two?"

Nicole's face was turning red. Unfortunately, there was more for Rebecca to cover.

"I'm also not sure I'm getting all the facts from Bethune-Peterson. The first time we talked, she dismissed the idea that anyone would care about her husband's rumored sexual orientation. Gloria Shaw, however, told me there were two members of the board who, if they believed it, would consider it proof that Peterson was unfit to lead."

"So, you're suggesting she essentially bought two no-votes by getting a kid to lie about being propositioned?"

"I'm suggesting that your friend knew the stance of these two board members on same-sex relationships. So, it's suspicious to me when she dismissed the rumor as irrelevant when, clearly, it isn't."

"Maybe she hadn't considered the implications of the rumor. Or maybe, she didn't know the position of these two people. Just because Shaw knows, or thinks she knows, that doesn't mean that Ellie does. Even assuming she did know, perhaps she didn't think it was relevant to your question. I can think of a hundred reasons why this didn't come up when you talked to her."

One of those hundred reasons, Rebecca knew, was because Bethune-Peterson admitting this knowledge was to concede that she knew how to push her husband out of office. But reasserting that possibility would get them nowhere, and she still had more to cover.

"We also have the issue that much of the case for Peterson's death being a suicide is based solely on Bethune-Peterson's word. She testified to his extreme depression. She verified that he wrote and signed the suicide note. Detectives hardly looked at the scene of his death because she said the house was exactly as she had left it. The autopsy ...."

"Enough," Nicole shouted as she ran a hand through her hair. "Why is it that you are so determined to blame Ellie? First, she was doing it for money, but I proved that wasn't the case. Then, it was love or lust that drove her, but I've noticed that idea seems to have fallen by the wayside. What, no eligible bachelor in her neighborhood? And now, it's a campaign to get Mr. Peterson to retire because she wants him all to herself? But the problem is, she's too stupid to know when to stop, and he ends up killing himself because of all the failures she staged. I've heard that detectives can become blind to every other possibility once they decide who the criminal is. I just never expected that from you."

And there it was—the crack in their association that Bethune-Peterson had wanted to exploit from the first day.

"You're right," Rebecca said after a moment. "Prematurely accepting a theory can blind investigators to other possibilities. I don't believe I'm doing that, but if you want, I'll drop this line of inquiry. It is, however, about the only lead I have, so dropping it means we are pinning everything on a few drops of blood, the possibility that Milgrom figures out what drove his unusual behavior, or finding some other dude who had a motive."

Perhaps it was the starkness of the options remaining to her, but Nicole squeezed her eyes closed and dropped her head. After a long moment in that position, she looked up. "Good summary. We've got a couple of drops of blood, which may or may not be in a database somewhere, but the police are working on that issue. And Mr. Milgrom may or may not have an epiphany about his earlier behavior, but neither you nor I will be involved in that process. And you forgot Dr. Spencer, who I'll be checking out. But when you look at the case that way, what stands out to me is the fact that you've become irrelevant. You're fired."

Logically, Rebecca had known that her termination was a possibility, and she thought she'd prepared herself emotionally for that eventuality. She hadn't. Anger took control of her mind. The impulse to tell the woman off, to tell her she was nothing but a ....

But the rest of that thought brought her imagined rant to an end. Nicole was nothing but a woman who had lost everything—her life, her friends, her memory. Since her escape from the kidnappers, she had regained her family, but no one else because she trusted no one else. Everyone was a potential source of pain, abandonment, or worse. She'd even constructed a new life where lasting relationships were impossible. None of the guests at Jen's Place would be around for long. They would be going on with their lives while Nicole remained isolated in her room at the shelter.

And then Bethune-Peterson had come along. The woman had, somehow, sensed Nicole's pain, if not the source. And equally mysterious, she had become a friend. She had become the sole refuge for Nicole in a sea of doubt and distrust. Maybe Doc would become that for her again, but he was nowhere close to that yet. And now, Rebecca was threatening to take Bethune-Peterson away. It was no wonder Nicole had reacted the way she did.

"OK," said Rebecca after a moment. "I'll be packed and out of here by tomorrow morning."

"You can stay through the weekend if you want," said Nicole. "I realize that you dropped everything in St. Louis to help me, and although you probably don't believe it, I appreciate that. Jen's Place is big enough that we won't have to see each other anyway."

THURSDAY, SEPTEMBER 1

Morning, Jen's Place

Rebecca stared at the open door of the dining room. Breakfast would be over in ten minutes and Nicole had yet to appear. She returned her gaze to the bowl of granola in front of her, a sprinkling of blueberries decorating its top. She pushed it aside, then pulled a half mug of steaming coffee into its place. It wasn't that there was a problem with the food, although it would be difficult to mess up fruit and cereal. Rather, it was a sleepless night of soul-searching that was robbing her of her appetite.

She didn't expect Nicole to suddenly change her mind, to welcome her back on the case. For Nicole to do that would be an admission that she no longer believed in the one person who had accepted her without reservation. That hadn't been the possibility that had kept Rebecca awake. Rather, she was wrestling with the question of whether she should risk another interview with Bethune-Peterson against her client's wishes or let Nicole live in a prison of her own design? The question felt a bit melodramatic, and yet, she couldn't shake the feeling that it was actually spot on.

If things stayed the way they were, Nicole would eventually have to face her doubt. Why hadn't her friend demanded that a handwriting expert examine the signature on the suicide note? How was Bethune-Peterson so sure no one had been in the house when the police hadn't examined the doors and windows for evidence of forced entry? Why hadn't she hired her own PI to look for the boy who had implicated her husband? Over time, this shadow of a doubt would grow until she could no longer trust Bethune-Peterson. That would only happen, however, long after she and Doc were exiled permanently from Nicole's world.

Interviewing Bethune-Peterson one more time, however, wasn't a guarantee the outcome would be different. If Bethune-Peterson had no hand in driving her husband to his death, perhaps Nicole would emerge from this situation with at least one staunch ally. And she might continue to explore her feelings toward Doc, leaving Rebecca the sole victim of this disagreement. She would take that outcome in a heartbeat. Unfortunately, she didn't believe that was possible because she was almost certain Bethune-Peterson was hiding something.

On the other hand, what if Bethune-Peterson had precipitated her own husband's suicide? Then, the effect on Nicole seemed to depend on the nature and extent of the older woman's involvement. If she had created the public humiliation and had emotionally abused her husband in private, her actions would serve to reaffirm a belief that Nicole was already battling—that at its heart, humanity was evil. Even though Nicole was strong, Rebecca didn't think anyone could live with that belief for long.

As to the immediate question—interview Bethune-Peterson or not—there were probably legal issues with a PI pursuing a case after a contract was terminated. Rebecca hadn't checked, and now she realized, she wasn't going to. That was because while legal problems could be costly, they were trivial compared to the cost to her self-worth if she walked away. With that thought, her choice was made.

Perhaps it was something in her peripheral vision or the result of coming to a decision, but Rebecca looked up to find Nicole entering the room. She figured she would nod a "good morning" but never had the chance as her former client navigated to a back table without even raising her head.

Nicole looked a little like Rebecca felt—tired and distracted. Perhaps it was nerves about her upcoming interview with Spencer? Rebecca knew she had lost a few winks on that account, too. She would have been apprehensive if they'd had a couple of days to prepare, but with no time, the interview could go wrong in so many different ways she couldn't count them. And now, with the contract terminated, there would be no last-minute words of advice.

* * *

Nicole stole a quick glance as she sat down with her cup of coffee, verifying that it was indeed Rebecca sitting on the other side of the room. She'd thought so but hadn't wanted to get caught looking when she first came in.

At least the PI had the good sense to stay where she was. One more word from the woman about Ellie or the interview and Nicole thought she might scream. Had Rebecca actually warned her not to try to seduce Spencer? It had sounded that way last night. What planet did she live on? Hadn't the woman noticed that she could hardly have someone come within ten feet of her, much less touch her?

And yet, Rebecca had noticed. She'd commented on her need for personal space. She'd shown restraint when Nicole knew she wanted nothing more than to reach out to her. So, what was Rebecca going on about Spencer and attraction last night? Nicole no longer knew, the late-night session blurring with the anger in her mind.

But she could handle herself in a talk with Spencer even without Rebecca's advice. After all, her task of getting the doctor to talk was nothing compared to the job Rebecca would have faced getting Ellie to spill her guts ... not that Ellie had anything to spill. Ellie wouldn't talk because she didn't like the PI, a fact that had become increasingly apparent over the last few days. Of course, her dislike wasn't because she had something to hide. That's what Rebecca would say, but it wasn't true.

"So, who am I trying to convince?" Nicole muttered to herself with a slow shake of her head.

At least she had accomplished one thing during her sleepless night—she'd checked into the common emotional reactions to having a pacemaker implanted. Basically, almost every recipient is somewhat anxious at first, but they adapt and return to a happier life. Some people, however, develop fears, depression, or dependencies. Unfortunately, she had found nothing to suggest that these medical devices could make people quick to anger, much less having that ire directed toward one specific person. Of course, if she had found anything like that, she suspected pacemakers would come with a warning: Beware as use of this device may cause you to turn on your best friend.

And yet, if the pacemaker-to-emotion connection was indirect and subtle, like the expression she'd used before—a butterfly flapping its wings in Peking producing rain in Central Park—a simple online search was unlikely to find anything. She needed to talk to someone who knew her story and who was versed in technology and psychology. Only Doc fit that description.

The appeal of a second phone call to him, however, had reversed itself since last night. Before her first call, she'd been incredibly nervous, a reaction she couldn't totally explain. But it had gone well, and at the time, she had looked forward to another one. But now that she understood Rebecca's true feelings about her friend, along with the near certainty she had shared her biases with Doc, Nicole dreaded talking to him. He, too, would be blind to any possibilities other than Ellie's guilt.

With no other options, however, she knew she would have to call Doc ... this one last time.

She looked up from her coffee to find that Rebecca had already left. It was time for her to get going as well. She'd use the remaining fifteen minutes or so to collect her thoughts in the peace and solitude of her room.

Morning, Dr. Nicholas Spencer's Office, Englewood, CO

Nicole sat in her car, watching a stream of pedestrians walking by on the sidewalk that bordered the parking lot. Many were dressed in scrubs, a reminder that there was a large medical complex composed of utilitarian brick structures only a couple of blocks away. Dr. Spencer's office, however, wasn't a part of that collection. Rather, his workplace was in a sleek modern building of steel and glass. She checked the time. Figuring five minutes to enter the building and find the room, she still had some time to wait.

Earlier this morning, she had received some disappointing news—two sets of it, in fact. First, when she called Miranda Milgrom, the woman didn't think that Spencer had given her husband any sample medications nor did Dan recall anything like that. And second, when she asked her to check their medicine cabinet for any leftover heart pills, she'd initially declined, saying it was unnecessary. But when Nicole insisted, Miranda looked, only to confirm that the shelves were bare.

The only bright spot in the call was Miranda's assurance that she could provide a full list of medications that Spencer had prescribed for her husband. She just needed to review the bills to make sure her list was complete, and then she'd email it to Nicole. To consider this a "bright spot," however, was a bit of a stretch. Even if he had prescribed something that had mildly disorienting side effects, it wasn't clear how that confusion was always expressed as anger directed solely at Peterson.

With little else to occupy her time, Nicole thought back to the crash course on interviewing that Rebecca had given her late last night ... at least, what little she recalled of it. It started with "plan the interview." Unfortunately, it ended there, too. There just wasn't enough time to work on the rest of the PI's suggestions: develop specific questions; identify the interviewee's likely responses; pay attention to body language as much or even more than verbal responses; and on and on.

As for the one part they had attempted, the plan, to call it succinct was too generous. She would ask about the model of pacemaker Spencer had used, watching for any features that might affect something other than heartrate. And she would ask what medications Spencer typically prescribed post-surgery. And that was it. Rebecca had emphasized the importance of staying within those boundaries, but in the light of a new day, the reasons for these restrictions weren't all that clear to Nicole. Maybe she would follow the PI's advice, but maybe not.

So, in the end, her planned questions sounded more like the topics two strangers might discuss while waiting for their drinks at a coffee bar than the interrogation of a possible accomplice to a case of defamation that resulted in death.

Nicole checked her watch again. "Showtime," she muttered to herself as she rolled up the window, donned her mask, and left the car. Her estimated requirement of five minutes to find the office was unnecessarily long by four. The Spencer and Associates office was on the first floor just to the right of the reception desk in the building's lobby. And if that wasn't easy enough, the name of the practice was displayed in brushed metal letters that were a foot tall if they were an inch. The building's receptionist simply nodded when Nicole looked toward Spencer's office, then yawned and went back to her magazine.

Nicole entered the suite, identified herself, and took a seat in an overstuffed armchair next to a large exotic plant and under an oil painting of dawn in the mountains. To describe the waiting area as opulent was only a slight overstatement, although she couldn't say she was enjoying the ambience. She was simply too anxious for most of it to even register.

She pulled her phone out of a pocket, planning to fake a few games of solitaire while she considered other possible lines of questioning. And since doctors are never on time, she figured she had anywhere between fifteen minutes and a half-hour to prepare. For the second time this morning, however, she was wrong. She had barely started her phone when she heard, "Ms. Veles, Dr. Spencer will see you now." Apparently, some doctors are punctual.

A woman met her at the door to the examination rooms. Her role in the practice, however, remained a mystery as she simply said, "Please follow me" in a well-practiced, if not warm tone. She turned and walked down the hall without a glance or another word.

The poshness of the surroundings didn't decrease appreciably from the waiting room. In fact, the only clue that she was in a medical office had been the signs on the door to the back area—"Masks Optional" and "No Handshake Zone." Well, at least that explained why none of the other visitors and staff were wearing masks, not that many people did anymore. For Nicole, however, it was a habit that would last for years, perhaps forever.

After a short walk, her escort knocked on a door with a simple brass plaque that read "Dr. Nicholas R. Spencer, MD." She opened the door and said, "Dr. Spencer, Ms. Nicole Veles to see you." Her officious tone hadn't changed. She turned and left.

With one look at his office, Nicole started wondering about the accuracy of something she had said to Rebecca: "He's not as well off as you might expect." But then, he probably held to the principle that to be prosperous you needed to look prosperous. His office was massive and lavishly furnished. An executive black lacquer office desk with a matching bookcase credenza dominated the center of the room. To the left, two plush upholstered chairs in dark gray sat facing each other with a small table and lamp between them. A matching sofa, table, and lamp were to the right of the desk.

"You never know when you'll need a nap between surgeries," Spencer said, apparently noticing the final direction of Nicole's gaze. Spencer stood from behind the desk, a smile on his face. "It's nice to meet you, Ms. Veles. By the way, the mask is really unnecessary. We've installed state-of-the-art air filtration systems in the offices. The air here is as safe as on top of Mt. Bierstadt," he said, naming one of the closer of Colorado's fourteeners, mountains that surpassed fourteen thousand feet. He came around his desk, hand extended.

Nicole took a step back, almost bumping into the closed door behind her, and removed her mask. "It's nice to meet you, too, Dr. Spencer. I can do without the face covering, but I'd like to stick with the no handshake rule."

"Of course," he said, then followed it closely with, "Ouch. That bruise on your cheek looks painful."

"It's not bad. Ran into a half-closed door in the middle of the night," she said, borrowing the lie from one of the women who had used it at Jen's Place.

"Well, I'm glad it's not as painful as it looks. And since this is more of a social call than a medical one, please, call me Dr. Nick." He paused a moment, perhaps to let her offer the use of her first name, but for the moment anyway, Nicole decided to keep things more formal.

"Shall we make ourselves comfortable?" Spencer asked as he raised a hand slightly toward the two chairs.

"Thanks," replied Nicole as they moved to the chairs and sat. "I was wondering about the model of pacemaker …."

"Sorry," said Spencer as he raised a hand. "I don't mean to interrupt, but before we get to the dry technical details, would you mind telling me a little more about yourself? I know you work part time for HealthVie. You mentioned that to my assistant when you requested a meeting. But I know nothing else about you. And, of course, I'd be happy to reciprocate if you have questions about my background."

"Oh, that won't be necessary," replied Nicole as she leaned forward in the chair. "Your credentials in heart surgery are well known. I doubt there is a name better known in the state of Colorado."

The effusiveness of her response took Nicole by surprise, but then, it was generally accurate. And flattery should facilitate the interview, shouldn't it?

Spencer nodded. "There are a number of great cardiac surgeons in the state who might wish to argue that point, but I appreciate the sentiment."

Nicole wasn't prepared for the man's modesty, but it only served to reinforce her positive opinion of his abilities. "As you mentioned, biomedical engineering is currently only a part-time pursuit. I'm fortunate that skilled manpower is in short supply, so flexible work arrangements can be made."

"Nonsense," said Spencer. "I'm familiar with HealthVie, and they wouldn't have allowed part-time employment had you not been exceptionally talented."

Nicole could feel her face warm. She wished she had an answer as smooth as Spencer's, but all she managed was, "Thanks." She found herself staring at her hands in her lap. When she looked up, she said, "My primary job is to manage Jen's Place, a shelter for victims of domestic abuse."

"Really," replied Spencer as he sat back in his chair and studied her. "I was prepared to say, what a loss for biomedical engineering, but I can think of few causes more worthy to have stolen you away from the field. Compassion and intellect. That's an impressive combination. And in a woman so attractive."

She had certainly tried to make herself look presentable, opting for a dress she hadn't worn since her working days in St. Louis. It was tighter and shorter than she remembered, but professional and flattering at the same time. But even so, his compliment was unexpected, and Nicole felt a warmth that spread from her toes to the top of her head. She was certain that a shy smile covered her face. How could it not after receiving such praise from a man of Spencer's stature? For the last two years, the sole expression she'd given to men was a glare that varied only in its level of hostility, and it felt surprisingly good to change that trend.

"I'm sure the goings-on at ... was it Jen's Place?"

"Correct."

"I'm sure that who stays there is not for public discussion, but perhaps you could tell me a bit about your work at HealthVie. Nothing company proprietary, of course."

"Since they just published a short description of my last project, I'm sure this is OK to discuss," she said. "It involved the design of an integrated suite of tools for monitoring the health of babies who are born premature. The key innovation in the suite is that the interface can be tailored according to the primary problems the medical team is facing, allowing a closer integration of work flow and the equipment supporting it."

"Sounds like an extremely valuable extension of the work you did before. And since heart problems are second only to breathing issues in preemies, I assume that heart monitoring capabilities were part of the suite?"

With her thoughts still focused on her description of the project—finally, it was a topic that she could address with some authority in front of a man she admired— Nicole nearly missed Spencer's question. But when it registered, she said, "Heart monitoring was a central feature, actually."

"Impressive," he replied. "But I suspect you'd like to get to the reason for your visit, the RM5700. Truly a state-of-the-art pacemaker."

For the second time, Nicole was slow to respond. This time, however, it wasn't because of anything she had said, but something in his words. It took her a moment to identify the reason for her unease, but when she did, she said, "How did you know my HealthVie project was an extension of work I had done before?"

Spencer looked puzzled for a moment. Or was that a look of guilt? Nicole wasn't certain.

"It must have been something that my assistant told me," said Spencer, as if he suddenly recalled the source.

"So, the fact that I worked part time at HealthVie wasn't the only thing you knew about me before this meeting. You also knew what I'd done before in St. Louis. Why the pretext?"

Spencer shrugged. "Just to ease into the conversation, to give you something you're comfortable talking about. I didn't mean it as any type of subterfuge."

Two possibilities immediately came to Nicole's mind. First, perhaps he was being truthful. Maybe he was as down-to-earth and as genuinely supportive as he appeared, and he just wanted to get to know her through some casual conversation.

She doubted that, however, which led to the second possibility—that he was playing her. He knew exactly who she was and what she wanted, and he was going to make her forget those objectives. If she ever had the need to describe the outcome of this meeting, he would be the older and wiser guide she needed to make her way in the world. Or perhaps this was all part of a seduction ploy—he was going to get the trusting girl in the dress that now definitely felt too short in a compromising position so no one would believe her. Nicole fidgeted in her chair reflexively while fighting against the bile that was starting to rise in her throat at the thought of his hands on her.

The trouble was, she wasn't sure how much of her suspicion was driven by Spencer's behavior and how much came from her acquired distrust of men? But with the question, something Rebecca had said came to mind. "Attraction—physical, emotional, or intellectual—can have profound effects on an interview. Don't get caught in that trap." At the time, Nicole had thought the PI was worried that she'd offer Spencer sex for information, and that was never going to happen. Now, she realized that Rebecca was concerned about exactly this situation.

The belief that Spencer was trying to turn the tables on her, make her the hunted rather than the hunter, also made one random detail that Nicole hadn't understood before fit into a now-clear pattern. When she'd called to make an appointment, she'd clearly been given the runaround at first. "Dr. Spencer is extremely busy, but I'll give him your message." She'd even wondered if she should have claimed a heart condition; maybe that would get her into his office. But it was only a couple of hours later when his office called back with an opening the next day. She had thought it great luck. Now, however, it was clear that it was just the opening gambit in Spencer's plan.

What had been suspicion became a certainty in Nicole's mind. "So, just how did the pacemaker you implanted in Dan Milgrom change his behavior so dramatically?"

Spencer drew back like she had slapped him. "I have no idea what you are talking about."

His response, however, was much too quick for him to have given her accusation any thought. "Yeah, right," she replied with as much sarcasm as she could manage. "Just call that zombie of an assistant you have because this meeting is over."

Perhaps he had already signaled her somehow because she seemed to materialize at the door almost instantly.

"Please show Ms. Veles out of the building," Spencer said, his tone flat. He turned his attention to his computer.

As Nicole followed Spencer's assistant down the hall, she wondered why she had called her a zombie. Sure, she was rigidly formal, but then, she might be afraid to show emotion in a place that now seemed as cold and sterile as it had felt opulent before. Her only excuse for the name-calling was that she was furious that she'd almost been taken in by Spencer.

Now, she had a reason to talk to Rebecca, although she might do it over the phone. She didn't like to think of it as gloating ... but that is exactly what it was going to be. She just needed to steel herself first for a call to Doc.

At the Same Time, the Peterson Residence

"I thought you'd be gone by now," said Ms. Eleanor Bethune-Peterson as she stood motionless in the open door to her home. It wasn't the friendliest of greetings, but then, Rebecca hadn't expected a hug. "When are you going to accept the fact that Randy's death was nothing more than age catching up with him."

"When age is packing a 9mm Glock," thought Rebecca, but she didn't say it. Bethune-Peterson was a strong, resilient woman—the phrase "tough as nails" had regularly been uttered in the same breath as her name. But even so, that didn't mean she had no feelings. Even the toughest, most experienced law enforcement officer might be brought to tears if forced to recount a particularly horrific case, and Bethune-Peterson discovering her husband's brains splattered on his office wall certainly qualified. So, Rebecca planned to handle her gently until she was certain a different approach was needed.

"Sorry, but my contract runs another eight days, so you're stuck with me for a while longer. But I do appreciate that you're busy and will keep these talks as short as possible."

"And I suppose you'd tell me you stand on principle and wouldn't leave, even if I doubled what Nicole is paying you? And don't repeat the lie you told me last Sunday. I've thought about it, and although I don't know why, Nicole's not going to hire anyone else. She wouldn't have driven halfway across the country if there was another option."

"I plan to complete my contractual obligations to my client." Rebecca ended her statement there, as to say more risked violating a confidence ... even if it was a confidence secured under a contract that no longer existed.

After Bethune-Peterson shook her head for a moment, she said, "Then, let's get it over with."

She turned on a heel, leaving Rebecca to close the front door. When they reached a room that appeared to be a study, Bethune-Peterson sat on a couch, then waited without a word for Rebecca to take the chair across from her.

"So, first I wanted to get some clarification about the times when your husband repeated a policy or personnel change announcement," said Rebecca. "I believe there was an instance involving some promotions and three others about changes in personnel policies?"

"I'm not sure there weren't a few more like that. Seems like I heard about Randy mentioning one of the standard holidays a few times."

"When these repetitions occurred, would he have actually stood up and made the same statement two or three times?" If he had, he looked forgetful; if he hadn't, then someone might have been creating that impression.

"Probably not. When the information is intended to go company-wide, he could have told his direct reports and waited for the news to trickle down. But he didn't really like that approach. Too slow. Too much chance someone forgets to pass on the news. So, generally, he would use HomeRight's weekly newsletter."

"And what's the process for getting something into that newsletter?" asked Rebecca.

Bethune-Peterson harrumphed softly. "Let me save you a whole bunch of questions. Things like promotions and policy changes are documented in formal memos for the company archives. If his OA typed them, then Randy probably told her to include the information in the newsletter. If the memo was prepared by another division, which was generally the case with promotions, then he'd tell her to include it in the newsletter or send her an email about it. And as to your final unasked question, yes, I could have left notes for Gloria so that these announcements appeared several times."

"That's Gloria Shaw?"

Bethune-Peterson's brow wrinkled for an instant, followed immediately by a shrug. "That's right."

"Wouldn't Ms. Shaw have noticed that she was repeating information unnecessarily?"

Bethune-Peterson reared back on the couch dramatically, her hand coming to her throat. "That's it, Ms. Marte. You've solved the case. Gloria did it. Oh, now wait a minute. There's actually no crime to solve, is there?"

It was time to push back, thought Rebecca, as the kid-glove approach wasn't making much progress. "I'm not sure if there was a crime or not. I'm only certain that the investigation of the incident was about as perfunctory as I've ever seen."

Bethune-Peterson waved a hand as if dismissing the notion. "That's because the police used common sense. And obviously, you have none."

"I've always thought of my imagination as my primary strength," replied Rebecca. "And in my mind's eye, I can imagine getting handwriting and forensic linguistics experts to examine the suicide note. You know, I still remember something from that note—your husband's quote about HomeRight being founded on bedrock and the wind. I just wonder how many dozens of other people at the company know it, too?

"And I wonder what the linguistics expert would make of the fact that he'd talked about his 'back-stabbing, one-time friends' nearly every day after he was removed from his position but never once mentioned them in his suicide note? Rather, he spent all his time railing against the board."

"I wouldn't know," replied Bethune-Peterson.

"And then I can imagine a computer technology expert examining the memory of your husband's computer to see if the note was actually typed on it. Right now, all we know is that it was printed on his printer. Surely, he wouldn't have gone to the public library to compose his farewell."

"His computer was pretty much wiped clean at HomeRight. I think they got carried away with what they considered business files."

"You'd be surprised what an expert can pull out of a computer even when the files have been deleted. There are all kinds of temporary and backup files, especially with word-processing software." Actually, Rebecca suspected that anything like that was long gone, but technological accuracy wasn't the point of this exercise. "And let's say the note was typed on his computer. Was the process a smooth flow of consciousness? Or was it written once, then edited to add some of your husband's favorite phrases after the fact. Wouldn't that be interesting?"

Apparently, the process was having the desired effect, as Bethune-Peterson just sat glaring when Rebecca paused. Maybe another nudge or two?

"Next, I can see your chief of police putting a little pressure on the media to find where they got the old marketing concepts document. Or why they even mentioned that your husband repeated some policy announcements. That's not newsworthy even in a struggling company on a slow news day."

"Why are you doing this?" asked Bethune-Peterson, biting off each word.

"You probably heard about the masked brute who visited Nicole and me last night."

"Yes, and I heard she's got a black and blue cheek this morning. What kind of PI are you?"

"The kind that steps in before your young friend gets carried away" was the answer, but Bethune-Peterson had no need to know that.

"I'm here talking to you because with all the doubts I had about this incident being anything other than aggressive business, that attack removed them. Someone is trying to stop us. And if the attack had that kind of effect on me, you can imagine what it did to galvanize Nicole's resolve. If we don't get some type of closure, Nicole will never find peace."

While she was talking, Rebecca wondered if this idea would fall on deaf ears. After all, she was here to accuse Bethune-Peterson of driving her husband to suicide, and now, she was making an appeal to her sense of loyalty to a friend? The callousness of the one and the kindness of the other weren't necessarily mutually exclusive, but they were at odds.

But against all those odds, the appeal was having an effect. Bethune-Peterson's posture, which had been stiff and defiant, had wilted under the weight of these imaginings. Her arms lay limply at her sides. Her glare was gone, replaced by a sad gaze that fell on her lap. Rebecca just hoped it was enough because this talk was her last hope to get to the bottom of things before she ran out of excuses to be in Colorado.

"OK," said Bethune-Peterson. Her pause after the word was so long, however, that Rebecca wondered if she had reconsidered. But after another moment, she said softly, "Yes, I killed my husband. While I didn't have my finger on the trigger, I set in motion the events that led to him taking his life. I hope someone gets peace from knowing these facts because Lord knows, I'll never find any again."

For Rebecca to claim she took no pleasure in pushing Bethune-Peterson to this point, although true, would be dismissed by the woman outright. Her words would be wasted, but she could proceed in a less accusatory tone. Apologies would come later.

"I think it would help to know just what events you're talking about. Were they designed to get your husband to retire?"

Bethune-Peterson nodded, but her gaze never left her lap. "They were. Retire from HomeRight, not from life." She released a sigh. "I thought he was going to retire five years ago when I backed away from the company, but it was almost like he had to fill up whatever void I'd left. He became even more fixated on success for reasons I could never understand. We had everything we needed and more. And while he said he wanted to travel and for us to spend time together, that dream lasted only until the next staff or board meeting."

"So, how did you start this chain reaction?"

Bethune-Peterson looked up at Rebecca. "I did three things. First, I had a copy of the original marketing report, and yes, it had a date on it. I removed the date and leaked it to the press with a note, supposedly from an employee concerned about the company's future. You see, when Randy wrote that original document, he not only sent it to a friend at another company, he shared it inside HomeRight. The story's always been that his friend's feedback was so harsh that he hired Dan Milgrom to cover areas where he lacked the background.

"Well, that's only part of the story. It was the rumblings inside HomeRight that really got Randy thinking that the company needed some fresh blood, even though we were only a handful of employees at that time. I was hoping that another rumor about employee unrest might do the same. I thought he'd beef up the communications and human resources areas. And since sharing his vision for the future had become a lot of what he did, retirement would suddenly seem less drastic. Unfortunately, everything went sideways almost immediately."

Rebecca wondered if a few disillusioned employees in what was now a massive company would cause Peterson the same level of heartburn that it had when he probably knew everyone by name? But even so, it was easy to see why Bethune-Peterson had thought it might. As to why the scheme had failed, she thought she knew.

"So basically, the press made the out-of-date marketing concepts the story rather than unrest among the working troops?"

"Exactly," replied Bethune-Peterson. "I was hoping some reporter would just call Randy and ask about morale in the ranks. That would have been enough to get him thinking. Or maybe, employee discontent could have been a footnote on a bigger story, but no. Ideas like giving out stamps that people could collect for discounts grabbed page one."

"Stamps?" repeated Rebecca, not sure she had heard correctly. "You mean like ones you'd paste on a letter?"

Bethune-Peterson shrugged. "I'm not surprised you've never heard of that. S&H Green Stamps were among the last to disappear, and that was in the 1980s. Nowadays, if it won't fit in your smartphone, no one wants it. So, anyway, because bad news sells papers and one unhappy camper in a workforce of hundreds wasn't enough of a tragedy, the paper ended up blasting the ideas in the report. I still remember the title: *Neanderthal Thinking Marks HomeRight's Marketing Future*. If they'd made a single call to the company, they would have found out the document was used solely for orientations for the new employees. And maybe they did because the op-eds disappeared after a day or two. But by then, the damage to Randy's reputation had been done. Want to guess what that accomplished?"

"Made him even more determined to stay on?"

"Correct, which is exactly the opposite of what I'd hoped," replied Bethune-Peterson. "After that fiasco, I wanted something that would get his attention but wasn't newsworthy—not that I thought the document was. Anyway, I thought a simple slipup at work would do it, so I wrote a note supposedly from Randy that asked Gloria to run a story about some internal promotions three times. And to answer your earlier question, no, she wouldn't have thought anything about it. For important safety and policy announcements, repetition was standard. And while she's intelligent and conscientious, she doesn't have time to analyze everything that goes into the newsletter."

"And you didn't expect the news to get outside of HomeRight?" asked Rebecca to make sure she understood.

"I didn't, but I was wrong. Maybe it was because this mistake followed so closely after the marketing report disaster because the paper resurrected that issue while adding the idea that Randy had started repeating himself without realizing it. Basically, it implied he was developing dementia without really saying so and offered only the one example of the promotions as proof. But that was more than enough for the public. Rumors about Randy's failing mental health started spreading. And as my luck would have it, a couple of weeks later he actually announced a new policy twice, only to nullify it the week after that."

"If there was something HomeRight wanted in the papers, is there someone your husband would have gone to? Someone he knew and trusted?"

"There was, but he retired ten or so years ago. I suspect there was someone else after that, but I don't know who. And besides, those kinds of issues would be handled by Communications nowadays."

At least in Rebecca's gut, getting a newspaper to cover some of these largely trivial business issues felt out of the norm. And Bethune-Peterson's version of events wasn't changing that feeling at all. Could the media actually be that starved for copy? And while the press might run with a minor story with the promise of a scoop later, she hadn't admitted to making that promise. Had someone else at HomeRight made that offer?

"And finally, the last thing I did was to delete a deposit email," said Bethune-Peterson. "I went into Randy's home office one day and the inbox for his personal email account was just sitting there open. And why not? He wouldn't be expecting a saboteur in his own home. And I figured if he thought he was becoming forgetful, he might push the date for his retirement up. I know my forgetfulness bothers me, and it gets worse every day."

Everything from Bethune-Peterson since the moment they had met at Jen's Place had fallen in the range of insulting to impersonal. Perhaps, her admission to misjudging people, primarily the media, was the start of a change to this pattern, but this concession was even more personal. To Rebecca, it felt like a shift in the rhetoric. Perhaps the same thought had struck Bethune-Peterson, as she paused a long moment before continuing.

"You have to understand. I didn't want to destroy Randy's confidence. I just wanted him to believe it was time that he relinquished some of the responsibility for running the company, and delaying the deposit of a week's receipts for a few days seemed perfect. Unfortunately, what I deleted was a thread of three emails. With nearly a month's worth of cash flow missing, the bank had to issue overdraft warnings. And somehow, once again, the reporters found out."

"So, you didn't tell the media?"

"No," replied Bethune-Peterson without hesitation. Then, she paused a beat. "The printing company that we use was the only one whose payment was actually delayed, so they knew about HomeRight's solvency problem. It could have been someone from there."

"What about the rumor concerning your husband's sexual orientation? Did you start that?" asked Rebecca.

"Absolutely, not," she replied, some incredulity registering in her face. "Some people believe that bad news comes in threes. I don't. It comes when it comes. It's just a coincidence that that boy felt he needed some additional attention about the same time I was creating problems for my husband. And besides, why would that rumor make Randy think about retiring?"

"It wouldn't," said Rebecca. "Are you aware that there are a couple of people on the board that probably would have seen your husband as an unfit leader for HomeRight if they believe the boy's statement was true?"

"I know who you're talking about, and you're probably right. If they came to believe the allegation, they might have voted no confidence on that basis alone."

Nicole had been right on this score. She hadn't explicitly asked Bethune-Peterson about how the boy's story would affect the board, and her omission, along with the woman's guilty conscience about what she had done, had made the episode irrelevant in her mind.

Bethune-Peterson stared for a moment as a frown slowly took over her features. "Are you suggesting someone hired that boy to claim Randy practically attacked him just to get a couple of votes from the board?"

Rebecca raised her eyebrows.

"Oh, my God. You are thinking that," said Bethune-Peterson as she stared incredulously at Rebecca.

"It could be a coincidence like you said, but it fits with someone trying to drive your husband out of the company. I just wanted to make sure it wasn't you."

"I wanted him to retire. I didn't want him to be publicly humiliated by being forced out. That's ... incredibly cold."

"So, the three things you mentioned were the only mistakes that you arranged?" For Rebecca, it seemed like there had to be more.

But rather than answering, Bethune-Peterson seemed to be having some trouble leaving the last topic. "I guess I'm not cynical enough to think the way you do. The idea that someone invented that whole sick story, that they got that poor boy to lie to the police for a couple of votes from the board? That's incredibly heartless." She paused a beat. "And frankly, the allegation wore on Randy. He wasn't sleeping well. At times, I wondered if that story wasn't a big contributor to his forgetfulness. But every time I had that thought, it was followed by the one that said I was just making excuses, trying to give myself an easy way out. I started his downfall, even if chance conspired to speed his descent."

"But the three things you mentioned were all you did?"

"Oh, yes, sorry," replied Bethune-Peterson. "The answer is yes, just the three things. After them, I felt snakebit and backed off."

"Did you ever speak to Dan Milgrom about the problems your husband was having?"

"I told you about the dinner the four of us had ... well, planned to have, anyway. That night probably would have made any discussion between us awkward, but the bigger problem was that I couldn't very well say, 'ease up on my husband because his faults are my doing.'" She paused a moment.

"Yeah, I could have said that, should have said it, but I was embarrassed." She shook her head slowly, her eyes becoming misty. "Let's face it, I was too damn proud to stop things when I had the chance. And when they started spiraling out of control, I couldn't stop them. The more problems that came up, the more Randy wanted to fix them. Dan tried to help him, but things got heated between them." She looked off into the distance for a moment. "Funny, but it was a lot easier for me to mess things up at work than it was for me to fix them. Anyway, the board finally had enough and voted him out."

From Rebecca's perspective, she had clearly made progress on the case. But equally clearly, this couldn't be the whole story for several reasons.

For one, if she had trouble believing that a year-long series of financial downturns, a soliciting allegation, and a hostile boardroom could drive a highly successful businessman to suicide, how could she believe that only three mistakes would? A man of Peterson's experience and stature wouldn't crumble so easily.

Second, would Milgrom really have become such a vocal detractor after only these three missteps? And why did his emotion come across as anger? Wouldn't a lifelong friend exhaust months of compassion and understanding before becoming frustrated enough to resort to vitriol? But perhaps most of all, Bethune-Peterson's version of events didn't explain why someone had come to tell Nicole to mind her own business just yesterday. That wasn't anything Bethune-Peterson's actions could have precipitated. And it wasn't a coincidence.

Of course, one possibility was that Bethune-Peterson hadn't fully revealed her involvement. Maybe she had done everything. There was, however, a factor that suggested she had come clean. Of the three things she had admitted to, two were events that Whitten had singled out as shattering his confidence in his old boss—the missing deposits and the marketing document. He wouldn't have mentioned her third action—causing a promotion announcement to be repeated—because that would have sounded ridiculous. It was simply too minor. So, perhaps he was surprised by the first two because he hadn't been party to them?

Whitten now moved to the head of her suspect list. He had the opportunity and the motive. But as she had concluded so often before, he lacked the means to turn Milgrom on his old friend. And that was a major hole in this theory.

"Ms. Marte?"

"It's Rebecca," she replied, feeling that Bethune-Peterson deserved the courtesy.

"Thanks, Rebecca. I have a question."

"OK."

Rebecca was expecting something along the line of "what kind of trouble will I be in when my actions are known?" Instead, she got, "Can you talk to Nicole? I'm not sure I could look her in the eye, after what I've put her through."

If voicing a sentiment over and over made it true, then Bethune-Peterson was definitely solicitous of Nicole's well-being. Repetition, however, didn't equate to truth, even if people acted as if it did. But on the chance that Bethune-Peterson was sincere, she could do her part. Besides, with her contract now terminated, she doubted she'd ever have the full story anyway.

"Yes, I'll talk to Nicole," Rebecca said. "But you should come see her in a day or two yourself. She's stronger than you think. And your desire to rebuild a connection with a man you'd felt you'd lost to his work will be a message that should help her."

By the look on Bethune-Peterson's face, she didn't understand the message. But it wasn't Rebecca's place to say more. If Nicole wanted her friend to know the rest, she'd tell her.

After a moment, Bethune-Peterson nodded. "OK, I'll do that."

Late Morning, Jen's Place

Nicole put her phone on speaker and placed it on the bed. "Hi, Doc."

"Nicole? Is that you? You sound far away."

"Yeah, it's me. I'm just not holding my phone. I felt like I might need to pace around my room a bit."

She thought it likely because the only other time she had called him, she'd practically walked a hole in the rug and left a red mark on her cheek from pressing the phone against it so hard. She wasn't sure she could stop the pacing, but at least, she could get the device away from her face.

She wasn't sure why she was so nervous talking to Doc that first time. Why should she care if they no longer had anything in common, assuming they once did as everyone said. It was a question she couldn't answer, but then, her life had been full of such issues over the last couple of years. But this time, she expected her anxiety to be worse, and she knew exactly why. She wanted something from this man, but there wouldn't be any repayment, not even a future call. He would be joining the ranks of the untrustworthy, just like Rebecca.

"OK, sure," Doc replied. "I'm something of a pacer myself. It helps me with thinking."

If her memory was correct—and that was an assumption of immense proportions—then his words were a significant understatement. Doc's pacing, walking, hiking, and jogging were constant companions to his hours of mentally sorting, weighing, reorganizing, evaluating, and combining data from everything from his company's new training technology to selecting a brand of toothpaste. And even if his legs were still, his mind never seemed to be. At least, that was how she remembered him.

"I have a rather unusual question ... or at least, it seems that way to me. I was wondering if there is some sort of connection between a human's heart and the brain." She was half expecting him to break out in uncontrollable laughter. He didn't.

"I assume you mean besides the obvious—that the heart supplies blood to the brain. And the brain, or the brain stem anyway, controls heart rate."

"Resting heart rate, yes," said Nicole. "But with the fight or flight response, higher brain structures like the hypothalamus get involved in changing heart rate."

Doc laughed. "I should have remembered who I'm talking to. Of course, you mean something besides the obvious. So, tell me. What exactly is it that you want to know?"

Exactly? Nicole wasn't sure she knew exactly what she was looking for. But if nothing else, she could try different types of connections between these organs. She'd start with the most direct one, the one that would make her case that Spencer was involved, even though the whole idea was too bizarre to be believed.

"Can changes in heart rate affect thought? And specifically, could it make someone angry?"

"Angry, huh?" He paused a moment. "Are we talking about a change in heart rate great enough that the person would notice it? Things like pulsing in the ears, maybe even feeling the face flush?"

"Yes, definitely."

"And just a change in heart rate? Nothing else like blood pressure or breathing rate?"

"No. At least, not initially," said Nicole. "I suppose if the person felt some emotion after the change in heart rate, other bodily changes might follow. Things like more rapid breathing."

"Yeah, I would think so, too. But initially, it's just a racing heart looking for a reason why it's going so fast? Hmm. Interesting, although as you said, a bit unusual."

There was another pause on the line, this one much longer. Nicole found herself staring at the silent phone on her bed, still wondering if a laugh would come next. But again, it didn't.

"Yeah, I think that might be possible. I'm thinking of some research that I ran across in school that dealt with why people sometimes pick the wrong emotional reason for bodily changes that they're experiencing. Maybe you've heard of the old saying that relationships formed under extreme conditions never last?"

"Sure," replied Nicole. "If two people are thrown together in some situation that's very exciting or very dangerous, they may develop an attraction to each other that disappears when things go back to normal." She paused, working out the details of how this might answer her question. "So, some of the bodily changes that are due to excitement or fear get misattributed to attraction. Is that what you're talking about?"

"That's the idea," replied Doc. "Hold on a second." She could hear the clack of computer keys in the background. "The theory is called the Two-Factor Theory of Emotion, and the basic idea is that emotions have two parts: physiological changes in the body—things like increased heart rate—and an emotional label that's assigned to these changes. That label is based on how the person interprets the situation."

"I assume this theory is based on something besides the old saying," replied Nicole.

"Of course. In some of the original research, people were given doses of adrenaline, which would cause a typical fight or flight response—higher metabolism, increased blood flow, elevated heart rate. Then, when these people were exposed to someone who was happy, they reported feeling happy; when they were exposed to someone who was angry, they felt annoyed. Basically, they looked at the situation to find a reason for their physical symptoms."

"Hmm, that sounds ...." She hesitated. Did she really want to poke holes in his answer when she was asking a favor? But then, she wasn't sure she had anything without some additional clarification.

"That study sounds kinda artificial. The adrenaline was probably injected with some cover story. It's a new flu vaccine or something like that. Then, they put these people with someone cracking jokes or someone who was complaining about being in psychology studies and asked how they were feeling? What are they going to say? I'm angry because the jokes aren't funny? I'm happy because this guy is upset with school? I don't know, but this study doesn't seem all that realistic to me. Like it would only work in the lab."

Doc chuckled, causing Nicole to start choosing her words to tell him off. But before she could, he said, "That's funny because I had exactly the same thought in school. And by the way, the cover story for the injection was that it was a new drug to test their eyesight, which I wouldn't have remembered except I'm reading it off the screen. That's pretty lame, too. But fortunately, the findings have been replicated in more realistic settings."

"Any of that research described wherever you are on the Internet?"

"No, not on this site, but I remember one study from school. The participants, who were all male, walked across two different suspension bridges. One was narrow, somewhat unstable, and high above the ground. The other was wider, more stable, and lower. On the other side, they were met by an attractive female experimenter who had them fill out a survey. Then, she said if they had any questions about the study later, they could call her, and she gave them her phone number. Since you've been ahead of me this whole time, you want to guess what happened?"

Doc seemed pretty good at explaining things because the answer seemed obvious to her. "The guys who crossed the more dangerous bridge called more frequently than the others. They misinterpreted some of their sweaty hands and racing heart as attraction rather than fear."

"Exactly," Doc replied. "While we tend to think that the emotion-producing situation causes the body to change, it can also work the other way around. The body changes and we find the reason for it in our surroundings."

"That's exactly what I was looking for," said Nicole excitedly as she picked her phone up off the bed and switched off the speaker function as she pressed it to her ear. "This is how they made Dan Milgrom feel anger on demand."

"Whoa," replied Doc. "Not every study has supported the theory and there are alternatives to it, as well."

"Which is just another way of saying that our knowledge of human emotions isn't complete or perfect. That doesn't mean this possibility is wrong."

"No, it doesn't. It just means you'll need more ...." He paused, a soft laugh coming over the line. "Of course, you and Rebecca know you'll need something to corroborate this theoretical possibility." He paused again. "But there is one thing I'm not following. You can't go around giving people adrenaline and expect them to wonder why they feel odd."

"No, but you can make their heart rate increase using a pacemaker."

"Outside of the operating room?" He sounded incredulous, which didn't surprise Nicole.

"With the new, high-tech models, absolutely. They allow for remote-control calibration after they are implanted. So, if you were unethical enough, you could use that capability to ramp up heart rate whenever you wanted to change their emotion."

"Unethical?" replied Doc. "I probably would have said criminal ... although I'm not sure what law covers messing with people's physiology? But even if that worked, this person—Dan Milgrom, was it?"

"Right," replied Nicole.

"Mr. Milgrom would have to look at his situation and believe that his heart drumming in his ears was because of something or someone in it that he disliked, rather than something that he feared or someone he felt attracted to or any other emotion that's associated with heartrate. And the timing of the heartrate increases and decreases would need to correspond to when this person or thing was in the setting. You think all of that could have been coordinated with Mr. Milgrom?"

"Well, here's the situation," replied Nicole. "It's a business setting involving Milgrom, his boss, and several others. Think basic staff meeting. And while I don't know everyone in those meetings, I doubt he would have attributed the change in his heart rate to sexual attraction. And fear seems unlikely, too, since he had worked with this group for years. But when his boss starts talking about his plans for the company and Milgrom gets agitated, he might well interpret that as anger toward the man and his ideas."

"And I'm guessing that this staff meeting is somewhere near the top of the company?"

"The very top of a good-sized company," replied Nicole, "meaning that wealth and power are the likely motives. And I think I know exactly who had his finger on the pacemaker's remote." Nicole paused. "Thanks, Doc."

In the excitement of the last couple of minutes, she'd forgotten Doc was ... well, not exactly the enemy, but someone who would share Rebecca's tunnel vision where Ellie was concerned. At least, he would once the PI had a chance to talk to him. She couldn't compete with that, so better to leave it at thanks and get on with proving Rebecca wrong.

"I need to run now. I need some time to organize my thoughts before I meet with Rebecca."

"Mind if I call you later, see how things turn out? All I know now is that you have someone messing with Mr. Milgrom's emotions, which somehow causes a shift in wealth and power in a big company. I'm not sure I can live with that cliffhanger."

"I'll try to call you when we have it figured out," she said, although she had no intention of doing so. But maybe she would send him a text explaining her falling out with Rebecca and that he was collateral damage. Perhaps she owed him that much. She disconnected.

An idle thought came to her mind. From the mirror in her room, Nicole knew her face was slightly flushed and she could hear her heart drumming in her ears. And when she thought about the context, she could have labeled the changes as the result of attraction to Doc. She knew better. She was excited that soon, she'd make that smug PI, Rebecca Marte, eat her words.

Afternoon, Jen's Place

When Rebecca thought she heard the front door to the Jen's Place office suite open, she leaned over to see who was in the reception area. Though the area was empty, the maneuver made her smile. She had performed the same one routinely in her own office back in St. Louis, as it, too, had an unmanned outer office. Her smile, however, was short-lived as a niggling concern that had long been in the back of her mind moved to the fore. Would Marte Investigative Services ever be more than a one-woman operation? Would there ever be anyone in the reception area?

It wasn't that she doubted her skills and abilities; rather, she was concerned about her location. Even before the mass exodus from major metropolitan areas caused by the COVID pandemic, St. Louis had frequently been high on the list of the fastest-shrinking cities in the United States. True, it also tended to top the list of murder capitals, but few of those cases called for a PI not affiliated with a high-powered law firm. And frankly, she wasn't sure she wanted to be the gofer girl for some criminal lawyer.

And now, she had an impulsive detour to a different state to investigate a non-crime resulting in her firing to add to the resume. Black eyes like this one had a tendency to resurface at the worst possible moment.

This time, she was certain she heard the door open and leaned over to see Nicole entering. Maybe she could rectify the problem this case had become right now. After all, she did have some game-changing information to share with her ex-client.

"I'm packing and can be out of here tomorrow if that's what you want after hearing my news."

Nicole's eyes narrowed. "Not if it's just more of your ... theories about Ellie. I've heard enough of them for a lifetime."

"Then, how about a confession from her?"

"A confession? To doing what?" asked Nicole. She crossed her arms over her chest, an expression of resistance that was becoming familiar to Rebecca.

"She admitted to removing the date and leaking the marketing document to the press, to causing a promotion announcement to be released three times, and to deleting the emails with the company's gross receipts before they were processed."

"You're lying. She didn't actually confess to that," said Nicole.

"Actually, she did. And she asked me to tell you because she's embarrassed that she let you go to so much trouble and expense. She said she'll call you later to apologize."

"And she did all those things to get her husband to retire?" By now, Nicole had uncrossed her arms and was standing with them hanging by her side.

"Please, have a seat," said Rebecca. "After all, it's your office."

Nicole did.

"I know these acts seem very poorly conceived now, but Ellie even talked about why, at the time, she thought each would nudge her husband closer to retirement. But when they all backfired, she stopped. Everything bad that happened to HomeRight and her husband after that was just bad luck or the logical progression of a trend she started. Or at least, that's what she believes."

"Ellie?" said Nicole.

At first, Rebecca didn't follow. "Ah, yes. We got on a first-name basis by the time the talk ended. But anyway, I can't see how that's the whole story. It's nearly impossible for me to believe that she sent that thug after you, for example."

"And you're having trouble figuring out how Milgrom's emotions were being influenced, right?" Nicole asked.

"Yeah, that's the sticking point because no one seems to think he would have listened to Whitten."

By now, Nicole's disposition had completely reversed. She was nodding her head, a slight smile coming to her lips. "What's going on?" asked Rebecca.

"I have the piece of the puzzle you're missing," said Nicole. "Well, Doc and I have a theory, anyway."

"You and Doc have a theory about Milgrom's about-face? OK, let's hear it."

"First, let's get things back the way they should be. If—and I realize this is a big if—but if you want the job to check out this last piece of the puzzle—and there are a lot of questions surrounding it—would you consider coming back on the case?"

"I'd much prefer finding out exactly what happened than going back to St. Louis with the case unsolved," Rebecca replied. "Yes, I'd be glad to work for you again."

"Excellent. The basic idea that Doc and I came up with is that someone was manipulating Dan Milgrom's emotional reaction to Randolph Peterson's business ideas. So, every time the boss spoke, Milgrom would fly off the handle."

"OK," said Rebecca slowly. "And what makes this possible?"

"His pacemaker." Over the next fifteen minutes or so, Nicole described her meeting with Dr. Nicholas Spencer and her later phone call to Doc. When she finished, she said, "You don't seem nearly as skeptical as I thought you would be. I kept expecting you to interrupt with all kinds of questions, especially when I got to the psychology part."

"Well, I'm not sure I would have ever come up with this idea. And if I had, it certainly wouldn't have been in the context of this Two-Factor Theory you talked about. But the basic idea isn't that foreign, and I don't think it will be for you, either, if we look at it a different way. You know what a polygraph or lie detector measures, right?"

"Sure. They usually measure heart rate, blood pressure, skin conductivity, and respiration rate. I also know that calling these devices lie detectors is considered a misnomer and that their results aren't usually admissible in court. People can learn to trick a polygraph."

"That's one of the limitations that's often mentioned. But more generally, polygraphs can only tell you that these physiological measures have changed. And since there is no specific pattern of bodily reactions from lying, the technician has to infer what the changes mean. So, distinguishing between someone who is nervous but telling the truth and someone who is nervous because they're lying is extremely difficult."

Nicole looked away for a moment. "So, Doc and I were talking about an old saying—that relationships formed under extreme conditions never last. It makes the technician's task sound nearly impossible. If the person who is experiencing the emotion can't tell if his heart is racing from attraction or from fear, what chance is a technician going to have?"

"Exactly. Attraction won't come into play in a polygraph test on a criminal case. But anxiety because someone is lying or because they are intimidated by the whole process will often be competing possibilities. Like any information we get in an investigation, we need to look for a pattern and not take any one result, from a polygraph or any other source, as proof."

Rebecca gave Nicole a moment to consider this information. And when she seemed satisfied, she asked, "So, tell me how this mysterious someone was ramping Milgrom's heart rate up and down in the middle of staff and board meetings without calling attention to him or herself?"

Nicole's brow wrinkled in a frown, and Rebecca would have sworn that the change in expression occurred at the exact instant when she used the word "herself." She thought they were beyond arguing about Bethune-Peterson's possible role in her husband's death, but now, it seemed like she might be in for another round.

"I need to apologize for being so defensive about Ellie … and all the other stuff I said earlier," said Nicole. "I didn't want to hear that she might be anything other than blameless. Apparently, I was the one who was blind, since she played a role in Mr. Peterson's downfall."

"An apology is completely unnecessary. You were protecting a friend, and loyalty is a strength in my book." And in one respect, Rebecca felt she might understand Nicole's reaction even better than she did. One friend that wasn't family was all the woman had.

"So, back to the original question," said Rebecca. "How does one change the settings on a pacemaker in the middle of a business meeting?"

"Well, with this model, the final adjustments are made after it's implanted. Everyone's different, so the resting and exercising heart rate may need a final tweak. All you need to do is locate the pacemaker's remote within ten feet or so of the device. It sends a signal to the pacemaker to increase or decrease heart rate ... and that's it."

"There's a remote for this pacemaker? Like a TV remote?" asked Rebecca.

"We call them that, but no. It's basically a modified laptop that can read the encrypted signals from the pacemaker and send encrypted commands back to it. For safety reasons, the encryption is specific to a pair of devices, and the distance limitation is another safeguard. The manufacturer wouldn't want one remote changing the settings of another pacemaker across town. So, the person controlling Milgrom's emotions would need the right computer and be at the staff or board meeting, rather than standing out in the hall, for example."

"So, we have Whitten or Shaw or some other person TBD on a laptop in these meetings, pretending to take notes, while increasing Milgrom's heart rate whenever Peterson takes the floor to discuss a new vision for the company or a new business strategy.

Milgrom interprets his state of agitation as a 'fight' response since there's no reason he'd consider fleeing from a business meeting. And with physical violence being inappropriate, it becomes verbal aggression."

Nicole nodded her agreement with Rebecca's summary, adding, "I think that covers it."

"In that case, we have one statement that needs a closer look," said Rebecca. "Bethune-Peterson described a meltdown between her husband and Milgrom at dinner one evening. Unless someone else was hiding in a back booth with a computer, Milgrom's emotions weren't being manipulated that night."

She and Nicole were both quiet for a moment. For her part, she was working on reasons why Bethune-Peterson might have misinterpreted the situation. Apparently, Nicole was doing the same.

"Bear with me a moment," said Nicole, "but Ellie never had any direct exposure to the shouting matches that occurred at work. She wouldn't know what they looked like. She saw an argument at the restaurant and thought, ah, this is what I've been hearing about." She paused a beat. "If you think that's possible, I'd be happy to go back to her and get some additional information."

"I think that scenario is completely plausible ... but let me suggest a different way to check it out. If we go back to Ellie, she'll just elaborate on what she's already said. But if we're building a possibility on this Two-Factor theory, then what's important is the label Milgrom put on the situation. Let's ask him about that argument."

"Perfect," replied Nicole. "So, if someone at the staff and board meetings was controlling Milgrom, who are we left with? I know Whitten, Peterson, Milgrom, and

Shaw would be there, although I thought you didn't like Shaw as a suspect. Anyone else?"

"As for the complete guest list to these meetings, I have no idea," admitted Rebecca. "Sounds like another good question for Dan Milgrom. And as for Shaw, yes, I struggle to find a motive for her to run Peterson off. It's just making her life much more difficult. I also sense compassion in her tone and expression every time his name comes up. But reading suspects isn't a science ... as we've already discussed."

After a moment of silence, Rebecca asked, "Can you do your thing with social media and look for any connections between Shaw and Spencer?"

"Absolutely," Nicole replied.

"I also think we should try to get the police to reopen the case, and to do that, we'll need Ellie to retract some of her statements. Or she could express some doubt about things she'd said before, like the speed that her husband was supposedly deteriorating."

"That shouldn't be a problem. You mentioned several when you were making the case we should be looking at her. Things like the content of the suicide note or the fact that the house was undisturbed."

"OK, but we can't be putting words in her mouth. Sooner or later, she'd get tripped up on some detail of the half-truth. So, let's see what she'd be comfortable saying."

"Right."

"Then, we need to give the police some reason to interview Spencer. He didn't exactly panic when you suggested he gave someone the ability to tug at Milgrom's heartstrings on demand ... but he wasn't exactly calm about it either."

Nicole chuckled. "Tug at his heartstrings? Quite poetic ... and strangely appropriate since, if all of this is true, someone was affecting his emotions via his heart." She paused. "But there's one thing I don't understand—why the police should interview him rather than you? I can't see that we have enough to interest the police, and you know exactly what to ask and where to look."

"True, I have a little more background, but you can't overestimate the impact of a police interrogation on someone like Spencer. He's probably never been inside a police station, much less inside a tiny interrogation room with nothing but a table, a few chairs, and a couple of detectives. And if we can't get enough to involve the police, then I'll interview him. So, can you make a set of your graphs for Spencer with special attention to the rest of our persons of interest, especially Whitten?"

"I've already picked up a little more about Spencer and Whitten," said Nicole. "Apparently, they play golf together at the country club on a fairly regular basis and have for years. That would have given Spencer lots of time to casually mention a wild idea he had back in medical school, which isn't that farfetched. Turns out, his undergraduate degree was in psychology. And then later, when he mentions that one of Whitten's coworkers, Dan Milgrom, is getting a pacemaker, Whitten comes up with the plan. He makes it sound generally innocent and Spencer needs the money. Voila."

"Psychology? Really?" asked Rebecca.

"Yeah, but it's not as incriminating as it might sound. Psychology is a fairly common pre-med major, but it fits. And I'll start checking into who besides Whitten interacts with Spencer."

"Good," said Rebecca. And it was good work, although it also worried her. The late-night visit the day before had been a warning, perhaps made worse because they hadn't cowered at the thug's words. But now, if Nicole was on to something, the stakes were even higher. The perpetrators would stop at nothing to hide the calculated ruthlessness they had practiced on Milgrom and Peterson. "You are being careful, right?" she asked.

"I think so," replied Nicole.

That wasn't the response that Rebecca had hoped for and she felt a knot form in her stomach.

"Spencer's bio was online and since I had a meeting with him, I didn't think looking at it would raise any red flags," said Nicole. "And generally, I'm still getting most of my information from social media. But the information on Whitten and Spencer's golfing is from a call to the country club. I picked a time when I knew Spencer wouldn't be there and then asked for him by name. When they confirmed he wasn't on the grounds, I asked for Whitten. That got a chuckle because the person on the line said she'd already checked since the two of them often played golf together, but he wasn't there either. I suppose the country club ended up with my phone number, but I doubt anyone is going to dig through their call logs looking for it."

The knot in Rebecca's stomach untied itself. She wasn't sure if Nicole had a long history of watching detective television shows and movies or if her commonsense precautions had become second nature in a world where she trusted few. But for now, anyway, her safety measures seemed sufficient.

"OK, but if you run into a situation where you're unsure how to proceed, we can talk it through."

"Sounds good," replied Nicole with a determined nod.

"So, any thoughts as to how we might get the police interested in interviewing Dr. Spencer? Something more than he was the surgeon of a friend of the suicide victim."

After a moment, Nicole said, "Well, the police would know that Milgrom and Peterson had been at each other's throats for weeks. That would be part of the background on the suicide. So, we could mention that people are often more emotional for months after surgery, and anger is one emotion that's been reported. And the reason they'd need to talk with Spencer is that his methods are different than most."

"Hmm, not bad," replied Rebecca. "Or more to the point, better than anything I could come up with. But just for my edification, are Spencer's methods that much different than any other surgeon's?"

"I doubt it," admitted Nicole. "But I'd bet he'd play up every little thing that's unique if you asked him."

"Good. We'll go with that if the need comes up. Different topic. You find out anything about that boy who said Peterson had propositioned him? Getting him to tell the police he'd been paid to lie and by whom could make short work of this whole case."

"Yeah, I did check, but I didn't learn anything useful. First, as you already know, there's not much in the police report because it was just an initial complaint and with the birth certificate they required later, it wasn't a crime. The address he gave is fake, which, interestingly enough, is the same one his mother gave me when they came to Jen's Place. Either they had planned this from the start or they routinely give a false address to protect themselves. But even more strange, the phone number she gave me was correct, which was how I spoke with her that one time. Of course, she never answered again and now, the number's not working."

"OK, we'll put that on hold for now," said Rebecca. "So, is there any reason we shouldn't start checking out some of these ideas? We could make a couple of phone calls."

Nicole seemed surprised, but covered it well with, "I'm game if you are."

Afternoon, Tucker Redd's Apartment

The cell phone that Whitten had given Redd lay on the dresser ringing. Only one person had the number. He checked the display anyway, hoping that some telemarketer had discovered it or reached him with random dialing. He wasn't that lucky.

"Hello, Mr. Whitten."

"You should have broken her damn jaw, you nitwit."

"Veles?" asked Redd.

"Have you been beating up other women?"

"No, sir." Redd knew that his failure to admit the fiasco at Jen's Place to his boss yesterday wasn't a permanent solution, but he had hoped it would give him more than a day. It hadn't. Now, he was probably going to be sent back to break some legs. That is, assuming he wasn't the one who ended up in the hospital rather than Veles. He'd tried to convince himself that her blow to his chest was just luck, but he kept coming back to the same conclusion. She was incredibly fast and much stronger than she looked.

And though his chest still hurt, it was the PI, Marte, who had done the most damage. He was sure his nose was broken and the bruising had spread to his eyes. Keeping a low profile in his current state was going to be impossible.

"So, Spencer called me claiming that Veles had accused him of murder." Whitten gave a mirthless laugh. "Of course, when I got to the bottom of it, she'd just accused him of messing with a patient's head. What a gutless twit."

"Spencer is that doctor?" asked Redd.

"Jeez, man. Can't you keep track of the people you beat up? Yes, he's your soft lily-white punching bag from a couple of days ago. Anyway, it looks like Veles isn't going to stop her meddling, so it's time we put an end to it. One thing, though. It has to be done soon, like yesterday."

"I can't kill a woman," said Redd.

"Who said anything about a woman? I meant Spencer. With him gone, she's got nothing but dead ends for her and her leggy PI to investigate."

Whitten was quiet for a moment. "What is it with you and women, anyway? No, wait. I don't care. But I am telling you right now—get over it. Sooner or later, you're going to have to deal with a woman, and when that time comes, I don't want any back talk. Got it?"

"Yeah, I got it."

"Good. I don't care how you get rid of Spencer, but like I said, it's got to be soon."

"What's the pay?" asked Redd. He was still irritated by the pittance he'd received for silencing Veles. True, he hadn't actually completed the job, but Whitten hadn't known that when he decided on a figure.

For several seconds, all Redd heard was silence. Finally, Whitten said, "Don't you trust me to compensate you fairly for the few minutes this job will take? After all, if you yelled 'boo' on a dark night, Spencer would probably keel over with a heart attack." Whitten chuckled. "Wouldn't that be apropos? A heart surgeon dying of a heart attack?" He chuckled again.

"I'd just like to know what I'm risking prison time for."

"You're not going to prison. I have some of the best lawyers that money can buy. So, look. Do the job and we'll come up with a figure that'll make both you and that wife of yours happy. But right now, I have to get going." Whitten disconnected.

"Murder?" Redd muttered to himself. After he'd seen the video of his assault on Spencer, he thought it might come to this someday. He just hoped that he would have more time to find a new job. He didn't. The time had come, and he knew what had to be done.

Redd took a few minutes to form a plan. He knew better than to make it too complex. Straightforward had always worked best for him, and this one was about as simple as a plan for murder could be.

He opened the dresser drawer and pulled out a cloth-covered bundle. After carefully unwrapping the contents, he spread three knives of varying lengths and curvatures on the bed.

"These should do the trick," he muttered as he looked down at the gleaming blades.

Afternoon, Jen's Place

"Hello, Miranda. It's Nicole Veles. I'm here with Rebecca Marte and I've got you on speaker. Is Dan there?"

"Hi, Nicole, Rebecca. How's the sleuthing going?"

Rebecca glanced across the desktop to the woman sitting on the other side, making sure that Nicole was handing off the question. "Good," replied Rebecca. "We just wanted to follow up with your husband on a couple of things."

"Of course. I just took him a cup of coffee and I'm enjoying one myself."

Rebecca looked at Nicole again, this time willing her to avoid any comments about their drinks. But then, Nicole knew them better than she did. Her client said nothing.

After a moment of silence, Ms. Milgrom said, "Just a second. I'll get him." They heard a muffled, "Dan, it's Nicole Veles and Rebecca Marte on the phone." A pause, after which they heard, "I don't know. You'll have to ask them." Then, back at full volume, "Do you mind if I stay on the line? This is investigation stuff, right?"

"Yes, it's related to the case," said Rebecca. "And, no, we don't mind if you listen in." She was increasing the chance of a digression—a debate between the couple that was more show than disagreement—but the possibility Miranda might remember something Dan didn't was worth the risk.

Shortly, Dan Milgrom joined them on the line. "What can I do for you ladies this afternoon?"

"Hi, Mr. Milgrom. It's Rebecca Marte, and Nicole Veles is here with me."

"It's Dan ... like I mentioned before."

Actually, Rebecca was fairly certain he hadn't suggested a first-name basis during their previous talk, even though the discussion had become more amicable by the end. But she could take him up on his offer now. "Sure, Dan. We're just looking for a little more information. I was wondering if you remember a dinner date with the Petersons about two years ago. As I understand it, you and Mr. Peterson had some type of disagreement, and you and Miranda left before the meal was served."

"You remember that, Danny," said Miranda. "It was the night you practically made me go hungry."

"We got the entrées from the kitchen and brought them home."

"Well, mine was cold and the conversation once we got here .... Well, there wasn't any."

"And like I said then, I'm sorry about that. But to your question, Rebecca, we obviously recall the night. It was the last time we tried dining with Ellie and Randy. What about it?"

"You've mentioned that some of your complaints with Mr. Peterson were, in retrospect, a bit harsh and you're not sure why you made so much of them. How about that evening? Did the discussion get heated that night?"

"You've got a very diplomatic way of putting things, Rebecca. Let's just tell it like it was at HomeRight. I was mercilessly brutal to an old friend and there's no way I can justify it."

"Honey, we've been through this," said Ms. Milgrom softly. "It seems like you were being tough on him now, but if you could go back, you'd find everything you said had a reason."

"That's the mantra," he replied slowly. "It's just tough for me to believe. Anyway, as to that night at dinner, it wasn't anything like the shouting sessions at work. We'd just learned that Randy had accidentally deleted the deposit emails, and I had a very clear objective in talking with him that night. I thought we should stop the practice of him reviewing the receipts. Randy balked, so I asked him how they'd gotten deleted. I thought if we knew, we could develop some kind of safeguard so that it wouldn't happen again. But all he kept saying was that he didn't remember looking at the numbers or deleting the email.

"Anyway, after a while, I got frustrated, somewhat with Randy, but mostly with myself. I couldn't seem to find the right question. I kept trying all these different situations, hoping something would jog his memory. Did he ever check his work email in the morning with his coffee? Late at night before he went to bed? Did he remember Ellie looking over his shoulder at the email? And on and on. Finally, I gave up. And because some of the talks at work had become ... well, like I said, mercilessly brutal, I figured it was time we got out of there before things got out of hand."

So, it appeared that the episode Bethune-Peterson had interpreted as one of Milgrom's inexplicable meltdowns was actually something different. Milgrom had a reason for the talk and he remembered it. Things had gotten tense, but the discussion never deteriorated to name-calling and finger-pointing. Milgrom even labeled his emotion differently. That night at the restaurant, he'd been frustrated with himself; when things boiled over at work, he was angry with Peterson.

Of course, proving that Milgrom had only become angry with Peterson inside the confines of a staff or board meeting would be next to impossible. All it would take to disprove that conjecture was one counterexample anytime during the year or so that the defamation had occurred. But Rebecca could accept this premise as a working assumption that would greatly reduce the number of suspects. And her next question should give them that figure.

"One thing we were wondering is, who from HomeRight would attend both Mr. Peterson's staff meetings and the board meetings?"

"Well, let's see. I would, of course, as well as Randy and Whitten. Tom Reynolds, head of accounting, and Trey Gonzales, head of logistics, would be at most of them. I think that's all the regulars."

"Not Gloria Shaw?" asked Miranda.

"Great. That makes me look like a male chauvinist," he replied.

"That's because you are one, honey," added Ms. Milgrom.

He sighed loud enough that Rebecca could hear it over the phone. "I often said that Gloria made HomeRight run, so I wouldn't think my slipup had anything to do with her gender."

"Anyone else?" asked Rebecca quickly, hopefully pulling the discussion back to suspects and away from sexism.

There was a significant pause on the line. Finally, he said, "Others might be called in when there were special topics on the agenda, but no, I think that's everyone who attended regularly. At least, during the last part of my tenure."

"Thank you," said Rebecca. "That's very helpful."

And it was. Under the assumption that someone was manipulating Milgrom's emotions and that this happened only during staff and board meetings, she might have as few as four suspects. What Rebecca needed now was a way to bolster this conjecture in case Milgrom had unintentionally omitted someone else, and she had an idea. Whoever was calling the shots for their late-night visitor was probably trying to keep a step ahead of them, which meant they were seeking information regularly. And the Milgroms were certainly a possible source for that leak.

"Have either of you had any visitors from HomeRight in the last few months?"

"Oh, not me, dear," replied Miranda. "I didn't really get involved with Danny's work friends."

"As for me," said Mr. Milgrom, "not a damn person has dropped by."

"Honey, language. And don't you think they'd be interested in your phone calls from work? There's been a steady stream of those."

"Steady stream?" The line was silent for several moments. "James Whitten is about the only one from work who still calls, and that's been maybe a couple of times a month."

"Not Gloria Shaw?" asked Rebecca.

There was a faint sound, and Rebecca could almost picture Milgrom slapping his forehead with a hand. "I did it again," he said. "Sorry. Yes, she calls occasionally. But even with the both of them, I'd hardly call that a steady stream."

"And Mr. Reynolds and Mr. Gonzales don't call?" asked Nicole. Internally, Rebecca smiled, hearing her client already checking into the pair of newcomers.

"What? Those two? Not a word."

"When Mr. Whitten calls, what do the two of you discuss?" asked Rebecca.

"Well, not how to run HomeRight, that's for sure. He has his own ideas about that ... and I suppose, they're OK. The company is bouncing back nicely." He paused. "Anyway, most of our conversations are just small talk. And the same for Gloria. It's how am I doing? Weather's sure bad. What keeps me busy in retirement? That sort of thing."

So, if one of their suspects was keeping tabs on the investigation via Milgrom, it was probably Shaw or Whitten. Maybe one of them was passing the information on to Gonzales or Reynolds. For that matter, they could have been passing on what they knew without even realizing it. All it would take was a casual question about their old coworker during a coffee break or over lunch at the office. That approach, however, wouldn't be the most timely or reliable—how would Gonzales or Reynolds know when he needed to make a casual inquiry? So, her primary suspicions remained with Shaw and Whitten.

Now, it seemed like the time to put Peterson's saying about bedrock and the wind into practice; it was time for Rebecca to take a shot in the dark. If she could pinpoint the time Milgrom and Shaw had last spoken to Milgrom and cross-reference that to Nicole's activities, perhaps they could figure out what had made the person or persons behind the thug so nervous. Given the number of assumptions underlying this question, it was truly a long shot.

"Dan, if you can, try to remember the last time you spoke with Mr. Whitten and with Ms. Shaw."

"I'm not very good at remembering dates," Milgrom replied.

"That's true," added Ms. Milgrom. "Something that happened three years ago he'll think was last year. And he never remembered our anniversary until he put it on the calendar on his computer."

"At least I remembered to put it in there," said Milgrom. "Now, wait a second," he said with a touch of excitement. "Nicole, when were you in St. Louis?"

"Third week in August," Nicole replied. "I was there from August 19 to 23. I got back home on the 24th.

"I last talked to Gloria the week before you went there, so during the week of August 12," he said. "I remember that call because your name came up."

"Nothing bad, I hope," said Nicole.

That, in Rebecca's mind, was the perfect follow-up. Nicole hadn't led him with a question—you weren't talking about my trip to St. Louis, were you? Rather, she was letting him provide the reason he remembered the call in his own words. That was starkly different from the myriad of memory joggers Milgrom had tried with Peterson to get him to recall how the deposit email had been deleted. Rebecca wouldn't have believed a word Peterson said after all those leading questions.

"Nicole, you couldn't do anything bad if you tried," Milgrom replied.

But, as Rebecca knew, even the best follow-up questions sometimes failed. She started thinking about a question of her own when Milgrom said, "Gloria asked how you were coming along in finding someone to look at Randy's suicide. That surprised me because I didn't even know she knew you were looking for a PI. Turns out, Tom Reynolds's wife had mentioned it to her."

"Do you know how Ms. Reynolds knew?" asked Rebecca.

"That probably came from me," said Miranda. "The whole case became a pretty common topic around here. Ellie and I don't talk that much, but she mentioned Nicole was thinking of hiring someone. And later, she said ... well, that Nicole was going back east to hire a PI. St. Louis is east to Ellie. A day or two after that, Lacy Stockmeyer asked me how the trip was going. I'm not sure how she heard. But I talked to Tom's wife—she goes by Babs, which probably is short for Barbara. Anyway, I mentioned it to her."

Well, this was going about as well as most of the long shots Rebecca had taken. Maybe Ms. Milgrom hadn't befriended her husband's coworkers, but she was friends with their wives. And the way information traveled in Lone Tree, a city approaching 15,000, it felt more like a hamlet of 200 ... or at least, it did in this neighborhood. But she decided to finish the inquiry anyway. "How about Mr. Whitten? When was the last time you talked to him?"

"Oh, not long ago at all. What was it, Miranda, Sunday?"

"It was Sunday, and it was starting to get late. Who calls so late on a Sunday night? James Whitten should really know better."

Sunday? Rebecca didn't think that tidbit would help at all. She'd check with her client, but she didn't think Nicole had done anything on the case until after her arrival Sunday evening.

"You know," said Ms. Milgrom, "after claiming I was your haggard personal secretary, greeting all your visitors and taking all your phone calls, you come up with what, Danny? Three, maybe four calls a month? But that's only because we limited it to HomeRight calls. The guys in his poker club call three or four times a week, and I'll bet his doctor calls close to once a week. Then, add in everything to keep the house clean and the occasional neighbor who comes by for coffee. Well, it adds up."

It wasn't the question she wanted to ask, but to be thorough, she did. "Dan, do any of your poker buddies work at HomeRight?"

"Naw. Poker has always been my escape from work."

"OK. What doctor is it that calls?" asked Rebecca, getting to the comment that had captured her attention.

"Why, Dr. Spencer," replied Ms. Milgrom. "I've never heard of any doctor as dedicated as him. Two years later and he still calls. And such a handsome and distinguished gentleman. Do you know him, Nicole?"

Nicole stammered for a moment, then replied, "Not as well as I'd like."

Rebecca concurred. They needed to know Dr. Spencer a lot better than they did. "And you said Dr. Spencer calls around once a week?" she asked, just to verify.

"Yeah, around that," replied Milgrom. "Maybe a little less."

"And he's been doing that for two years?"

"Pretty much, although it seems like the frequency has gone up recently."

"Have you had any problems with the pacemaker?" asked Nicole.

"None at all. Well, after I got used to the idea, anyway. You know, it's a little creepy having some machine keeping your heart going."

"So, what do the two of you discuss?" asked Rebecca.

"A little small talk, and then the usual doctor stuff. How you feeling? Appetite OK? Getting your sleep? But he always seems to get around to Randy's death and how I feel about it. And he's not a shrink." He paused, then continued with some bite in his tone. "One time, he asked if I felt bad about what happened. What a stupid question. Of course, I feel bad. I was really tough on my old friend."

Most would find Spencer checking on Milgrom's mental state after such a long period unusual, although admirable—Miranda Milgrom certainly felt that way. But if what Rebecca now thought was true, his interest in his patient was self-serving and despicable. He was using his doctor-patient relationship to find out if Milgrom suspected anything about his past behavior and if so, was anyone listening to him?

"I think we've covered everything," said Rebecca. Although she had planned to ask Milgrom if he was still being followed, if they were as close to breaking this case as she thought, that concern would soon be history. "Is there anything you'd like to ask or add?"

"Not from me," said Milgrom.

"Danny seemed to think you might drop by sometime for coffee," said Ms. Milgrom. "Anytime you have a moment, the pot's always on. You, too, Nicole."

Rebecca doubted the pot was ever off, but she said, "Thanks. I'll try."

"Me, too," added Nicole.

Once they had disconnected, Nicole said, "We got him!" accompanied by a fist pump.

Most of the time, Rebecca would have found Nicole's gesture somewhat humorous, but in this case, she was going to need to bring the woman back to Earth. "Yes, most likely," she replied. She picked up her phone and started typing.

Nicole held out a hand. "What are you talking about? Whitten pulled Spencer in with the promise of a huge tax-free payday. But when the doctor saw how it turned out, he started panicking, looking for reassurance that his secret was safe by calling Dan Milgrom all the time. Whitten, on the other hand, was using Milgrom to keep tabs on us. And when he didn't like what we were up to, he hires some thug to warn us off."

"Or maybe the doctor is working with Shaw. She learned my name when Whitten mentioned it at work, but otherwise, he's not involved. And she or the doctor hired the thug."

Nicole's face fell.

"Look, I agree that your scenario is easily the most likely. But let's work the case like we planned and get the police involved as quickly as possible. That means your next action is to look at the common connections between Spencer and the other two people we just learned about. You OK with that?"

"Yeah, I am," said Nicole. "And I suppose you're right. After all, you're just telling me not to do what I accused you of doing—settling on a theory too quickly."

"Which is always good advice." Rebecca read something from her phone's display. "So, an important first step in our plan was to see if we could get Ellie to recant some of her earlier statements and have the police reopen the case. I just texted her to see if we could drop by. You up for a talk with Ellie?"

"You bet."

Afternoon, The Peterson Residence

Ms. Bethune-Peterson opened her front door and immediately drew back. "Nicole, your cheek looks really painful. Let your PI handle the fight next time."

"It was just a slight miscalculation. I bobbed when I should have weaved," said Nicole. But by the confused look on the older woman's face, the boxing jargon didn't make any sense to her. "The goon who visited us yesterday evening got in a lucky punch before we ran him off."

"What did he want?"

"We're not sure. All he said was that we should keep our noses out of his business, but we think it might be related to your husband's death. We think we might be close to something and that's making them nervous."

Bethune-Peterson frowned. "Well, I hope that's not the case because I already have enough to feel guilty about. Did Rebecca tell you what I did?"

"She did. And ...."

Bethune-Peterson didn't wait for her to finish. "Sorry, Nicole, but I need to say this. I am so terribly sorry for everything that I've put you through. If I hadn't been so proud and stubborn, we could have gotten to this point a lot faster and with a lot less expense. It's just that I couldn't admit that I had stirred up the hornet's nest, especially with everything that followed."

"It's OK," said Nicole. "We've made it this far, and the important thing is to keep moving forward." Nicole summoned all the resolve she had, stepped forward, and embraced the older woman.

When she stepped back, Bethune-Peterson had a hand pressed to her chest. After a moment, she simply said, "Thank you," as a sad smile spread across her face.

"The reason we're here is because you're still trying to shoulder too much of the responsibility for your husband's death," said Nicole. "We believe there are others involved."

The woman's smile faded, and she paused a moment. "I'm going to have trouble believing that, but you two should come in so we can talk it out."

As Bethune-Peterson led them to the study, Nicole cast a worried glance at Rebecca. But if the PI was as concerned as she about the need to "talk this out," she wasn't showing it.

When the women were seated, Rebecca described what they had in mind, making it sound quite simple and completely logical. They just wanted Bethune-Peterson to question some of her earlier statements to the police that had made her husband's death look like an open-and-shut suicide. With the additional doubt she would create, they would reopen the case.

Nicole noticed that the PI said nothing about the psychological theory on which their request rested, but she knew why. Bethune-Peterson's reaction to that part of the puzzle would probably be something like, "What crackpot came up with that?" And besides, it wasn't information the woman really needed to play her part.

When Rebecca finished, Bethune-Peterson said, "You want me to retract what I said before? You want me to say things like someone else might have written the suicide note?"

Her gaze as she talked kept shifting between the two women.

"Only if you feel it's possible," said Rebecca.

"Of course, it's possible," snapped Bethune-Peterson, her focus now on the PI. "Lots of people knew the way Randy talked and half the staff at HomeRight could probably forge his signature. Sometimes that was necessary."

She paused, perhaps to let some of her disappointment in this turn of events to dissipate.

"Look, everything you mentioned is possible, but I'm not going to say any of it to the police. I know what happened, and having a bunch of detectives crawling all over my home and harassing my friends isn't going to change anything. I started Randy's deterioration and nothing I tried could stop it."

Nicole wondered if her friend could really be as rock-solid in her position as she sounded. "Are you certain that you and bad luck were the only things working against your husband? Isn't it possible that there was a planned, systematic effort to run him out of the company? To make him appear to be the cause of all of HomeRight's financial downturns? To make him appear incompetent? Are you certain that Dan Milgrom's anger was just him protecting the company? All of this just doesn't add up to me."

Nicole thought her impassioned plea might be working as Bethune-Peterson sat motionless for several moments. Finally, the woman said, "We didn't have much growing up. My parents had to work long hours on the land just for us to survive, and the experience, many would say, made me hard. But, Nicole, whatever you've been through must have been worse, which is why I've always felt a strong connection to you. But that said, I can't do this for you or for Randy. He's gone and you're ... well, frankly, strong enough to live with my failings."

"Then, do it for yourself," said Nicole. She paused a moment. "Why is it, based on a few hours talking with you that I doubt we know the full story of your husband's death? And yet, after weeks to consider everything you know, you're certain nothing is remiss? Isn't there some doubt in your mind that you'd like removed once and for all?"

"No, Nicole, there isn't." She paused, releasing a long sigh. "There isn't because there's something I haven't told you, something I haven't told anyone. And it seems like this isn't going to end until I confess everything."

Nicole glanced at Rebecca, wondering if the PI felt as taken aback as she. But Nicole couldn't tell anything from her face. So, she turned back to her friend, wondering if the three things she had admitted to were just the tip of the iceberg. Had Ellie orchestrated everything, right up to her husband's death?

"The morning that Randy killed himself, we argued," the woman said softly. "That stubborn, delusional old man wanted to go back to HomeRight, take back his company. That would have destroyed him ... and us. And I told him so before I walked out. When I came back, he was dead. The mistakes I'd made over a year earlier were miscalculations. That morning, however, I was completely blind. I had no inkling of what I had done."

Nicole thought she understood how Bethune-Peterson felt about that moment in her history. She had just crushed the last hopes of a man who had withstood a year of shame and scorn. She had destroyed him. But to Nicole, there was a much different possibility, and apparently, Rebecca had the same thought.

"So, I assume over the years that you and your husband have had disagreements?" said Rebecca.

Bethune-Peterson turned to the PI, her expression blank. "All married couples do."

"And some of those disagreements had been bitter?"

"Of course," said Bethune-Peterson, her eyes now starting to narrow.

"And after each, Mr. Peterson would fall into a depression?"

"Don't be ridiculous. Randy was a strong, confident man." After a moment, during which Bethune-Peterson probably recognized her contradictory claims, she said, "That morning was different. He'd been through a year of hell. So, what did I do? I heaped on more guilt."

"And perhaps you did push him over the brink," said Rebecca. "I can't say for certain ... but neither can you. What we can say with certainty, however, is that Mr. Peterson was planning a comeback. Who makes plans like that and then kills themselves?"

"That .... That wasn't a plan," said Bethune-Peterson. "It was just desperation talking." But rather than waiting for either of her visitors to answer, she put up a hand and dropped her gaze to her lap. When she looked up, she asked, "Are you saying that someone killed Randy? Murdered him in his own office?"

"I'm saying that it's possible," replied Rebecca. "And the first step in getting an answer is to give the police a reason to take another look at the case. Your husband's intention to retake his leadership role at HomeRight is about as strong of a reason as I can imagine."

Bethune-Peterson got up from her chair and walked to the fireplace. After a few moments rubbing her hand over the wood of the mantle, she turned back to her guests. "You've been implying that someone was forcing Dan Milgrom to attack Randy, but you can't or won't tell me who it was or how it was done?"

"Sorry, but we can't," said Rebecca. "We have a solid possibility, but it's incomplete. With what we have, however, and with the police investigating, we should be able to get to the bottom of this quickly."

"Nicole?" said Bethune-Peterson.

"I had a hand in developing this idea. Well, I and an old friend did. And, yes, I believe Dan Milgrom was being manipulated without his knowledge."

Bethune-Peterson became quiet again. It seemed like five minutes to Nicole, but it was probably less than two. Eventually, the woman spoke. "I need some time to think about all of this. If I decide to go to the police, I'll let you know." She started toward the door of the study.

"But ...," started Nicole.

Bethune-Peterson turned back to her visitors. "I need to sleep on it."

And since that was apparently all she was going to say, Nicole and Rebecca followed her to the front door. Once outside, Nicole turned to Rebecca. "Do you really think Mr. Peterson was killed in his own home?"

"Think about it. If you had set up this entire scheme—the rumors, the faked mistakes, the manipulation of Milgrom so he'd smear his friend—and you learned that Peterson was planning to make a return, what would you do?

"For Bethune-Peterson, the knowledge of his plan was irrelevant. After months of blaming herself for his deterioration, the only pertinent fact that morning was her unwitting delivery of the final blow to her husband's self-image. To reveal that fact to anyone would serve no purpose except to make her look bad. What it does in my mind, however, is to make someone else look guilty of murder."

Evening, A Back Road in Lone Tree, CO

Redd pulled the bundle of knives and a bag with a roll of duct tape and some gloves from under the passenger seat and exited his car. He'd never been here before, but from online maps, he knew he had about a two-hundred-yard walk through an open field before he got to the lawns of the neighborhood beyond.

He started, walking slowly, quietly, while idly bouncing the cloth-covered knives in his hand. He didn't care for them. He wasn't a knife-fighter, but they had their purpose. Killing, of course, but they could also be used for persuasion, and he needed these blades for both of those uses tonight.

He didn't know exactly what he'd gotten himself into, but the job certainly wasn't the bodyguard-in-training position he'd expected. Somehow, things had escalated from personal protection to the occasional strongarm persuasion and finally, to murder. He wanted to know why. So tonight, before he killed his prey, he'd get his answers.

The walk to the agreed upon location took him about twenty minutes, mostly because he had to move with stealth. Even though he was in an open field, his direction of travel, black clothes, and tools of the trade would leave no doubt about his intentions. So, every time he thought he heard something or believed he'd seen motion out of the corner of his eye, he'd stop to reconnoiter. Fortunately, nothing ever materialized out of the dark of the night.

The outbuilding where they were to meet sat at the back edge of the man's expansive lawn just beyond the field. Redd arrived there almost ten minutes early. He used only about 30 seconds of that extra time to pick the padlock on the door. Even so, by the time he turned to look, he could see the man coming across his lawn.

Apparently, the story he'd used to lure him here was working even better than he'd hoped. His bait had been information. Just the insinuation that Veles had stumbled onto something new about Randolph Peterson's suicide was enough to bring him out here to his death.

When he was still ten yards away, Redd said, "Inside. I need to show you something." He stepped through the door without waiting for a reply and turned on a light. With the reassurance of the illuminated room, he was confident that the man's curiosity would bring him the last few steps.

"How did you ...."

He never got to finish his question, however, as Redd's fist crashed into his temple. The man slammed into the wall behind him from the force of the blow and slid slowly to the ground.

Redd taped the man's hands together and placed a piece of tape over his mouth. He didn't think there were any houses close enough to hear the calls for help that might escape the closed room, but he didn't want to take the chance.

There was no chair in the shed, which would have been Redd's first choice, but the joists in the ceiling were exposed. There was also a length of chain on top of a workbench. Redd looped the chain between the man's taped hands and threw the other end over a joist. Although the links of the chain didn't slide over the wood easily, in a matter of a few moments, he'd raised the man to his tiptoes. He took the knives out of the cloth, put them on the workbench, and then used one to cut away the man's shirt and pants.

After a few minutes, the man woke up. It only took a moment for him to evaluate his situation and even less for him to panic. He was already begging with his eyes to speak. But Redd knew better. Take off the gag now, and he'd be screaming for help.

Redd took the leather gloves out of the bag and slowly put them on, flexing each fist in front of the man's face as he did. The man began struggling against his restraints as tears started running down his cheeks. With his first blow, Redd was sure he felt a rib crack. He didn't stop until he felt it twice more. Now, the only pain worse than his knives removing the man's flesh would be the agony of him trying to fill his lungs for a scream.

"I have questions," Redd said. "And I'm going to keep asking them until I'm convinced I have the full story. Whether that takes ten minutes or ten hours, it's completely up to you. But every time I think you're lying or holding out on me, I cut away a little more of you." Redd held up a knife. "Understand?"

The man nodded, his face twisting in pain from even that slight motion.

Redd took the phone that Whitten had given him out of a pocket and propped it up on the bench. "For the record," he said. "Now, I'm going to take off the tape, and you can start talking." He turned on the phone's video recorder and ripped off the tape.

"The floor's all yours, Mr. Whitten."

FRIDAY, SEPTEMBER 2

Afternoon, Jen's Place

Nicole looked up from her work and massaged the tight muscles in her shoulder with a hand. It had been a long morning spent on the computer searching for connections between Dr. Spencer and their remaining persons of interest—Shaw, Reynolds, and Gonzales. She had, however, come up empty. And of the three, she was doubting there was anything to find on Gonzales or Shaw. Both had modestly active social media presences, and after she had gone back as far as records allowed, she hadn't found even a hint that they'd crossed paths with Spencer.

The doctor was from the East and had gone to school there. Gonzales haled from Seattle. Shaw was from Los Angeles. Neither Shaw nor Gonzales had any connection to medicine, and as far as she could tell, Spencer had few other interests in life save finding a glamorous wife who could further his mystique. Shaw and Gonzales didn't travel in the same social circles as the doctor nor were they members of the same organizations. In short, there was no commonality in the rather long and extensive public history of the three.

Nicole was somewhat less sure about Reynolds, but only because he generally kept his private life exactly that—private. At first, his lack of a social media presence raised a red flag in her mind, but as she studied what breadcrumbs there were, she began to relax.

Under the assumption that many documented their life online to share with family and friends, it made sense that Reynolds would have little to post. He was single, an only child of parents who had passed away several years ago, and a three-year resident of Colorado. When Nicole went back to his days in Tucson, his hometown, she found a slightly more prolific presence, though still paltry by most people's standards. Currently, he maintained a profile on a business-related social media site and appeared in pictures that others, mostly from the HomeRight accounting department, had uploaded. He wasn't hiding from the world; he just didn't have much he felt he needed to share with it.

A lack of connection between any of these people and Spencer wasn't a problem for Nicole. Well, it wasn't except for one thing. She was having difficulty not concluding Whitten was their man, even though she knew she shouldn't settle on a theory prematurely. But while that thought rankled her slightly, the absence of Rebecca was starting to worry her a lot. The PI hadn't been at breakfast. She had missed their workout, and she hadn't shown up at lunch, either. And when Nicole went to the office, there was no indication she had been there all morning. Had the goon from earlier in the week returned with new orders? If he had, she'd find him if it was the last thing she ever did.

Nicole could feel her anger growing in lockstep with her concern for the PI, but perhaps that was for the best. If she could expend that emotion now, perhaps she could deal with this thug dispassionately when they met. Perhaps …. She didn't finish the thought, however, as someone knocked on her door. Rebecca's face appeared as the door cracked open.

"Please, open the safe. I need my firearm. And get a jacket. It's still pretty cool this afternoon."

"Your gun?"

"Just in case."

"And just where are we going that you might need it?"

"We have an appointment with Dr. Spencer. Or with someone at his office anyway. I'll explain in the car."

* * *

From her vantage point in the passenger seat, Nicole cast a sideways glance at Rebecca. "So, Ellie did call the police this morning," she said with a shake of her head that meant she didn't envy the police. "With her long-standing place in the community, she can raise a stink when she wants to. But if they're looking into Mr. Peterson's death again, why are we going to visit Spencer? And how the heck did you get him to meet with us?"

"Maybe I should concentrate on driving," said Rebecca, feigning a tone of seriousness. "This stretch of road's jammed, and we wouldn't want anything to happen to us this close to wrapping things up."

Nicole shook her head in disbelief, only then remembering that her reaction was lost on a driver whose eyes were locked on the road as part of her self-entertainment. "Why did I have to hire the one PI with a sense for the dramatic?"

Rebecca smirked. "I'm sure I'm not the only one. But to answer your question, I'm not certain we're meeting with Spencer. All I really know is that his office texted me saying that the two of us should get there ...." Rebecca paused to check the time on her dashboard. "Within the next fifteen minutes. After that, the police will be there and we'll have to read about it in the papers. And I'm guessing the sound's off on your phone."

Nicole knew it was without even looking. She always turned it off when she needed to concentrate, so instead of checking that, she went directly to her text messages. First, she found one from Bethune-Peterson, explaining her plan to call the police. Then, she found the one from Spencer's office. After reading it, she said, "I suppose it was too much to hope that my text would be a little less cryptic than yours. But if it was from Spencer, you think he's going to confess?"

"I think a confession is more likely than confessing to us."

"I have no idea what you mean," replied Nicole.

"You remember when we had the Milgroms on the phone, and Dan confirmed that Whitten had called him last Sunday?"

"Sure. I figured that was so he could stay one step ahead of us."

"Which is pretty much the same thing I thought. And no doubt you remember that later in that same conversation, we found out that Dr. Spencer was calling Milgrom almost every week."

"How could I forget that?" After a moment, Nicole said, "Ah, they don't trust each other. They were both calling Milgrom for basically the same information."

"Right. I'm thinking that distrust has become fear in Spencer's mind. So, I can see him wanting to confess but not to us. What good would that do? He probably thinks that if he gives the police a statement, he'll be safe from Whitten. Unfortunately, I don't think he's the forgiving type, and with the money Whitten has, Spencer probably won't be safe even behind bars."

"So, if not to confess to us then why the summons?"

Rebecca's phone announced that they had arrived at their destination. "We'll know soon enough." She stopped the car in one of the aisles of the parking lot, staring at the building. "This is where Spencer works?"

"Yep, first floor, just to the right as you enter. And with their sign in foot-high letters, there's no way to miss his office."

Rebecca chuckled. "I was picturing a labyrinth of hospital rooms, dead-end halls, locked up labs, and tiny storage areas—basically, the kind of place where ten-year occupants still don't know their way around. But I don't think anyone is going to waylay us in there. I'll just leave my gun locked up in the car."

The women parked and went inside. The scene was quite different from the first time Nicole had been there. The building receptionist was sitting at attention at her desk—gone were the yawns and her magazine. She was flanked by a man in a uniform, apparently part of the building's security. "May I help you?" he asked.

"Rebecca Marte and Nicole Veles to see Dr. Spencer," Rebecca said.

The guard glanced at the receptionist who nodded. "Please, go on in."

The scene inside Spencer's office suite was similar to the lobby, although this time, they had to show their identification. Soon after passing muster, Spencer's "zombie" assistant appeared at the door to take them back to his office. Nicole, however, hardly recognized the woman. Gone was the cold, aloof exterior. In its place was a disheveled woman with a tormented tissue in her hand and mascara smudged below one eye.

"You're not from the police," she said, stating the obvious since Rebecca was displaying her credentials.

"No, I'm a private investigator, Rebecca Marte. And I believe you know Nicole Veles." But if she recalled Nicole, she was too preoccupied to say so. "We received a text from Dr. Spencer's office."

"Oh, yes. The text was from me."

Rebecca extended a hand. Nicole put hers behind her back, but neither gesture had an effect on the woman. She was looking over Nicole's shoulder as if waiting for someone to burst through the door, guns blazing. After a moment, she glanced at her watch.

"Yeah, still ten minutes," she muttered to herself, then looked at her guests. "Sorry, things are a bit chaotic this morning. I'll take you back to see Dr. Spencer now."

She never noticed Rebecca's proffered hand.

"So, what's going on?" asked Rebecca after they had passed into the backroom area.

Nicole half expected the assistant to offer an excessively polite refusal, which really meant, "None of your damn business." But instead, she said, "You'd think I would know, wouldn't you? But I don't. All I know is that yesterday afternoon, Dr. Spencer had me cancel all of his appointments for the rest of the day. Then, he asked me if I'd stay around for dinner, and he ordered it delivered. I expected .... Well, dinner wasn't what I expected as he paced and hardly ate anything. Then, around 9 o'clock, he asked me to leave, but I think he spent the night here.

"When I came in this morning, he asked me to cancel all his appointments for today and all of next week. Then, he had me call the police and ask that they send a marked car here at 1 o'clock. Why a marked car, I don't know, but he was adamant. He said he'd be leaving with them to make a statement. What about, I have no idea. None of this is like Dr. Spencer. He's usually so calm and organized, but he's been nothing but frantic since yesterday."

Perhaps at that moment, she realized her statements hadn't put Spencer's practice in the most flattering light. "Of course, I'm probably mistaken. I'm sure Dr. Spencer has everything in hand."

Nicole found the woman's reassurance almost comical, considering the state of alarm in the lobby and the office suite. But rather than mentioning that fact, she turned to Rebecca.

"Do you think Ellie called Dan Milgrom yesterday afternoon? She might have wanted to give him a heads up that she was going to the police and that got back to Dr. Spencer."

"Maybe, but I'm still thinking he just realized how precarious his position was."

"So, you have some idea what's going on," said the assistant. "Dr. Spencer's obviously concerned for his safety, but from whom?"

"We're not sure, either," replied Rebecca. "Until everyone has made their statements to the police, it's just speculation on our part."

Speculation that needed only one more piece to the puzzle, thought Nicole. Who was Spencer's partner? And while her money had long been on Whitten, Rebecca had easily woven a scenario that implicated Shaw. She suspected that the PI could do the same for Reynolds or Gonzales ... or some other dude. Hopefully, however, she'd be entertaining these four other possibilities for only a few more minutes.

They arrived at Spencer's door and the assistant knocked. A voice from within said, "Is that you, Charlene?"

"Yes, and I've got Ms. Marte and Ms. Veles with me."

Nicole could hear the sound of a lock being thrown, and then the door opened a crack to show Spencer's face. "Come in," he said, quickly closing the door and locking it behind them.

"Thank you for coming," Spencer said.

Nicole noticed that his coat and tie had been tossed onto a chair. His shirt was wrinkled with one sleeve rolled up to the elbow while the other seemed to have been pushed up his arm to the same spot. A blanket lay rumpled at the foot of his couch. His eyes were bloodshot and his hair was a mess. It had obviously been a long night for the doctor.

"We don't have much time, but that's fine. I have everything ready for you."

Nicole and Rebecca exchanged glances. "You have what ready for us?" asked Rebecca.

"Well, not so much for you, Ms. Marte, but for Ms. Veles. I figured she might want you here. You know who James Whitten is, right?"

"We do," replied Nicole.

"Well, the man has gone mad. He thinks that somehow, I got one of my past patients ...." Spencer glanced at a piece of paper as if he couldn't remember the name. "A Mister Daniel Milgrom to turn on his boss, maybe even kill him. I couldn't really make too much sense out of his ranting, but that's what I got out of it."

"So, Mr. Whitten called you? When?" asked Rebecca.

Spencer didn't look too happy to have his story being questioned. "All the details are in the statement that I've prepared for the police. Of course, I can't give you that statement."

He turned around to pick up a couple of pages from his desk, and while he did, Rebecca held a finger up to her lips.

When he turned back to the women, he said, "But I also prepared one for Ms. Veles." He held out two pages and a pen. "It's just what we discussed when you were here yesterday."

If Rebecca's gesture didn't mean 'Be quiet,' then her next action—more technically, an inaction—would probably appear strange to both of them. Nicole just looked at the man and said nothing.

"You can change anything in your statement if you don't think it's accurate." He paused. Nicole remained quiet. "Your cheek looks a lot better today. That bruise is going to be gone in no time." Again, Nicole was silent.

Spencer turned to Rebecca. "I don't know what difference it makes, but Whitten's call was Monday, a little before lunch."

Rebecca nodded. "You know, the police can tell the difference between incoming and outgoing calls."

Spencer frowned. "I've been trying to help him, you know, with his delusions," said Spencer. "Maybe that day I called him. It's hard to remember."

"And how about this morning?" asked Rebecca. "Have you been helping him today?"

"I'm not sure what you're getting at, but I don't think I want to answer."

"OK. Nicole, shall we be going?"

"Wait a second. I don't know what this has to do with anything, but yes. I called last night and again this morning, several times, but he hasn't answered. He's probably gone off the deep end."

Rebecca nodded. "OK. Since you've met us halfway. Nicole, do you want to take a look at what Dr. Spencer has prepared for you?"

She took the pages from Spencer's hand and started skimming them. When she was finished and looked up, Rebecca turned back to the doctor.

"So, not having Whitten to reassure you that everything is going to be OK seems to be weighing heavily on your mind."

"It is. He's a troubled man, and him not answering for more than half a day is very concerning. He may have harmed himself. I'm sure you understand."

"Yes, I think I do," replied Rebecca. "Without Whitten's assurances, you're thinking he'll be sending his associate to finish the beating he started a week ago. Unfortunately, you won't be walking away this time."

If Rebecca had slapped the doctor's face, Nicole didn't think he could have looked more shocked. His mouth literally fell open. "Get the hell out of my office," Spencer snarled.

Nicole tore the pages in half and tossed them in the air as they turned to leave. Once they were outside, Nicole asked, "How on Earth did you know Whitten had Spencer beat up?"

"James Whitten can't resist the temptation to prove he's smarter than everyone else. You remember I mentioned a call he received while I was interviewing him?"

"Yeah, the call where he almost hung up and then later, told you it was a doctor friend who had done him a favor. Who could forget those contradictions?"

"He was just trying to prove we couldn't catch him even after he gave me those hints. You couple that information with our belief that Spencer and Whitten don't trust each other and the fact that Whitten has a penchant for having his hired muscle deal with problems, it made sense that they weren't having a nice dinner on a Friday evening. Also, when he reached for your statement on his desk, he winced. He moved like someone with sore ribs."

"I thought Spencer was going to have a stroke when you said that."

"By the way, that was a great job making him fill the silence. A lot of people find that difficult to do, but you did it well. So, what about the statement he prepared for you?" asked Rebecca, as they passed through the lobby of the building and out the front door. The women paused a moment as not one, but two marked police cars pulled to the curb. "Looks like his ride is here." They started walking toward their parking spot.

"The statement wasn't totally fiction, but the wording had a definite slant toward fantasy. Where he had written that the meeting was a professional discussion between colleagues in allied fields, he'd actually called the meeting a social visit and said I should call him Dr. Nick. Or where he said that we shared our professional backgrounds, it should have said that he faked ignorance of mine so he could gush over my past work. And then my last accusation—that the pacemaker he had implanted in Milgrom had drastically changed his behavior—became some rumor I'd heard."

"He's not stupid," said Rebecca. "He stuck fairly close to the truth, making it more of a question of your interpretation of the discussion versus his. So, when his attorney asks you if you claimed that a pacemaker could change a person's emotions, you're going to have to say yes."

"But there's research that says it does." But as soon as she said it, Nicole started shaking her head.

"What am I thinking? I can just hear the defense lawyer asking the jury, 'Can you believe that you're supposed to convict my client because some college sophomores asked a girl out after crossing a suspension bridge?'"

"I think you have your answer."

"So, Spencer thinks he can get away with this?" asked Nicole. "He thinks he can pin everything on Whitten?"

"I'd guess he thinks a confession will keep him alive, and with an enemy like Whitten, that would be an accomplishment. So, shall we go home and watch the news for Whitten's arrest?"

"Sounds good. I might even order a pizza delivered so I won't miss a minute. You interested?" asked Nicole.

"Pepperoni is my favorite."

SUNDAY, SEPTEMBER 4

Late Morning, Jen's Place

Nicole pushed back from the desk in her room and stretched her arms over her head. It had been two days since Spencer had turned state's witness in the case of the murder of Randolph Peterson, and now he was probably thinking it was the worst decision of his life. Had he known Whitten was already dead, he could have walked. Now, at a minimum, he'd never practice medicine again, and he had a fair chance of ending up in prison.

For Nicole personally, the last two days had been a time when she emerged from the dark prison of her past—perhaps not all the way, but further than she had ever escaped before. Now, she was certain there were people she could trust, people who might one day become friends. And maybe, just maybe, there was someone she could love ... again.

Her emergence began with Eleanor Bethune-Peterson's confession and her call to the police. The woman had made mistakes in judgment, which was only human. But then, she had compounded those errors by placing too much faith in her version of reality. Everything Ellie saw and heard only served to reinforce her belief that she and she alone had destroyed her husband. And that, too, Nicole knew was the nature of humanity. But in the end, Ellie had dared to believe there was another possibility. She had sacrificed her pride and had given the police a reason to reopen the case. Nicole was a mere youngster compared to her friend, but she couldn't have been prouder of Ellie.

As for Rebecca Marte, Nicole now knew that the PI had acted in good faith from the very beginning. She had confided her suspicions and theories to Nicole at every step. And while the doubt that she had gotten the full story from Ellie had driven a wedge between them, Rebecca had been right. That fact alone would have drawn Nicole further from her world of distrust. But when Rebecca also jeopardized her career in her determination to find the truth, to force Ellie from her carefully constructed world of self-blame, the subtle pull had become a force of immense proportions.

And Doc? Well, Nicole was still in a quandary over him. Emotions, it seemed, found their meaning in a person's interpretation of the world around them, and at the time her revulsion formed, the reasons were obvious. Her only memories of him were filled with abuse and cruelty. Logically, she questioned those memories. The few people she trusted told her they were false, but that knowledge had done little to change her feelings. But now, she had at least one memory of him that she knew with certainty to be true. He had been there to listen and to suggest that one last, missing piece of information that had caused all the other pieces of the puzzle to fall into place. That memory, she hoped, would be the start of a new world that included her one-time fiancé.

Perhaps it was time to start building those memories. She scooted her chair back to the desk and started to reach for the phone when someone knocked on her door. "Come in."

"Sorry to interrupt, but the police have asked if I can stick around for a few more days," said Rebecca as she leaned in through the partially open door.

"Come on in. Have a seat. I'm sure we can work something out."

Rebecca stepped inside and sat. "You'd think after ten hours of interviews over two days, they'd know everything I do, but I suppose they want to make sure. So, any chance I can crash here a little longer?"

"Absolutely."

Rebecca laughed. "Well, as far as working something out goes, that was pretty easy. I'll get everything out of the office so you can move in. Or turn it into another guest room. Or whatever you have in mind."

Nicole hadn't thought this through completely, but suddenly, it seemed obvious. "I have a better idea. Just stay in the office ... permanently."

Rebecca hesitated. "I don't think the business base of Marte Investigative Services warrants two offices, much less one that's nearly a thousand miles from my home. And I can't just walk away from my obligations in St. Louis."

"So, go back, close up the books, and get rid of your apartment. How soon is your lease up?"

"But I have family in St. Louis."

Nicole was still a little new to reading between the lines, but Rebecca's change in topic caught her attention. Did she already know her lease was almost over? "OK, but think of all the great vacations your family can have out here. You do like Colorado, don't you?"

"I love hiking. The mountains are so beautiful. And the sunsets—unbelievable."

"Well, your family will feel the same. And you can hike every weekend along with biking, skiing, snowshoeing, rock climbing, horseback riding, and a dozen other outdoor activities I'm forgetting." Rebecca seemed to be thinking about it, so she added, "Tell you what. If you want, I'll charge you a nominal fee for room, board, and office space in exchange for your security and investigative services for Jen's Place."

Rebecca laughed again. "I'm not sure how nominal you're thinking, but you'd be getting the short end of that deal. I've seen the prices of housing and office space around here, and they're quite a bit higher than St. Louis."

Maybe her earlier guess was right. Maybe Rebecca was already considering the option of staying. "So, my advice is to take advantage of me before I come to my senses."

"You're serious, aren't you?"

"Never more. You'd have at least the start of a built-in customer base. Most of the families that stay here need legal services, and after you meet some of the local lawyers, I'd bet they'll direct some work your way. There are lots of big companies around Denver that need background checks done. And I'm sure Ellie, Miranda, and Gloria will give you glowing recommendations. And, of course, I will, too. So, what do you say?"

"You make a very convincing argument, but what do you get out of it? I mean, besides me maintaining your security system? I can only polish camera lenses so many hours a day."

"Peace of mind, good optics for the shelter, protection for my guests, and a friend." Nicole hoped she wasn't pressing her luck but decided she should get everything out on the table. "And maybe you'll let me tag along on another case someday."

Rebecca looked at Nicole for a long moment. "I'm not sure what to say."

"Then say you'll give it some serious thought."

"Of course, I will … that is, if you'll start those nominal fees now. And regardless of where I end up, you'll always have a friend in me."

"Thanks. That means a lot. But as for charging until you decide, thinking time is on the house."

Rebecca studied her long enough that Nicole was starting to feel self-conscious. Eventually, the PI said, "Maybe this is too personal—and just say so if it is. But from the start, money has not seemed like much of an issue for you. You hardly looked at my fees before signing the contract. You've fed me and given me a place to work. You even covered all the expenses of getting my Colorado PI's license."

"The answer to that isn't personal at all; it's part of the public record. I'm sure you know that criminals can be sued in civil courts. Well, I was part of a suit against the kidnappers. They left behind a considerable estate, and while the jury was generous with everyone, they apparently felt especially sorry for me. A lot of the money went toward buying Jen's Place. And with what was left, I should be able to live comfortably even with the meager income produced by the shelter. Well, I will if the stock market starts behaving itself."

Rebecca smiled. "Well, I better get out of here. After all, I have some heavy thinking to do, and there's no better place to do that than the mountains. I'll see you tomorrow and maybe we can work out." She stood to leave.

"Brien going along?"

Rebecca grinned. "See you at breakfast, Nicole."

When the door closed, Nicole felt a wave of melancholy pass over her. Other than when she had to say goodbye to family after a short visit, it was a feeling she hadn't experienced in more than two years. It was, she recognized, the mirror side of friendship. Rebecca would always be a friend, as she had said, but it wouldn't be the same if she lived 850 miles away. And yet, she had no doubts that the warmth of even a distant friend was worth the sadness of the miles between them.

She reached for her phone, but it started ringing before her hand got there. She checked the display.

"Doc, what a nice surprise on a Sunday morning." She looked at the phone display again. "Well, early afternoon for you."

"Uh, yeah. Quarter to one, I guess. I took a chance calling, so if you're busy, no problem."

"No, it's pretty quiet here." But then, she realized that's not all he was asking. She'd built some substantial walls between them, no phone calls being one. That one needed to be the first to fall. The rest? Well, she would see.

"I know I haven't been available a lot, but I'm going to be around a lot more often." She figured he'd read between the lines.

"That's …. You're not sick, are you?"

Nicole laughed. Apparently, he had read between the lines and found another possibility there. "No, I'm fine. I just meant it might be nice if we talked a little more often. That is, if you want to."

"That would be great. So, idle curiosity is a good enough reason for me to call?"

"If we cut out those calls, I might never hear from you again." That made him laugh, which was a relief. The first wall was already crumbling.

"Good, because whatever's happened out there the last couple of days has me stumped. Some guy named Whitten killed his last boss, although he had tried to make it look like a suicide. A doctor named Spencer seems to be involved in that. And then someone, maybe Whitten's bodyguard, killed him?"

"All true, but let me add the connections your papers seem to be missing. Dr. Nicholas Spencer and Mr. James Whitten were working together to defame the last President and CEO, Randolph Peterson, so that the board would remove him from office. Then, Whitten would take his place.

"But about seven weeks after he was voted out, Peterson decided to try to get his company back. The police knew of a call he made to HomeRight Human Resources five days before his death. The HR representative said that they'd discussed Peterson taking the figurehead position he'd turned down earlier; he thought the chance of a successful return was better from the inside. He was even willing to refund a severance package of nearly a million dollars that the board had given him, so he was obviously determined to give it a try."

"I'm surprised that call didn't have a bigger impact on the police investigation," said Doc. "It certainly puts the alleged suicide in a different light."

"It might have, except that the suicide note came down pretty hard on the board members. The police decided that Peterson had changed his mind about a comeback because of their intractable opposition, as he called it. But when his wife said he was still planning a return the morning he died, that got the police to reopen the case.

"Word that Peterson wanted a job got back to Whitten. He, however, couldn't risk the chance that the old president would uncover his plot if he was back in the company. So, he presumably paid Peterson a visit and staged his suicide. It would have been easy enough since Peterson had no way to know he should fear his old chief operating officer."

"Rebecca is rubbing off on you," Doc said. "He presumably paid Peterson a visit rather than we caught the perp red-handed?"

"You're no one to talk, the way you over-qualify everything," Nicole replied with a laugh. "I'm not sure I've ever heard you make a simple declarative statement." In fact, if her memory was right, she had teased him about that more than once.

"Guilty as charged," he said. "But after the staged suicide, the story gets even murkier here. It sounds like Whitten was then murdered by his own bodyguard?"

"Well, that's the theory. All we know is that Dr. Spencer decided to give the police a statement to protect himself, but when the police went to pick up Whitten for questioning, they couldn't find him. That is until they checked the outbuildings. He'd been tortured to death. They found a video of him on a phone at the scene in which he confesses to Peterson's murder. He also tells the police who he was getting to print some not-quite-newsworthy stories at the papers, documentation of his payment to the mother and the boy who framed Peterson for propositioning him, and personal notes on how he'd adjusted the timing of the losses reported for the business."

"Sounds like Whitten was behind most of the problems that brought Peterson down, but you didn't mention some missing deposits," said Doc. "The papers around here made a big deal about them."

"And they were a big deal," replied Nicole. "But those missing deposits and a couple of other problems were honest mistakes that just happened at about the same time as Whitten launching his smear campaign." She figured that was a good way to summarize Ellie's role in her husband's downfall and death.

"So, this Dr. Spencer admitted to his part in the plot before he knew his accomplice had been killed?" asked Doc.

"You have the timing right, but Spencer never admitted to being an accomplice. Most likely, he got pulled into this whole thing unwittingly but didn't do anything to stop it. So now he's claiming that Whitten was delusional. Oh, and I should mention that Whitten smeared his boss, at least in part, by getting the company's CFO, Dan Milgrom, to turn on Peterson using Milgrom's pacemaker to alter his emotions."

"So, that worked," said Doc.

"Apparently. Spencer gave Whitten the laptop he used to adjust the pacemaker's settings, and that fact as well as the location of the laptop was in the video. So now, Spencer has to explain why he gave a laptop to a delusional man that just happened to have the encryption key for Milgrom's pacemaker on it."

"That should make for quite the courtroom drama," said Doc. "So, back to this bodyguard who supposedly killed Whitten. Why are the police having such a hard time finding him?"

"It looks like it was an under-the-table arrangement between Whitten and this guy, so no employment records to check. No one knows who he is." Actually, she did know a little more about him, but the police had asked her and Rebecca to keep quiet until later. That request, however, was now causing her some unease. "Sam, I don't want to start off keeping secrets from you, but anything else I might know about this guy—can we discuss it later?"

"Sure. I understand. And if you can never say anything, that's OK, too. Even without an ending, it's a helluva story."

They were quiet for a while. Finally, Nicole said, "I think this is part of our shared history. It was around Christmas. You were sent on a business trip to someplace in Nevada and I was in Kansas City for most of the time."

"Don't forget the ski trip," said Doc. "You were on it for a week or so."

"So, it did happen?"

"It did."

"One of the things I remember most about that time is all the phone calls and emails we sent to each other. It was just day-to-day stuff, but it ...." It took her a moment to find the right words. "It made you seem more real. Like I knew you, rather than us just being the strangers that we were."

"I'm hoping you're suggesting we do that again."

"I am."

"Who first?" asked Doc.

"You, of course. And I'd like a story about something you've done or something that interests you. And something that takes an hour or so to cover. I just want to listen for a while ... if that's OK with you."

"Nothing I'd like better. So, let's see." He was quiet for a few moments, then said, "Of course. What am I thinking? I have the perfect story. It's got everything. Intrigue. Romance. Even a few laughs. It all started about six months ago when ...."

The End

ACKNOWLEDGMENTS

This book would not have been possible without the help of a number of talented individuals, and I've been fortunate to work with several who have continued their support of my writing, book after book.

First, I'd like to thank Ms. Janet Harrison for all her helpful comments on an earlier draft of the manuscript. A number of people saw sections of this work before her, but she was the first to review the tale, start to finish.

I try to "bend" the psychological theory and research used in my books as little as possible. I find the fictional worlds built that way much more tension-eliciting than just making up how people perceive, learn, and recall. Dr. Liz Gehr has been very generous with her time and expertise to keep me closer to that objective.

The diligence of my editor is greatly appreciated. Most would have given up trying to teach me the use of commas in coordinate vs. cumulative adjectives, but she persists.

And finally, thanks go to my talented daughter, Ms. Courtney Perrin, for the design and creation of the cover art. When I "brand" the series by asking her to use the same fonts, color schemes, and human silhouette on each, she still finds a way to keep the covers fresh and interesting.

ABOUT THE AUTHOR

Bruce Perrin has been writing for more than twenty-five years, although you will find most of that work only in professional technical journals or conference proceedings. After receiving a PhD in Industrial/Organizational Psychology and completing a career in psychological research and development at a major aerospace company, he's now applying his background to writing novels. Not surprisingly, most of his work falls in the techno-thriller, mystery, and hard science fiction genres, examining the intersection of technology and the human mind now and in the future. Besides writing, Bruce likes to tinker with home automation and is an avid hiker, logging nearly 2,500 miles a year in the first nine years of Fitbit ownership. When he is not on the trails, he lives with his wife in Aurora, CO.

Thank you for reading *The Beating Heart of a Mind*. If you'd like to help others find this story, please consider leaving a review on Amazon, Goodreads, or the website of your favorite bookseller.

For all the latest on my new releases, promotions, and book reviews, please subscribe to my newsletter at BruceMPerrin.com